TOO MUCH INFORMATION

AN AWKWARD LOVE NOVEL

MISSY JOHNSON

CHAPTER ONE
LAURA

I TAKE a deep breath and glance at the courier e-mail again. It's well past their allotted "four hour" time frame, and I've got better things to do than stand around my apartment waiting all day. Okay, so maybe that's not true. Maybe I'd be here regardless, but for the love of God, put me out of my misery and deliver my damn sex toy. My heart pounds as I repeat that sentence in my head, because I'm already wishing I'd never ordered the stupid thing.

I blame Becca for this.

When I complained to her that she never puts enough thought into my birthday gifts, she presented me with a gift card for Diddle Me Softly. It had been sitting in my drawer for nearly six months. It was only last week when I decided to do a spring clean that I found it. I was all alone in my apartment, so naturally, my mind began to tick over. I'm a twenty-six-year-old single woman with a healthy sexual appetite who was experiencing somewhat of a drought when it came to men. So why did looking at toys and vibrators make me feel so embarrassed? I mean, who was going to know what I got up to in the privacy of my own home? So long as I didn't whip it out in the middle of the local coffee shop, I thought it was a pretty safe assumption that nobody would ever know.

One glass of wine was all it took for me to load up that site and have a look.

The first thing that surprised me was the sheer variety of toys available. Was there really that big a market for this kind of thing? Maybe I'd gone into the wrong profession with medicine because obviously sex toy development was the way to go.

As I ran through page after page of toys, I became more overwhelmed and curious at the same time, until I stumbled across the Clitmaster7000. Despite its slightly terrifying name, it actually looked pretty tame compared to some of the other things on offer, so I thought it was a safe option for a beginner like me. I mean, forgive me for being a prude, but the idea of something bigger than my forearm going anywhere near my vagina was *not* getting me all hot and sweaty. So, I took the plunge and ordered it.

I unlock the door and peek outside. A thought hits me as I glance down the hallway and my gaze falls on my neighbor's door. My eighty-year-old widowed neighbor.

God, please don't let it have been delivered to Iris by mistake.

The number of times she brings me my half-opened mail, because she didn't think to check the name on the label before opening it... Well, I wouldn't put it past her to have signed for my package, opened it up and assumed it was a toy for her cat, Milton. I cringe as I picture him swatting that bad boy from one end of her apartment to the other. I slam the door closed and lean against it.

I cringe because how would I explain that?

I feel like I need to put it all into perspective because I'm probably coming across as that annoying, whiny girl that nobody wants to be friends with. While there may be an element of that, panicky and jumpy isn't who I am.

I'm a doctor, for God's sake. I deal with situations that push me to the edge on a daily basis. I can handle a medical emergency any day of the week, but a situation that I can't control? Even something as simple as a potentially embarrassing package arriving, I struggle with. I'm the first to admit I have flaws and worrying about what other people think of me is probably my biggest.

The knock on the door comes so suddenly that I jump about a meter in the air and nearly give myself a heart attack. *This thing is already trying to kill me, and I haven't even tried it yet.* When the thudding of my heart has subsided, I brush myself off and stroll over to the door, casually opening it like I'm expecting a delivery of toilet paper.

The delivery guy stands there, smiling at me as he cradles the brown wrapped box like it's a new baby. I frown, my paranoia kicking into overdrive. Is he looking at me funny? He glances down at the box in his hands, and then back at me.

"Package for a Lauran Black," he says.

"Laura," I whisper.

I go to snatch it out of his hands and fumble, then we both watch in horror as it falls to the floor—well, I'm horrified; he looks mildly amused.

"Hope there's nothing breakable in there," he says leaning down to pick it up. "Underneath all that brown paper. I always try to guess what little treats people have bought themselves." He winks at me and my heart stops beating. "And you know what they say about brown paper."

God, the delivery guy knows I bought myself a sex toy.

He hands it to me again, along with a form that I quickly sign and thrust back to him. I send him on his way and slam the door closed, leaning up against the door. I slide down it until I'm sitting on the floor, where I carefully examine the box. All I want to do is throw it out, but it's here now, so I might as well take a look.

I carefully peel away the brown packaging and examine the box. With shaking hands, I open it and then reach inside. The size of the box is deceiving because the actual product is small enough to fit on the end of my finger. Which is the whole idea, I guess. I carefully pull it out. I'm both curious and suspicious that this is going to do anything for me. Even so, I am starting to wonder if I'm missing out on something—like Becca seems to think I am. Enough that I'm considering taking it for a test drive right now.

I wander into my room and sit down on my bed, carefully inserting the battery. I press the button, giggling like a twelve-year-old when it comes to life in my hands. I shake my head, because Becca would die if she knew what I was about to do. I'm sure she got the gift card, fully expecting me to never use it, but what else am I going to do with my Sunday afternoon? I take a deep breath and turn it on, then I slide it onto my finger and dive under the covers.

It's not like I'm going to be broadcasting this on YouTube or anything.

Here goes nothing... *Oh my.*

I groan as it vibrates against me, surprised at how good it actually feels. I bring my knees up and spread my legs a little farther apart, massaging my clit with my new buzzy friend. I clamp down on my lip, stifling a moan as I tease my entrance, pushing my finger just a little farther inside. I gasp, clutching onto the sheet with my other hand as my body begins to react. This is happening faster than I thought it would. I'm ten seconds in and already close to coming. Maybe I have been missing out.

"Oh, holy *fuck...*"

I groan, my head snapping back as I thrust it back and forth inside me. I gasp as my hips buck forward and push my finger deeper inside me until I...

My eyes fly open in shock.

Oh no, no, no. Please not this.

I frantically shove my hands out in front of me, like I need confirmation that this is really happening. Because the hands-free buzzing in my vagina isn't a dead giveaway.

Frantically, I try and dig it out, but it's no use. If anything, I think I've made it worse. I groan and grab a

5

handful of sheet as the toy rubs against my clit, driving me crazy.

"Oh lord, fuck, fuck *fuck*," I hiss.

I bite down on my arm to muffle my cries as my heart pounds out of control in my chest. The last thing I need is for Iris to hobble in here to check that I'm okay. Damn me for giving her that key to water my plants while I was away last weekend for my cousin's wedding.

"Oh *God,* make it *stop.*"

Struggling to catch my breath, I clench my thighs together, and groan, squeezing my eyes closed. I climax again, number five in as little as ten minutes. The worst thing is, they don't seem to be letting up. If anything, they're becoming more intense. *Oh, my fucking lord.*

I lower myself onto the floor and reach for the box, which has half rolled itself under the bed. My body aches, begging for relief, or at the very least, five minutes where I'm not climaxing. I fumble for the box, dropping it twice, before I get a firm enough grip on it to hold it up to my face. My hands shake as I struggle to read. Then I see those four little words that make me feel like I'm going to pass out.

For external use only.

Who the hell designs a vibrator for external use only? Doesn't that defeat the whole purpose? Am I the only one who thought letting my finger do a little traveling wasn't going to do any harm? Or am I just the only one unlucky enough to have their vagina decide to inhale it? Maybe I should've gone with the forearm sized one, because this tiny little thing is well and truly stuck inside me.

I should call an ambulance.

I laugh, dismissing that as an option. And say what? That's out of the question anyway because of which hospital they would take me to. I'd rather die a slow and painful orgasmic death than be wheeled into the ER of the hospital I'm supposed to be starting work at next week.

Groaning, I fall forward against the bed, fumbling for my phone as another orgasm rips through my body. Sweat covers my forehead as I close my eyes and clench my thighs, my vagina throbbing as I struggle to breathe. Panting, I resume my search for my phone, finally finding it hiding between the pillows. I somehow manage to get Becca's name up on the screen. I sigh, relieved, because this is *not* the time to be calling the wrong number.

"Hello?"

"Get over here," I sputter. "*Now.*"

"What? Where are you? What's going on?" she asks.

"Becca," I cry, barely able to focus on what I need to say to her. "Get. Over. Here. *Now.*"

"Okay, I'm coming."

Apparently, so am I.

I wheeze and drop the phone, crying out as the toy plays me like a violin.

I crawl across the floor in the direction of the living room. She's got to be at least ten minutes away, but that's probably how long it'll take me to get over there. I can barely manage a few slithers at a time because it's at the point where it just hurts. The orgasms themselves feel incredible, but those few minutes in between are just pure torture. I'm not sure how much more of this I can take. On top of everything else, I'm completely exhausted. This has to be the most intense workout I've ever had.

———————

BECCA POUNDS on the door just as orgasm number six tapers off. I can barely move by this point, but I made it to the door to unlock it before number six and that's the main thing. Now all I need is for her to get this thing out of me.

"It's me," she calls out. "Are you going to let me in?"

"It's open," I manage to get out.

She walks in, her eyes widening at the sight of me hunched over the couch, thighs clenched, rocking back and forth on the floor. *At least I'm not naked.* I managed to half squirm my way into a dress that I found lying on the floor in my room—though I must look a mess—with only one arm through the hole and the skirt bunched up around my waist. Now that I think about it, I'm not sure why I even bothered. She sprints over to me, crouching down beside me.

"Jesus, are you okay?" She glares at me as I let out a strangled sob. "Tell me what's wrong?" she says. She looks me over, her eyes wide with concern. "Were you attacked? Did someone break in and rape you? Talk to me, Laura. Should I be calling an ambulance? The police?" Her dark eyes study mine as I struggle to form words to answer any of her questions. "For God's sake, Laura. Say something."

"No ambulance," I mutter.

I groan and clamp my legs together, gasping as my body begs for relief. This is a nightmare. I point to the bedroom, where the box is still lying on the bed. Becca stalks through to my room, returning a few seconds later with the box in her hands. Her eyes widen, to the point where they're nearly ready to fall out of her head.

"No fucking way," she hisses.

I nod, sweat pouring out of places I didn't know sweat could form. She clasps her hands over her mouth and stifles her laughter, before quickly kneeling down next to me.

"What do you want me to do? Dig it out? I'll do that for you," she says as I glare at her. "Wait... I should've asked before offering. Front or back?"

"Becca," I growl, my voice high noting at the end.

"What? I'm sorry, it was a legitimate question," she cries, holding her hands up in defense. "You know I don't handle poop. How on earth did you manage to get it stuck in there in the first place?" she asks, shaking her head.

"Can we discuss this later, *after* it's been removed from my vagina?" I beg her.

"Yes, yes, I'm sorry. Okay, let's get you down to my car."

"Car?" I say, alarmed. "What happened to you offering to help me—"

"You seriously want me digging around in there like I'm looking for loose change down the back of the couch?" she asks

9

seriously. Then she giggles, but she stops when she sees my expression. "Sorry. Disturbing mental image. You understand this is pushing the friendship boundaries, right?"

I nod weakly. *Oh, I understand it, all right.*

She sighs and helps me climb up properly onto the couch while I try to steady myself as my body begins to convulse. *God, not again.* I wipe a layer of sweat off my forehead and rock back and forth, riding out the orgasm as I whimper into the cushion. Then I gasp, clenching my thighs again, until it passes.

"You're coming already? But I haven't even worked my magic hands on you yet," she jokes, flexing her fingers. "Hey, do you have any kitchen gloves, or—"

"Just get it out," I beg her.

"Fine," she grumbles as she gets down onto her knees. She lifts up the skirt of my dress and peers between my legs. "Hey, you smell really good. What kind of body wash do you use?"

"*Becs.*"

"Right, sorry," she mutters. "Focus."

I close my eyes, my toes curling as she slides a finger inside me. I groan, thrusting my knees together, because just the feel of her fingers inside me is driving me insane.

"This kind of feels like that game we used to play at Halloween, where we had to find the balls in the slime, while blindfolded," she muses.

"Except with less balls," I mutter.

She spends the next half a minute feeling around inside me, then she jumps to her feet and backs up so far, she's standing against the wall on the other side of the room. She shakes her head, a mortified look on her face.

"I'm sorry, I love you, but I can't do this. I can't feel it anyway and what if I damage something or pull the wrong bit out?" she demands.

I laugh, even though I want to cry, because the situation is so helpless. My hands shake as I lift them to my head and cover my face. I'm so tired, and I can already feel another orgasm beginning to develop.

"Do you want me to call an ambulance?"

"No!"

"Why not?" she asks, surprised by my sharp tone.

"Because they'll take me to Mercy," I say, gritting my teeth.

"Yeah, because it's the closest... *Oh*." She pauses and at least tries to fight the smile forming on her lips. "It's also where you start your residency next week. I guess this isn't the kind of first impression you want to make."

"You reckon?" I say, on the verge of tears. "Please, Becs, just *help* me."

She frowns at me. "Can you walk?"

"No," I whisper. "I crawled from the bed to here and it took twenty minutes."

"Then I'll have to carry you." She turns around, bending her knees as she taps her back. "Jump on," she urges me.

"What?" I protest. "I'm two inches taller than you," I say, laughing in spite of how desperate I feel. "You can't piggy back me all the way downstairs—"

"Unless you have a better idea, shut your trap, and get on," she demands. I climb on, wrapping my arms around her neck as I hold on for dear life. "You know, I always dreamed that one day, you'd be having repeated orgasms while riding on my back," she jokes, leading me into the elevator, which, thank God, is empty.

By some miracle, she manages to carry me all the way down to her car, while passing minimal people. I hurl myself across her back seat and whimper. She shuts the door and gets in, glancing back at me with a frown on her face.

"You know, I'm totally regretting getting you that gift card right now," she grumbles.

"Really?" I mutter, grunting as a stab of pain slices through me. *That can't be good.* "Well I think I'm regretting it more."

How did this go so wrong? I picked the least scary looking toy on that damn site. Who could mess that up?

Me. Apparently, I can because here I am vibrating my way to the emergency room, instead of heaven, like I was promised on the box.

I insist we go far enough out of downtown LA that there's no chance of running into anyone I know, and forty minutes later, we're finally nearing the exit for the Orange County Hospital. As Becca takes the exit, the severity of the situation starts to sink in. I feel like passing out. *What the hell am I going to say?* How am I going to explain to a doctor that I, a medical professional, have managed to lodge the world's smallest vibrator inside me?

"Here we are," Becca soothes as she cuts off the engine. "You wait here; I'm going to race inside and find you a wheelchair."

I nod, resting my head against the seat as she disappears. All the worst possible outcomes are racing through my head right now. What if I need surgery? Forget about the pain or explaining this to a doctor, how I do explain it to Mom and my brother, Matt? I'm such a shit liar, too, so if I concoct some story, they're going to see right through it and badger me until I confess the truth, which pretty much happened with every lie I told during my childhood.

The door opens, and I look up, expecting to see Becca. Instead, I see a middle-aged male orderly smiling sympathetically at me.

"Your friend said you might need some assistance getting out?"

"Thanks," I say, not sure what else to say to that.

Becca's face appears behind him, mouthing *I'm sorry*. I brace myself and carefully slide my butt across the seat to the door. I moan, my thighs twitching as I bury my face in the seat, pressing my legs together. I sob softly as I come for what feels like the thousandth time.

After this, I don't think I'll ever want to orgasm again.

Of course, I know I'll stop thinking that the moment this is over. It's like gorging yourself with Easter eggs to the point where you're physically sick. You swear off chocolate for life, and it lasts for two hours. Or maybe that's just me.

"There we are," he says as I sit down in the chair. I nod, my heart racing as I lower my head. "Let's get you inside now, hey?"

He hasn't asked what the problem is, which makes me wonder how much Becca told him. Usually orderlies talk your ear off, asking you all sorts of invasive questions. Not this guy, though. This guy is even avoiding eye contact.

He wheels me into a cubicle and helps me onto the bed. I clutch his arm as the movement triggers another orgasm. They're getting shorter now, which is good, but it's just constant pain. All I can think is how I'm on my knees, clutching some strange man's arm, while he supports me through an orgasm. When he starts trying to soothe me like he's comforting a crying baby, I nearly lose it—in more ways than one.

"You're okay. We'll get you checked out and get this pain under control," he assures me.

I nearly faint with relief. Pain. He thinks I'm in pain.

Oh, thank God for that.

Rolling myself over, I lie back on the bed and smile, my heart pounding erratically in my chest. I close my eyes and focus on my breathing, trying to slow down my heart rate. I find the best position is to lie flat on my back with my legs slightly parted. The less I move, the easier it is to handle, even though there's no relief from the constant discomfort.

I listen to Becca thanking the orderly for his help. I wait

until he's gone before I crack open my eyes to see Becca leaning over my face. Her eyes are laced with concern.

"I'm sorry," she whispers. Her usually bright eyes are laced with worry as she clutches my hand. "He insisted on helping when I asked for the chair. I told him you had an exploding cyst."

I laugh at that and even manage a smile.

"It's fine."

She touches my forehead and frowns. "You're sweating bucket loads, Loz. Maybe I should go and find—"

"Please don't," I say grabbing onto her arm. "I want to avoid talking about this for as long as I can." I glance at her, a horrible thought suddenly hitting me. "Actually, can you request a female doctor for me?" I ask. "I don't think I can handle telling this story to a male."

Especially if he's young and even remotely attractive.

"I'll see what I can do," she promises.

She walks out, leaving me alone as another orgasm hits. I'm exhausted as I cry out, my hands grabbing hold of the sides of the bed I'm lying on. I groan, my back arching as my body starts to tremble. Finally, it subsides, leaving me breathless and nearing my limit. I wipe my eyes because I'm not sure how much more of this I can handle.

What if they never stop?

"Laura Black."

My head whips around. I stare at the deliciously sexy doctor standing in front of me, staring down at a clipboard. I want to die. My breathing shallows as panic takes over.

Oh God, no.

This guy is perfect in every way. From his well-defined muscles that are peeking out of his scrubs, to his messy, but stylish dark hair, right down to those dreamy, chestnut colored eyes... He looks like a freaking model, and he's *definitely* not someone I want to discuss this with.

Where the hell is Becca with my female doctor?

"Hi. I'm Doctor Dillon, one of the resident doctors here." He smiles warmly at me, but I don't smile back. I'm in too much shock to do anything other than gawk at him like an idiot. He glances down at his clipboard and then back at me. "So, you have an exploding cyst. How bad is the pain, on a scale of one to ten right now?" he asks. "And have you had cysts in the past?" he adds, flicking through his notes.

His brow furrows when I don't answer either question. He steps closer to the bed. I jump, causing my body to react in the one way I don't want it to in front of him. I blink back tears, squirming as I squeeze my thighs closed while doing my best to ignore him as he looks at me in surprise.

"I can't talk to you. I need a female doctor," I puff, my face flaming.

"I totally get that, Laura. I'm more than happy to request that for you, but we're severely understaffed tonight so you might be waiting a while." He clears his throat. "I can assure you I'm very professional. I take the safety and privacy of my patients very seriously, and I'll do everything I can to make sure you're comfortable."

He speaks earnestly while I lie there, defeated. I know I

can't put up with this for much longer. So what if he's hotter than a Calvin Klein model and in five minutes, he'll be elbow deep inside me, probably while I'm in the middle of an orgasm?

As soon as this is over, I never have to see him again. The important thing right now is to get this out of me. I take a deep breath and nod.

"Fine, let's just get it over with," I mutter, gritting my teeth.

"Okay, can you tell me more about the cyst?" he asks. "Has it been diagnosed previously?"

"I..." I swallow, my heart pounding. I close my eyes and force the words out. "There is no cyst. I had a mishap with a toy."

"I'm sorry?" he says, frowning at me. "I don't understand what you—" He stops mid-sentence and stares at me, his eyes widening. "*Oh.*" After a moment of reflection, he quickly moves on. "So, it's stuck? *Inside* your vagina?"

"I wouldn't be here if it wasn't," I snap, close to tears again.

"Right," he replies.

He shakes his head, looking a bit lost at what to do next. Given that he's a resident, this could well be his first disappearing vibrator case. *Yay for being his first.*

"Okay, so have you attempted to get it out?" he asks.

I nod. "I've tried, but I can't get myself into the right position. Every time I do, it triggers an orgasm."

"Do you have a phone?" he asks.

"No, why?" I say.

I have no idea where this is heading. He reaches into his pocket and hands me his phone. I stare at it, confused. Does he want this on video to show his friends later? That doesn't sound very professional to me.

"I want you to google a picture of the toy. When I go in, it will help if I know what I'm looking for," he explains.

He explains it like I've asked him to go to Toys "R" Us on black Friday and he doesn't know what he's looking for. I sigh and snatch his phone from him. I'm past the point of being embarrassed about this. I just want it over with, and if he needs more of a visual than what he's about to get, then I'll give it to him.

"There," I growl, thrusting his phone back to him.

I look up in shock when the curtain is whisked back, and Becca appears.

"There aren't any female..." Her voice trails off as she stares at my doctor. "Oh."

"Hi," he says, frowning at her. "We're kind of in the middle of something here."

"Right, I'm her friend."

She edges closer to me, her eyes growing wide when she catches sight of what's on his phone. I close my eyes and groan.

"This might get fairly invasive," Doctor Dillon says to me. "I'm not sure it's an activity you want your friend here to witness?"

"Oh, trust me, I've had a good old feel around up there." Becca laughs. Her face falls when I glare at her. "Still, I might wait out here, just in case," she whispers, backing up. She gives me a big thumbs-up as she disappears behind the curtain.

He turns back to me, his eyes locking on mine.

"I'm going to examine you if that's okay?"

"Knock yourself out," I say, my voice weak.

Thank God I waxed last week.

Being such a new doctor, I'd only had the one patient experiencing sexual gratification gone wrong, but he was male, and it was a TV remote up his anus, so it wasn't quite the same. I'm not entirely sure what this examination is going to entail, and I'm not looking forward to finding out. Of course, I don't have much choice.

I take a deep breath as he lifts up the gown to reveal my pelvis.

"Okay, let me know if you feel any pain or tenderness." He presses various points, studying my face for my reaction. I shake my head because all the pain and discomfort is much farther south. "No pain at all?" he asks.

"There's not really pain associated with you pressing down," I say, trying to explain what I'm feeling. "It's more constant," I finally say. "And much, much lower."

"That's good news," he says. He smiles encouragingly. "I think I can retrieve it manually without the need for surgery if you're okay with me trying?"

Manually. As in, with his hands. I close my eyes and make peace with the fact that there is no saving this situation. At this point, I might as well roll with the punches and get it over with.

"Sure," I say, a small smile on my lips. "But at least tell me your name before you penetrate me?"

He chuckles at that. "Luke."

He disappears for a moment, then comes back in wearing

gloves and carrying a large bottle of lubricant and the biggest set of forceps I think I've ever seen. If I wasn't freaking out before, I certainly am now. Remember what I said about needing to be in control? My heart pounds as he pulls on his gloves and then sets up a wound care kit on the table next to the bed.

"So, how many lost toys have you retrieved?" I whisper, my throat dry.

He glances at me, amused. "Enough to know what I'm doing," he assures me. To me, that translates to none. "I'm going to start with just an internal exam. I promise you, if I'm not confident I can get it by hand, I'll stop and do an ultrasound. Okay?"

I nod, swallowing the baseball sized lump that has formed in my throat. I flinch as he reaches for a speculum and greases it up. He smiles sympathetically at me.

"Any discomfort or if you need a break, just tell me, okay?"

I nod and squeeze my eyes shut, jumping at every tiny touch. *It's just like having a pap smear. There's nothing to be concerned about.*

"I'm going in," he says.

I groan as he slides the instrument into place, bracing myself as it triggers another orgasm. I've lost count of what number we're up to, but this one feels much more intense. Probably because there is an insanely hot man only inches from my vagina. And in a few minutes, that insanely hot man will be placing his fingers inside me.

Oh God.

Wrong thing to think about. I arch my back slightly, the combination of him and the vibrator pushing me over the edge. I throw my arm over my mouth, trying to smother my moans. I'm so embarrassed, but apparently, my body doesn't care too much about that. At least, not enough to stop me from climaxing twice in the space of a minute.

Panting, my hands shake as I come down from my high—which is ironically also my lowest point of the day. I feel like crying. I want to get up and run out of here and never look back. The only thing stopping me is that I know I'll get probably as far as the nurse's station before it all starts again.

"Keep as still as you can, Laura. I know this is hard, but I can feel it. I just need to get a little deeper..." I whimper at the thought of anything of his going deeper inside me. "There. Got it."

My eyes fling open. My heart pounds, waiting for the next orgasm to begin, but nothing happens. Still, I brace myself and wait, and... nothing. I smile at him, tears welling in my eyes. I'm not even fazed that he's grinning from ear to ear while holding the buzzing little sucker out in front of him, like it's a prized fish he's just caught.

"Oh, thank God," I hiccup. I'm crying like a baby because the relief is incredible. *Now all I need is to sleep for a week, and I'll be fine.* "I can't thank you enough," I add, resisting the urge to hug him. *God, I'm so emotional.*

"You're welcome. I think this is the first time I've ever had a woman be grateful that I've stopped her from orgasming," he quips.

"I'm more than grateful. I'm thrilled," I say.

I sit up and swing my legs over the edge of the bed and stand up. He lunges forward to steady me when I struggle to keep my balance. I wince and rub my stomach. I clearly underestimated how sore I'd be.

"You really shouldn't be leaving yet," he says, frowning at me. "I'd like to keep you in for a few hours, so I can monitor you."

"Thanks, but I really need to get home," I say. All I can think about is getting as far away from here as I can, and I know for a fact that he can't make me stay.

"Okay, well if you insist on going, I can't stop you," he says. He reaches into his pocket and pulls out a script pad, scribbling on it. Then he rips it off and hands it to me.

"So, that's it? There's no other... aftercare needed?" I ask.

"Come back if there's any bleeding or pain, but you should be fine," he assures me. He manages to address me without smirking, but I can see the amusement in his eyes. "You'll be tender for a few days, and you might want to avoid using your toys for a few weeks."

"Damn, however will I cope," I mutter, narrowing my eyes at him.

He probably thinks I've got a kinky dungeon thing going on in my basement.

"Intercourse is fine once the tenderness has eased," he adds, a twinkle in his eyes.

"Trust me, *nothing* will be going near my vagina for a long time," I assure him.

"Sɪᴛ," Becca insists.

She arms herself with the wheelchair after I've signed all the forms, agreeing that I'm going against doctor's orders by leaving so soon. I'm just thankful this ordeal is finally over.

Much to Becca's surprise I willingly sit down. I'm still quite unsteady on my feet, so I'm all for her wheeling me out of here. Once at the car, she helps me into my seat and heads back into the hospital to return the chair. I breathe out, enjoying the moment to myself. All I have to do is think about what happened, and I die with embarrassment all over again. I think what makes it worse is that I know the kind of shit doctors say about their patients behind closed doors. I'm in that environment every day, where getting a patient like me is like winning the lottery.

Becca climbs in the car slamming the door shut. She takes one look at my face and bursts into laughter. I glare at her, which just makes her laugh even harder. If I had the energy, I'd get out of the car and walk home.

"I'm sorry, but I've been holding that in all day," she splutters. "I know it's not funny, but oh my freaking God, Loz, it could only happen to you." She forces the words out through her laughter and tears. "You're the only person I know to visit the ER with a toy lodged inside you. They make shows about people like you. Then, if that wasn't bad enough, you manage to get yourself fingered by the sexiest doctor I've ever laid my

23

eyes on," she says as she shakes her head. "Maybe I need to order myself one of them."

"What he did to me was closer to fisting than fingering." I scowl at her. "And thank you so much for the rundown, but I'm well aware of what just happened because in case you don't remember, I was there."

She nods furiously. "You're right, I'm so sorry. I'm a terrible friend, but I just had to get it out." She glances at me, biting back either tears or laughter. I'm not sure which. "I'm sure you know what that's like, right?"

She erupts into another wave of giggles, while I glare straight ahead.

"Are you done?" I snap.

"I think so." She takes a deep breath and straightens herself up. She looks at me, trying to disguise her grin as sympathy. "At least you don't have to see him again, right?" She points out.

Thank God for that.

CHAPTER TWO
LAURA

IT'S BEEN a nearly week since the incident, and I've finally worked up the courage to leave my apartment. Okay, so maybe I'm being a little dramatic, but this event came close to scarring me for life. Even though there were no long-lasting ill effects, other than a little pain and tenderness, the emotional trauma was proving a little harder to get over.

For the last six days, every time I've closed my eyes, I've been right back there on that bed, making small talk with the hottest guy I've ever met while he casually fingered me. I even had a nightmare last night where I ran into him in the middle of Walmart. I had to awkwardly make small talk with him, surrounded by vibrators and talking dildos—which they don't even sell—while my mom stood next to me, asking me what was going on. Maybe lying in bed, staring at the ceiling, bored out of my mind didn't help my emotional state, but I wanted to make sure I got plenty of rest like the doctor told me to.

None of that matters now, because it's all over. I'm back to being me, that little vibrating monster is buried safely at the bottom of a medical waste dumpster, and I never have to think about it again. Well, at least until I see Becca, because I know she's not going to let me forget about this anytime soon.

It's Friday, and I've been out for most of the morning, running from one end of the city to the other, trying to catch up on a week's worth of errands. I'm so behind on preparations for my new job that most of my time is spent chasing up medical forms, my uniform, and parking permits. It's all these last minute little things that are making it sink in that this is really happening.

I did my first two years of residency at Seattle Hospital, near where I did my pre-med. Seattle was a great hospital with an excellent program, but my dream was always to come back home. I'd have loved to have done it all here, but the program Seattle was offering was superior, and with what I wanted to specialize in, I knew I'd need all the help I could get. Moving away from my family was hard, considering how close I am to Mom and Matt, but I just kept my eye on the prize. It finally paid off when I was accepted into Mercy for my final year of residency. It's next year's fellowship that I have my sights firmly set on, though. It's such a tough program to get into that I thought my chances were better if I already had my foot in the door.

By the time I'm done with my errands, it's nearly one in the afternoon. I'm exhausted, hungry, and not that far from Matt's place, so I text Annie to see if she wants to meet me for lunch.

Annie is my sister-in-law. At twenty-three, she's a few of years younger than me, but we get on really well. She came over from London for a three-week vacation with a friend and never went back. That was four years ago, and she and Matt have been together ever since. I was so happy that he found someone like her, because as fun and laid-back as she is, she's also one of the toughest, bluntest people I've ever met, which is exactly what my brother sometimes needs, and I find her direct-ness hilarious. Listening to her curse, I imagine that's what the queen would sound like, yelling at the corgis for eliminating on her Persian rug.

I look up as she waddles into the cafe and over to the table where I'm sitting. She huffs as she struggles to get herself comfortable in a small wooden chair that was obviously designed without pregnant women in mind.

Aside from Becca, Matt and Annie are probably my closest friends. It's kind of funny we're so close, considering we're complete opposites. Matt is the guy who knows and loves everyone—the guy everybody wants to spend time with. Growing up, being his sister was hard because everyone assumed that I was like that too.

Instead, I was the shy, awkward girl who buried her nose in books to avoid making eye contact with people. I put myself under so much pressure trying to live up to his reputation and what people expected of me. It didn't help that I was missing weeks and weeks of school at a time. I think I was away more of eighth grade than I was there, because of a condition I had that meant my body produced painful, large uterine cysts. I would have gone crazy if it weren't for Matt and Becca keeping me company.

When I was fourteen, one of those cysts burst, which very nearly killed me. After two weeks in intensive care and two major surgeries, I ended up with no uterus, no ovaries, and no chance of ever having my own children. At the time, it didn't really hit me what that meant because having children was so far off my radar, but now it's beginning to sink in.

I turn my attention back to Annie, sympathizing as she winces and struggles out of her jacket and tries to stuff it behind her back for support. I take mine off, too, and hand it to her, which she gratefully stuffs behind her back. She sighs with relief. I suppose everything is difficult when you're nearly nine months pregnant.

"Get this fucking thing out of me," Annie exclaims in her proper English accent. I chuckle to myself because I'll never get sick of listening to her curse. "I cannot think of one tiny little thing that I enjoy about being pregnant," she adds. Then her eyes grow wide, and she claps her hand over her mouth. "Gosh, I'm sorry. That was completely insensitive of me, wasn't it?" She shakes her head and waves at herself. "Just ignore the daft pregnant woman over here."

"Seriously, you and Matt need to stop acting like you're going to upset me with every little comment," I say, laughing. "Let me enjoy this with you guys."

It's been like this since the day they told me she was pregnant. After three weeks of severe, constant morning sickness, Annie had jokingly asked me if I wanted it when it came out. Matt had glared at her, and the two of them got into a shouting match, while Annie profusely apologized and I tried to convince them I was fine.

I just wish I could make them see how resilient I am, and that just because I can't have kids, I'm not going to fall apart at the mention of a baby. I'm best friends with Becca, for God's sake. She's the queen of offending people. If I can handle her, I can handle anything. Though to be fair, I think being friends with Becca has significantly decreased my ability to be offended.

"Oh, I almost forgot. Matt wanted me to ask you over for dinner tonight." She stabs a tomato off her plate and pops it in her mouth, her lack of eye contact only mildly concerning me. "We're having a dinner party and one of my friends—Raina —can't come."

"Sure," I say. "So long as this isn't another attempt to try and set me up," I add, my suspicions stirring. I hold up my hand when she starts to protest her innocence. "It's fine, I'll come. Oh shit." I'd already made plans with Becca. "I forgot. Becs and I are going to see a movie."

"Can you get out of it? Matt's already arranged the menu, and it will just look odd if we're one person short," she pleads with me.

I grin because she really takes her dinner parties seriously.

"Okay, I'll text her and see if we can make it tomorrow

night. I'm sure it'll be fine." I pull out my phone to message her before I forget. "Am I excepted to dress up?"

She frowns at me. "If I say no, is there a chance you're going to turn up wearing that hideous snoopy shirt that should've been thrown out years ago?"

"One time," I say, laughing. "And only because you failed to mention the part where you'd invited a guy to our weekly pizza and slouch on the couch night."

"Yes, well, I was only trying to help." She sniffs. "Lord knows you need all the assistance you can get when it comes to finding a man."

I giggle. See what I mean?

AFTER WE FINISH LUNCH, I head back home, using the short drive to think about what I'm going to wear to the dinner party. I already know my options are limited since I've been putting off doing laundry for the last few days. After racking my brain, I admit defeat and surrender to the fact that I'll need to put in a load as soon as I get home.

I find my cream shirt with the lace cap sleeves in the bottom of a pile of clothes in the bathroom, then I trudge down to the basement of my complex and throw it in the only empty machine left, along with a few other clothing items. I turn it on the fastest cycle and impatiently wait the twenty minutes until it's done, then throw it in the dryer. Rather than waste more time waiting, I go back upstairs to check on Iris.

"Iris? It's me," I say, knocking gently on her door.

I hear her moving around inside and then the door swings open. She smiles, and places her soft, wrinkled hand in mine, yanking me inside. I laugh because she's much stronger than she looks.

"Are you going to stand there looking silly, or are you going to sit down?"

She's already on her way into the kitchen to prepare our usual tea without waiting for an answer. It might seem strange that I'm such good friends with my eighty-year-old, widowed neighbor, but if you met her, you'd understand why. She's fucking hilarious.

My own grandparents died when I was little, so I never really got to experience that kind of relationship. I'm not sure that's what Iris and I have, but whatever it is, I love it. I've only been living next door to her for a few weeks, but I feel like I've known her forever. I'm always at her place, catching up on the latest gossip from the world of reality TV, and every week, I've tried to take her out somewhere, just to get her out of her apartment.

We don't talk about her family, though I know she has a daughter who lives locally who she never sees. That makes me sad because she's such a great person and so much fun to hang around.

"So, what are we watching?" I call out to her, making myself comfortable on the couch.

Like I even need to ask.

Milton, her cat, runs over to me, jumping into my lap, meowing. I pet him and glance at Iris as she walks back in, carrying a tray.

"He loves you so much," she says fondly. She places my tea on the table, along with the homemade biscuits she knows I love. "It's strange because he can't stand people most of the time. Me included."

"Milton and I are very alike," I joke as I pet him under the chin.

I can't stand being around people either, sometimes.

He jumps off my lap and runs out of the room. I reach for my tea, smiling as I take a sip. It's so comforting. Is it offensive to say that there's something special about tea made by an old person that makes it taste better? I can have the same brand of tea and make it at home, and it wouldn't make a difference. It's like going to a café and ordering a sandwich. You can get all the same ingredients at home, but it's never going to taste the same.

Iris sinks down into her chair, turning her attention back to the TV. She shakes her head and nods toward the screen, annoyed.

"I can't believe he's chosen this biddy over the one with the legs that go on for miles," she snaps, shaking her head in disgust.

I chuckle to myself because she's hysterical. She's a reality TV junkie. There's no other way to describe it. I've never met anyone with such an appetite for conflict and drama, much less someone in their eighties. She has that channel running day and night. In fact, I'm pretty sure she sleeps in that chair.

"They're advertising for contestants for next year, you know." Iris turns to me and narrows her eyes.

"What?" I laugh, a blush creeping across my cheeks. "Me? No way. I could never go on anything like this. Besides, I don't need a TV show to embarrass myself in front of someone. I can do that all on my own." I glance at the screen and shake my head because this show is such a load of crap. "How many of these people do you think actually end up together?"

"What are you saying?" Iris asks, frowning at me.

"You think they actually get married?" I laugh at her horrified expression. "They'll be engaged at the end of this, sure, but two weeks later, it'll be off. And last season? Yes, they made it to the wedding, but I heard that he slept with the third runner-up on his wedding night. *After* saying their vows."

God, I'm crushing the hopes and dreams of an eighty-year-old.

Iris frowns and then sniffs as she shakes her head.

"I don't believe any of it," she snaps, turning her attention back to the TV. She points at the door, glaring at me over the rims of her glasses. "If you're going to sit there, picking it to bits, you know where the door is, missy."

I stand up, still laughing and lean over, kissing her on the forehead.

"Unrelated to this, I do have to go."

Iris looks at me, shocked I'd want to go anywhere and miss the end of *The Bachelor,* never mind the fact that it's a three-year-old episode—I'm disappointed in myself that I know that.

"Where are you going?" she demands. "You better be leaving me for a date."

"I hope not." I frown. "Though, if I know my brother and Annie, they're probably trying to set me up with someone."

"Good," she snaps. "You need a good kick in the butt."

"Thanks," I say, laughing. "Though I could say the same about you."

"Pfft." She sniffs. "Who would want to take this old thing out?"

"I think you'd be surprised," I say with a grin.

Remind me never to introduce her to the world of Internet fetishes, or it won't be the sounds of *The Bachelor* I'd be trying to block out at night.

I WALK BACK into my apartment, panicking when I see the time. *Shit, it's later than I thought it was.* I race down to the basement, gather my laundry, take it back upstairs and toss it on my bed. Then I have a shower. I wash as quickly as I can get away with, then I jump out, and quickly dry myself. After a short deliberation, I leave my hair down to dry naturally, then I dab on some makeup and shuffle my way into my black skirt, along with a low pair of heels.

On the way out of my room, I grab my shirt from the bundle of washing and throw it on, ignoring the way the still damp material makes my skin crawl. I don't have much choice but to wear it since the snoopy sweater is out of the question. Sighing, I grab my phone in my purse and race out the door. I haven't even left, and I already regret agreeing to this.

I DIDN'T EXPECT so much traffic getting across the other side of town, so by the time I pull up outside their house in Pasadena, I'm really late. My phone beeps as I unbuckle my seat belt. I fumble through my purse, already knowing it's Annie or Matt. I'm right.

> **Annie:** *Where are you? You're still coming,*
> *right?*
> **Me:** *Yes, relax. I'm outside, about to come in.*

I pound on the front door. Matt answers. He shakes his head and glances at his watch.

"What?" I say. "It's not like you gave me a whole lot of notice about this dinner party," I say with a frown. I push past him as he chuckles and then shuts the door.

"Like that would've made a difference," he scoffs. "So, what was it this time?"

"What do you mean?" I ask.

"Well, you're always running late, and you always have some half-assed excuse ready to go, so hit me with it."

I glower at him. He knows me too well.

"I got distracted with my eighty-year-old neighbor watching *The Bachelor,*" I say with a sheepish grin. He shakes his head and groans.

"If it were anyone else, I wouldn't believe that, but you..." He smirks at me. "The funny thing is, for somebody so anal, you suck at time management. How does that even work?"

"Anal?" I glare at him.

"You know what I mean. You like control," he says. "So why don't you control your time better?"

"Shut up," I say, poking my tongue out at him.

"You shut up." He grins. "Now get outside. Everyone's already sitting down, and you're ruining my dinner party."

I hear a distinctive laugh that sounds like a hyena wrestling a polar bear that can only be Raina.

"I thought Annie said Raina couldn't come," I say suspiciously.

"Did she?" Matt's voice lifts to a high pitch, and I groan.

"Matt."

"What?" he asks, shaking his head. "I didn't tell you because you'd think this was a setup, and it's not like that this time, I promise."

"Then what is it like?" I say.

"I've just got a friend staying with us and everyone else coming tonight is a couple, so I felt bad for him. And you're the only other single person I know at the moment. I needed things to balance," he says, speaking quickly.

"Balance?" I shake my head. "You owe me for this. If he tries to hit on me, you owe me double."

"Fine. I've got to go back and check on the risotto," he says, waving me off.

I shake my head then take a deep breath, glancing at my reflection in the hallway mirror before I walk out onto the patio.

"Laura," Annie exclaims, getting to her feet. Her dark eyes examine me as she leans closer for a kiss. I narrow mine slightly, letting her know that I know what this is. "Don't hate me. Matt made me ask you," she whispers in my ear.

"It's fine."

Life's too short to be angry at a heavily pregnant woman. The last thing I want on my conscience is her stressing out so much that she pops out a baby. And who knows? Maybe this guy and I will have something in common.

"I think you know nearly everyone," Annie says. "Raina and Dave, Lisa and Dan, Phillipe and Cassie..."

I smile at everyone as I sink into the only empty seat at the table. I wait until the last possible moment to turn my attention to the person next to me because I hate how awkward those first few seconds of a setup are. I smile and then lift my gaze to meet his.

And then I stop breathing.

I literally stop breathing.

God, no. Please, anyone but him.

My sexy doctor is sitting in the seat next to me.

I can't tear my eyes away from those gorgeous eyes or that lightly tousled hair that I just want to drive my fingers through or that tiny smirk that's only just visible on those full, red lips that look like they'd feel incredible to kiss.

"You must be Matt's sister," he says. His voice snaps me back to reality, and I glare at him as his glittering eyes lock firmly onto mine. "Laura, was it?"

"Yes," I say.

I swallow, forcing moisture back down my dry, constricted throat as I force my gaze away from his. I stare straight ahead and take a sip of my wine, which quickly turns into half the glass, while my other hand sits in my lap, clenched into a tight, shaking fist.

"Can I be honest with you?" he asks me.

He leans over, so his mouth is almost on my ear. Like any closer and he'd be sucking on my earlobe. I cringe at what that thought does to me.

Please don't.

"When I arrived and saw all these couples, I thought fuck, this is another one of Matt's schemes to try and hook me up." He pauses long enough for me to soak up his words. "But I have to admit, when I saw you walk out, I was excited." He pulls back and takes a sip of his beer, his dark eyes sparkling. "I'm getting a really good vibe from you, Laura. I think I'm really going to get a buzz out of talking with you tonight."

Oh God.

This is going to be hell.

CHAPTER THREE
LUKE

WELL, tonight just took a turn for the better.

I smirk at Laura as I watch her gulp down the last of her wine, before nodding at Annie to top her up again. She won't look at me, which I can't really blame her for, considering the compromising position she was in when we last saw each other. To be honest, I feel quite sorry for her. This has got to be torture for her. What are the chances of your brother trying to set you up with the doctor who saved you from a runaway sex toy?

When I first saw her walk out onto the patio, I couldn't believe it was her. She didn't notice me at first which gave me a chance to really study her without any limitations. When she's in control of herself and not mid-orgasm, she's actually very hot —not that she wasn't hot last time I...

Yeah. I think I'm going to quit that thought while I'm ahead.

Her long dark hair hangs around her shoulders, twisting into a mass of loose curls, and those deep blue eyes are full of such warmth that you can't help but smile back. Only when I smile, hers disappears, which brings me crashing back down to reality.

"So, Laura," I say.

She turns to look at me, knowing she can't ignore me when I'm talking directly to her without raising questions. Sure, some might say that I'm forcing her to interact with me, but if it gets us past what happened, why not?

"Do you live around here, too?"

"No, I live in downtown LA," she replies. "On the south side."

She doesn't even look at me as she speaks. Maybe I brought that on myself by using terms like vibe and buzz, but I really was just trying to lighten the mood and make a joke out of it. I guess we're not at that point in our relationship yet.

I frown, a thought hitting me. *If she lives closer to the city, then why go to Orange County?* There had to have been closer options for her to go to. Mercy's literally on her doorstep, for starters. I don't dwell on that too much. Instead, I try to talk to her again and again, but every time, she shuts me down.

"Laura?"

I say her name so loudly that it gets the attention of half the table. Oh well. She can't ignore that at least. She turns and glares at me.

"What?"

"You really need to cut me a break," I say in a lower voice.

"People are going to start asking questions if you toss one more dirty look my way. People being your brother and Annie," I add, unable to resist the temptation of another dig. "I'm going to take a wild guess and say they're... *uninformed* over your recent hospital visit?"

"And it will stay that way if you shut up. Maybe you can start with stopping the comments that make me want to give you dirty looks?" she suggests sweetly.

"Sorry, I didn't realize offering you a cushion to sit on would be so offensive," I protest, holding my hands up in defense. "Most women would be flattered if a man considered their comfort, like I just did," I add.

How was I supposed to know how well she'd recovered?

"There is a nearly nine-month-pregnant woman sitting opposite me, and you're offering me a pillow? How about you offer it to her instead?" She shakes her head, lowering her voice. "You don't want to draw attention to what happened? What the hell do you think offering me a pillow is going to do?"

She makes a good point, but still... chivalry is chivalry.

"So, you didn't tell anyone anything?" I ask her, scooting a little closer to her.

As a doctor, I'm genuinely curious, because it had to have hurt for a few days after the incident. How did she explain it to people?

"I would've expected at the very least, a funny walk for a day or two with that kind of penetration—not to mention the multiple orgasms," I muse. "By the way, did you keep track? I'm

41

pretty sure I counted five in just the short time I was with you. You could be up for a record."

"Are you done?" she explodes. "It's none of your goddamned business how many times I came."

She tosses her napkin down on the table and glares at me, mortified she just said that aloud and just as Matt happened to wander out onto the deck. He catches the tail end of her rant and raises his eyebrows at me and then shrugs as if to apologize. I shake my head and rub the back of my neck, knowing it's more my fault than hers. Okay, it's completely my fault.

The worst part is that I'm not intentionally trying to wind her up. Well, maybe it is intentional, but I swear I'm not trying to offend her. But somehow, I'm managing it repeatedly. Things keep popping out of my mouth before I realize how bad they sound. I think it's the nerves talking more than anything else because seeing her again reminds me that she's the kind of girl I'd usually go for.

It was hard enough keeping things professional when I was examining her, but I did it. The number of times my mind started to wander... I'll even go as far to admit that after my shift, she may have filtered into my mind once or twice while I was jerking myself off.

But here? She's not my patient. She's just Matt's sister, looking especially sexy in that short black skirt. It's hard to turn my emotions off and not react because that's what I should be doing. I mean, she's still technically a patient, right? I'm confused about how I should be acting, and when that happens,

I lose control of my mouth. I know I need to stop talking, but I can't.

"You know, I would've expected Matt's sister to be a little more outgoing," I tease her.

"Yeah, well I guess I'm not feeling all that talkative," she mutters.

I'm about to respond when Annie knocks over a stack of glasses she's attempting to balance and then carry. I smirk and get to my feet. I take them from her, and she sighs with relief.

"Thanks, Luke," she says. "Isn't he the sweetest?" She directs that comment at Laura, who stares daggers back at her.

"So sweet my teeth are rotting," Laura grits out through a smile.

Chuckling, I scoop up the rest of the empty glasses and carry them into the kitchen. I place them down on the kitchen counter and let out a large breath. God, she's killing me out there. I feel like I need a power nap before I get back out there. Or, at the very least, a pep talk. Matt looks up and winces. He walks over and slaps me hard on the back.

"Man, what's going on out there? I don't think I've ever seen you strike out as much as tonight." He chuckles. "I know my sister can be hard work, but I've never seen her this uptight."

"You're referring to the sister that you're *not* trying to set me up with?" I retort.

"Hey, this wasn't a setup, but it doesn't seem to have stopped you from trying."

"Sure, man, whatever helps you sleep at night," I say, not believing that for a second.

I wander back outside, pretending not to notice how Laura visibly tenses when I sit back down. For both our sakes, I keep pushing the conversation, trying to ease the awkwardness between us. I mean, she eventually has to lighten up, right? I figure the more I try and wear her down, the less of a big deal what happened will seem. Hey, she might even decide she likes me, if she gives me a chance.

THE REST of dinner goes by in much the same way. I'm inappropriate, and she either ignores me or glares at me. The party eventually breaks up, and as soon as Annie and Matt go to walk the last couple out, Laura jumps up. I watch her with interest as she rushes to clear all the plates from the table. She really wants to avoid being alone with me. Matt walks back out and shakes his head.

"No, you go and sit back down. Enjoy yourself," he says, gently chastising her. "I didn't invite you so you could clean up after us."

"No, you invited me so you could..." She shakes her head. "Never mind." She sinks back down into her seat and scowls at Matt as he walks away.

"You really can't wait to get away from me, can you?" I question.

"Do you blame me?" she asks. "It's nothing personal. I'm just really embarrassed about..." She shakes her head and glares at me. "No wait, it is personal. You've been an asshole to me all night."

I wince because I deserve that.

"I'm sorry. I think I was trying to make it so that the incident wasn't the worst thing to happen between us," I finally say. "I thought by making that seem less of a big deal, that this would be easier for you."

"What? That's the stupidest thing I've ever heard," she says. Then she lowers her head and laughs. I stare at her. Holy shit, has my plan actually worked? "That's really what you were trying to do?"

"Of course," I say, with a wounded expression. "I mean, if I really wanted to make you feel uncomfortable, I'd comment on how your voice isn't hitting the high notes it did last time we met."

She glares at me, and I laugh. "Okay, I'm sorry. I've been holding onto that one all night. I promise it's completely out of my system now," I call out to her, but she's already stalking off inside the house.

I groan inwardly and rub my head, then I give her a few minutes head start before I saunter back inside too. Matt glances at me as I walk through the door. He laughs and shakes his head.

"I'm not sure whether to be concerned or impressed with the way my sister just stormed out of here, cursing your name," he says.

I chuckle and run my hands through my hair, because if only he knew.

"What can I say? It's a talent. I'm going to call it a night, I think. Thanks again for letting me stay here. I appreciate it."

"Anytime, man."

I walk down the hallway to my room with the look on her face when she realized I was at that dinner party stuck in my head. She'll get over it eventually. Sure, it must have been embarrassing for her, seeing me there, but the memory won't always be this raw. I mean, it was only a few days ago. I really do hope I see her again, but I'm not sure the feeling is mutual. I could ask Matt to help me. I'm sure he would, and she'd have trouble explaining why she didn't want to be around me. Of course, there was one major flaw in that plan.

Making sure it never came up in conversation that I'd told Matt about the girl in cubicle nine.

"WELL, what do you want me to do? Put them up at a hotel?"

I look up as Annie storms into the kitchen, cursing Matt's name under her breath. Matt follows and stands in the doorway, not helping the situation by laughing at her.

"Well, yeah. If they'd given you the right dates in the first place, then we wouldn't be standing here, arguing over the fact that your parents are flying in tomorrow and we have no room to put them up."

"Well, what do you want me to do, put them up at a hotel?"

I wince, because they've been like this all morning, and I've just about had enough, especially when the solution is so blatantly obvious that it's staring them in the face. I slam my fist down on the table, causing them both to turn to me in surprise. It's like they'd forgotten I was even there, which is easy to do when you're at each other's throats, I guess.

"Guys, relax," I say, shaking my head. "There's a very easy solution. I'll just go and stay in a hotel."

"Really?" Annie sighs with relief.

"No way, man," Matt protests at the same time. Annie glares at him. "What? He's our guest, and I said he could stay. We can't just kick him out."

"We can when the alternative is kicking my parents out." She winces and clutches onto her stomach, then reaches behind her to balance herself against the counter. Matt races over to her, full of concern.

"I'm sorry." He sighs and walks over and wraps his arms around her waist. "I'll sort something out, okay? Don't worry about it. The last thing we need is you stressing out more."

Annie smiles, kissing him on the lips.

"Hey, what about Laura?" she asks.

"Laura?" Matt repeats her name, like the idea never even entered his mind. I laugh because this should be entertaining. "Hey, that's not a bad idea. She's thinking about leasing out her spare room, anyway." He nods his head slowly, looking more into the idea by the second. "This is perfect, actually. She's lives just around the corner from where you'll be working. In fact, she starts there next week too," he says, looking at me.

"At Mercy?" I say, my eyebrows shooting up.

"Yeah, I told you that, didn't I? She's a doctor, like you."

I start to laugh. *This just keeps getting better and better.*

"What's so funny?" Matt frowns.

"Uh, were you not at dinner last night? Your sister doesn't seem to like me all that much," I point out.

"True, but what's to say she'd like anyone she let her room out to?" he says with a shrug. "At least you're a safe bet. You're a known evil." He nods, as though it's been decided already. "No, this is a great idea. Trust me."

I shake my head and let him go with it.

It's a fucking fantastic idea, but one that she's never going to agree to.

CHAPTER FOUR
LAURA

"UGH." I climb into bed, still fully clothed. I face plant onto my pillows and then lift the covers over my head, wanting nothing more than to forget the last week. Tonight, was a disaster—from start to finish. Walking in there and seeing him sitting there at that table was like fate shitting all over me. That's the only way to describe it because why else would this happen? How unlucky does a person have to be to go through this sequence of events? I mean, what next? What else can be thrown at me?

It's like every time I actually manage to forget about what happened, something happens to throw it back in my face. I roll over, ignoring my phone as it vibrates madly on my bedside table until I can't listen anymore. I reach over and switch it onto silent because even the soft vibration of my phone is making me cringe. I can see whoever it is isn't giving up, so I give in and answer it.

"Hello?" I don't even bother to lift my head as I speak into the phone.

"Hey, it's me." Becca. I burying my face farther into my pillow and mumble something incoherent. "Are you okay?" She laughs. "How was the dinner party?"

"Bad." I swallow and force myself to sit up, so she can understand me. "Really bad. In fact, it couldn't have gone much worse kind of bad."

"Oh, it probably could have if you think about it hard enough," she says, attempting a joke. "You could've been set up on a blind date with that hot doctor from the other night."

Silence.

"*No!*" I can tell she's trying to hold back both her shock and laughter.

"Yes. Just come over. Bring a hammer or a bag to suffocate me or something because I'm done," I grumble.

"I really feel for you," she admits. "I want to tell you it's not that bad and how much worse things could be; but hell, I've got nothing." She chuckles. "I will come over though if that's okay? I think you need something that will take your mind off this."

"And what's going to do that?" I ask suspiciously.

"This."

I stare at Becca and laugh as she holds up the copy of *Mean Girls* that I got her for her twenty-first birthday. Tucked neatly under her arm is a jumbo bag of buttered popcorn, with extra butter. She hands me the DVD and tosses the popcorn on the couch, then walks into the kitchen. I smile as I examine the cover because I'm already feeling better.

This movie has been our go-to flick since Becs sneakily—and illegally—filmed it on her dad's camcorder for me when I was too sick to go and see it at the theatre in 2004. We watched the fuck out of that tape right up until her parents accidentally recorded themselves having sex halfway through the movie. It was the best way to recover from my fourth major surgery in twelve months. I nearly died laughing, while poor Becca was distraught. She couldn't look her parents in the eye for weeks. I knew that camcorder was trouble the moment I saw it.

"I'm surprised you can watch this without cringing." I giggle.

"Don't even go there." Becca groans, covering her face with her hands. "You know, I don't think they even realize to this day that we saw that." She gives me a sympathetic look as she pours us both a drink. "So, what happened?" she asks. "Because you totally made it sound like Matt tried to set you up with Doctor Hottie."

"Yep," I say, nodding grimly. "Even worse than that, it was a dinner party. Couples hell and no escape."

"No way!" She giggles, her eyes growing wide. "I'm sorry, but this is gold, Loz. This even beats slouch on the couch night."

"Oh, it gets better. You know what he said to me? He's getting a good *vibe* from me that I'm a *buzz* to be around."

Becca clutches a hold of her stomach as she dissolves into

laughter, tears streaming down her cheeks. She shakes her head and puts her hand out as if saying she's sorry. Hell, even I'm smiling, because I can almost see the funny side of it now. *Almost...*

"He said that? Loz, I love him. If you're not going for it, then I sure as fuck am."

"Keep your panties on. Nobody loves anyone," I assure her.

"So, what did you do?" she asks.

I shrug helplessly. "What can you do when your brother tries to set you up with someone who's been elbow deep inside you before the first date? I panicked and ignored him."

"It's okay," Becca says. She takes my hand, locking hers around mine. "This feels like a much bigger deal than it has to be. You said yourself that he's only staying with your brother while he gets set up, right?"

"A few weeks," I tell her.

"So, this really is only a short-term problem, then," she reasons. "He's obviously not that close a friend, or you would've met him years ago."

"True," I say, nodding my head.

"So, once he leaves, you'll never have to see him again. Until then, just don't hang out at your brother's house." She shrugs. "Problem solved."

"You're right," I say, feeling better. "Just a few weeks and the problem solves itself."

"Exactly." Her eyes shine. "Now if you actually *wanted* to see how dirty that doctor—"

"Becca."

"I'm kidding." She giggles, winking at me.

I smile at my friend because, crude comments and all, she always manages to cheer me up.

"Thanks for coming over to calm me down."

"Anytime." She shrugs. "Besides, it's a great excuse to watch trashy movies that we really should've grown out of years ago."

I get up and put the movie in, then sink back down into my spot, resting my feet in Becca's lap.

"You know what I find really amusing?" She giggles as she rubs my feet. "You avoid situations that make you uncomfortable like the plague, yet you keep finding yourself submerged in them. It's kind of hysterical."

"And then there are people like you, who'll do anything and everything and never have to deal with any of the consequences, at all," I tease her. "You're like the female version of my brother."

She shakes her head ruefully.

"Speaking of which, how are he and Annie doing?"

"They're doing well, although she hates everything about being pregnant," I say with a grin.

Becca is silent for a moment. "Hey, does it make you jealous at all?"

Her voice is soft as she studies me. I shrug knowing that I can't lie to my best friend. As much as I deal with it because I have to, it's still a sensitive subject for me.

"Sometimes, it does..." I pause, considering how I'm feeling for a moment. "I don't know that *jealous* is the right word. Bittersweet, maybe? Most of the time, I'm genuinely happy for them, but every now and then, the selfish part of me comes out, and I get really angry at them for getting something I want so badly, so easily."

I reach up and wipe away a tear that I didn't even know had formed. Just when I think I've come to terms with not being able to have kids, something makes me see that I haven't.

"It's okay to be sad," Becca says, frowning at me. "Bottling it up isn't good for you. You can be happy for someone and sad for yourself at the same time, you know."

I shrug. "I know, but it's not going to change anything. Being upset that they get to have a baby doesn't mean that I can, so why bother being angry? It is what it is. Deal with it and move on."

She pushes my feet off her lap and climbs over to me, wrapping her arms around me.

"That's a very mature way of looking at it," she says, smooching me on the cheek. "You're the strongest person I know."

I smile at her.

I wish I felt that way.

BY THE TIME the movie's over, it's too late for Becca to go home, so I convince her to stay. We curl up in my bed talking about nothing until I can't keep my eyes open anymore. I roll over, asleep before I've even had a chance to properly snuggle into my pillow.

I wake up the next morning with Becca's arms draped around me. I giggle as I listen to her snoring sporadically in my ear because this isn't exactly what I had in mind when I said that I wanted someone in my life. I hold my breath and slither out from her arms, careful not to wake her, but I'm not careful enough, because she stirs, her eyes springing open. She looks around, dazed and still half asleep.

"What time is it?" she murmurs.

"Around eight. What time do you have to be at work?" I ask, knowing she works most Saturdays.

She shakes her head. Her eyes are sleepy.

"I'm off today. I've got all day tomorrow on set, so this is my day to relax."

Becca is an animal handler, so she's always on and off movie sets and TV shows that require pets. It's a pretty cool job, and she's met loads of famous people through it. I've even gone along with her once or twice. It's amazing to watch her at work because she's a natural when it comes to animals.

"Great, want to do something, then?" I ask, throwing my robe over my pajamas.

She shrugs. "Sure. What do you have in mind?"

"Anything that will make me forget about Luke Dillon sounds good," I say hopefully.

She laughs. "I'm sorry, but even his name is perfect."

I sigh because she's right. He sounds like a movie star.

"So, what do you want to do?" she asks. "Because I'm not fussed. Whatever floats your boat."

"Hey, would you mind if we take my neighbor somewhere?"

I feel bad with work starting next week that I might not have as much time for her because I can see how much our little day trips mean to her. Earlier this month, we went out for lunch and to see an anniversary screening of *Sabrina*. She had a great time, and to be honest, so did I.

"She spends so much time cooped up in that little apartment watching TV." I shake my head. "Some nights I swear I wake up at three in the morning to the sound of her abusing Canada's *Bachelor* from about three seasons ago."

Becca giggles. "This is your eighty-year-old neighbor, right?" she asks, her eyes sparkling.

I nod. "It's both hilarious and adorable to watch," I admit.

"I've got the perfect day for her, then." Becca grins.

I SHAKE my head and smile at Becca. "You're a legend, you know that?"

She nods, looking pretty proud of herself.

"Yeah, I hear that a lot. I mean, it's not *The Bachelor*, but it's the next best thing, right?"

I glance over at Iris, who is eagerly watching on the sidelines, shouting abuse at the director, while she watches the filming for *Date Me at Dinner*, a new show that's filming its first season at the studio where Becca works. I cringe when she starts offering two of the contestants some friendly advice on how to be less slutty.

"Maybe you should go over there and pitch a new concept to the director." I giggle to Becca. "Eighty and doing it."

Becca grimaces, covering her face with her hands as she laughs.

"Honestly, I'm not sure any man her age could handle her. My granny is eighty-one and a big day for her is finishing the crossword puzzle," Becca jokes. "Iris isn't exactly your ordinary eighty-year-old."

I laugh because I certainly don't need anyone to tell me that Iris is exceptional.

After the screening, we head out for lunch, but not before Becca receives a firm word from the director promising that she will never bring Iris back to the set again. They had to reshoot most of the scenes, which will cost them a small fortune. I feel terrible about it, but at the same time, I haven't seen Iris looking this happy since *Sabrina*.

We eat our sandwiches in a café not far from home. Becca and I listen to her tell stories of the men she used to date. Apparently, she was quite the little minx before she settled down and married Walter.

"Do you miss him?" I ask her.

I don't know much about him, other than he's been gone for nearly ten years.

"Of course, but when you get to my age, you miss every-thing. I miss being continent overnight," she admits, a rueful smile on her face.

Becca and I burst out laughing because it was such an unexpected comment.

"You didn't have any kids?" Becca asks. I give her a look, and she winces.

"I have a daughter, but she's too busy to find time for me. She's done quite well for herself, but that means she works long hours. She has a family of her own now. I understand how hard it is to find time to visit Mom."

I bite my tongue because I hate that she's making excuses for her daughter. I don't care how busy you are, you always make time for family.

It's been a long day, and once Iris is safely back in her apartment, Becca and I head back to mine. We walk inside. I head straight over to the couch and collapse in a heap.

"Thanks for today. I think I had as much fun as Iris did." I laugh. "Sit down," I order her, lifting my feet up to make room.

She shakes her head. "I'd love to, but I better get my ass in gear and get home. I have a few things to get ready for tomorrow."

"Okay. I'll call you later in the week, then."

I've no sooner walked her out when my phone rings. I fish it out of my pocket, wishing my jeans weren't so tight because the damn thing stops ringing as soon as I go to press answer. It was Matt, so I call him straight back. It's always in the back of my mind that Annie might have gone into labor or that something is wrong.

"Hey, it's me. Mind if I come up? I'm downstairs."

"Sure," I say, surprised. "I'll buzz you up."

I let him up and open the door, then I walk back into the kitchen to pour myself a glass of wine. I smile when I hear the door open just as I'm twisting the cap off the bottle.

"Want a glass of wine?" I call out.

"Make that two."

I laugh and prepare a glass of water, knowing Annie is in no condition to drink alcohol. I take a sip of my wine as I peer around the corner into the living room. I nearly choke when I see Luke—not Annie—standing next to Matt. Jesus, I was not expecting him. I cough and splutter for a few more minutes, wincing as my chest burns, until I'm finally able to take a breath without feeling like I'm going to die.

They both stand there, looking amused.

"Good thing I brought a doctor with me," Matt quips.

"Hilarious," I say, making a face at him. I slink back into the kitchen to both compose myself and pour their drinks, then I walk back into the living room.

"Thanks," Matt says, taking a glass. "I need to ask you a huge favor." He glances at Luke in a way that makes me really nervous.

"What?" I ask.

I hand Luke his drink, still distracted by what Matt could want. Whatever it is, it has to involve Luke, or why would he be here?

"You know how Annie's parents were coming over for a few

weeks? Well, it was supposed to be next month, but they apparently told us they changed their dates to *this* month."

"Okay..."

I sit down on the couch, feeling faint. I'm not sure what this has to do with me.

"Only they didn't," he continues. "Annie swears they didn't tell her, but she's been forgetting everything lately, so who knows—"

"Matt, just get to the damn point," I snap impatiently. "What are you trying to ask me?"

"I want to know if Luke can crash here for a few weeks," he blurts out.

"Here?"

My heart races. I can't think straight. I can't look at Luke. God, I can't do anything.

"You have no idea how much it would help us out," Matt says, his eyes pleading with me to say yes. I look away because I've always struggled to say no to him. "We'll never hear the end of it if Annie's parents have to stay in a hotel and you have a spare room right here, so I thought it wouldn't hurt to ask," he pleads. "And you said to me a few weeks back that you were thinking of renting out your room, right? This would save you the trouble. And I'm sure Luke would be happy to pay you."

"Definitely," Luke agrees. I jump, his deep, sexy voice startling me.

What do I say to that?

"Sure, you can stay here," I hear myself say. I smile tightly at Matt, but not Luke. No, I can't even bring myself to look at Luke at the moment.

"Really?" Relief floods Matt's face. "Thank you, Laura. You seriously just saved my marriage," he declares. He slaps Luke hard on the back, pushing him toward me. "Besides, I'm sure you'll love having Luke around. And having him here will be handy for you since he starts at Mercy next week too. Maybe you can carpool or something."

"Mercy?"

I whisper the word, the blood draining from my face. I feel sick, but I still can't work up the courage to look at him.

"Yes, Mercy," Matt says, eyeing me strangely. "Luke's a doctor too. I told you that, didn't I? I'm sure I did." He shakes his head. "Anyway, you two will have heaps to talk about while he's here."

"Maybe we can exchange patient horror stories," Luke suggests lightly.

His eyes gleam with amusement as they connect with mine. I glare at him, mortified he just said that and in front of my brother, no less. Not that Matt knows anything, but still...

"Oh yeah," Matt chuckles. He nods enthusiastically as he gets up and walks over to the kitchen to put his glass in the dishwasher. "Make sure you ask him about cubicle nine girl. It's a fucking classic."

My head snaps sideways as I glare accusingly at Luke.

"You told my brother about it?" I hiss.

"I had to tell *someone*," he protests. "I didn't know you were his goddamned sister."

Matt walks back, oblivious to the fact that he's interrupted our heated discussion. I don't even listen as he and Luke chatter because I just keep going over in my head that he's staying here. With me. For three weeks.

This is a bad, *bad* idea, but I can't figure out a way to get myself out of it.

There's no backing down from this in a way that isn't going to raise questions. Maybe what I need to do is be prepared for those questions regardless because eventually, this is going to backfire.

"Well, I guess I should get going, pregnant wife on the warpath and all," Matt says, clasping his hands together. "I figured it would be just easier for Luke to stay here from now on."

"What about his things?" I protest.

I follow Matt to the door and peer out, shaking my head when I see Luke's luggage.

"What? I knew you'd say yes. Thanks again for this," he says as he kisses me goodbye. "I owe you big time."

"It's fine," I say, smiling so wide I'm at risk of my face breaking.

I wait until he disappears down the hallway, then I walk back inside. I feel sick. On the outside, I'm all smiles, but inside, I'm freaking out like crazy. My heart races as I walk back into the living room to Luke. I meet his eyes for the first time since he got here.

"Look, I'm really sorry about this," he says.

He sounds genuine enough, but I'm waiting for the follow-up comment. When it doesn't come, I lower my guard a little.

"It's not your fault," I reply.

"No, but I can imagine how uncomfortable this is for you. He said you wouldn't have a problem with me staying, and I couldn't exactly tell him why you would," he says. "I always planned to go to a hotel as soon as he left here."

"Only you can't because he'll find out and he will want to know why." I frown at him, knowing my frustration is misplaced directed at him. None of this is his fault.

"So, I'll make something up." He's the voice of reason. "I really don't want to impose on you."

"It's fine." I sigh, even though I'm so tempted to take him up on that.

I know that if I do, it will come back to bite me on the ass. The moment the questions start, Matt will know because I can't lie for shit. And while it might not seem like that big a deal, I know I'll never hear the end of it from Matt if he found out I was cubicle nine girl.

"Besides, it's the perfect location for you since you're starting at Mercy and all."

"Okay, that looks much worse than it is." He winces and runs his hands through his hair. "God, it probably looks like I'm going all *Single White Female* on you, but I promise I'm not going to chop you up and wear you like a second skin," he jokes as he laughs. He winces when I react to his comment by crossing my arms over my chest. "Ouch. Tough crowd tonight."

I shake my head because he's right about one thing: I do have lots of questions. I don't think he's stalking me, but I can't turn around without him being there ready to invade some other part of my life. Is he going to be there next time I have lunch with Mom, too?

"I know how bad it looks, but I applied for that job way before I had any idea who you were." He sits down on the arm of the chair, his earnest expression making me believe him. "I heard back on the morning of the dinner party that my interview was successful."

"So why didn't you say anything then?" I ask.

"Firstly, would you have listened. Second, why would I? I didn't know that you worked there or that you were even a doctor so it would be an odd thing to work into the conversation. Why didn't you tell me you were a doctor when you came in the hospital?" My eyebrows shoot up. He flushes. "Came *into* the hospital," he corrects himself through gritted teeth.

Great, now I look like the unreasonable one.

"Okay. We'll call that a coincidence. So, what are you doing at Mercy, anyway?" I ask him.

"I'll be doing a surgical fellowship in a special cardiac program," he says. "You?"

"My third-year residency."

"It's a big hospital," he tries to reason with me. I raise my eyebrows. "Fine, it's actually pretty small, but you'll be all over the place, while I'll only be in the one, tiny area."

"I'll have a spare key ready for you tomorrow," I say stiffly. "I'll show you the spare room. Towels are in here." I open up the cupboard just inside the bathroom door, snatching down my lacy underwear, which is hanging from the shower rail. *I wish I'd tidied up.* He smothers a laugh. "Help yourself to whatever you find in the kitchen. If you don't mind, I might go to bed."

"Sure." He smiles at me, and I force one back, then turn on my heel and stalk down the hallway. "Laura?" I turn around. "Thanks for this. I appreciate it."

"You're welcome."

CHAPTER FIVE
LUKE

I WON'T CHOP you up and wear you like a second skin?

What the fuck was I thinking? No wonder she's avoiding me.

At least, I'm pretty sure that's what's going on because she's gone when I get up and never there when I'm home. It's Wednesday night, my fourth night here, and given our hectic schedules, it would be easy to believe that we're both just very busy, but considering our history, I think it's more than that. In all the long hours we've both been working, I've seen her twice at the hospital. The first time, she didn't even acknowledge me. The second time, she managed a tiny smile, so I guess that's progress. Still, I can't force her to like me after what happened, but I'm hoping it'll become less of an issue the more she gets to know me. *If* she gets to know me because, the way this is going, she's going to keep avoiding me until I leave.

It's a shame because I think I could really like her. She's

smart, witty, sexy, and the fact that she's not obsessed with her looks is a major turn-on for me. I want to put her at ease, but aside from not knowing how to do that, I'm so overwhelmed with work that I don't have time to worry about anything else. Hell, I don't even have time to breathe at the moment.

I've been looking forward to this fellowship for a long time, and I'm frustrated that it's taking me longer to settle into it than I thought it would. The hours are long, and I feel like I have no idea what I'm doing. I never realized how good I had it where I was, until now. I'm sure that once I get used to the workload, things will be better, but it's not just that I'm struggling with.

I've been on the kid's cardiac rotation all week, and it's really getting me down having to work with patients who have barely had time to live between their doctors' visits and lengthy hospital stays. I can't stand watching them suffer through something that might end up killing them anyway. Sickness is never easy, but at least you can almost justify it in someone who's eighty or ninety because they've lived a full life. They've done things and seen things that some of these kids haven't. They don't deserve this. I guess that's what makes it so satisfying when you do manage to help them. Knowing you've done something to improve their quality of life is what makes it all worthwhile.

Today has been a particularly rough day because I've been working alongside Professor Lincoln Lewin, one of the best children's cardiac specialists in the country and one of the reasons I wanted Mercy. Working with sick kids is hard enough, but when you throw in working with one of your professional idols—who also happens to be as intimidating as hell—it's a whole new set of pressures.

"Are you keeping up with me?" Lewin asks as we head toward our next patient—our last for today. "Because I've saved the best till last."

"I'm ready." I nod, as we stop outside a room.

"Ben Saunders," Lewin begins. "Eight years old. He's been in and out of the hospital for most of his life, thanks to numerous medical issues. They were being controlled by a regime of medications until last month when his heart started failing. He's on the waiting list for a transplant, but with his rare blood type, finding a match is proving difficult."

I nod and follow him into the room, already feeling sorry for this poor kid.

"Linc," the boy says, his face lighting up.

"Ben, my man. How's my best patient doing?" Lewin asks, ruffling his hair.

Ben nods and holds up an Xbox controller, a triumphant smile on his freckled face. He brushes his dark hair back into place and smiles a toothy grin, but behind that happy attitude is a very tired and sick little boy.

"Top score again. You wanna try and beat me again or are you too chicken?" he taunts.

I glance at Lewin, a small smile on my lips. *Again?* I can't picture Lincoln Lewin doing anything remotely fun. Lewin catches my look and winks.

"What?" He shrugs, a ghost of a smile on his lips. "I'm a natural. I kill it at Mission Corpse Three."

"Uh-huh." I grin.

While Lewin plays Mission Corpse Three, I run through Ben's care plan, checking his stats, his latest blood results, and the results of his recent scans. They're all indicating the same thing: that this transplant needs to happen soon, or it might be too late.

My heart pounds as I watch this little boy and Lewin argue about their technique for bringing down a particularly nasty zombie. I admire Lewin for being able to just sit there and focus on making this kid's day just a little bit brighter. I'm snapped out of my thoughts by Lewin slapping me on the back. He walks out with me close behind him.

"You okay?" Lewin asks.

I nod, forcing a smile. "Just sick kids, you know?"

"Sure. It does get easier. I mean, it's always hard, but you learn to internalize it." He glances at me. "Take a break now if you like, then we can finish up by going over the reports together."

"What will happen to Ben?" I ask suddenly. As if I even need to ask.

Lewin shrugs. "We hope like hell we find a donor soon."

I walk away, thinking about Ben and Lewin. I appreciate the break more than he knows. He could be riding me even harder and pushing me to break, like many of the specialists at his level do, but he's not. He's recognizing that I'm struggling, and he's giving me the chance to take a breath. Any apprehension I had about working with Lewin has long gone because now all I have left for this guy is admiration. If I can be half the doctor this guy is one day, I'll be happy.

I grab a coffee and something to eat from the cafeteria, and then I head up to the roof. I don't know why I thought that I would have more time moving into this fellowship program, compared to residency. I don't think I was expecting just how fast-paced and full-on this program was going to be. I don't regret it for a second, but it's a big adjustment.

I walk out onto the roof, breathing a sigh of relief when I see that I'm alone. I've been out here a few times, thanks to Lewin's pack-a-day addiction. Both times it was quiet, so it seemed like a good place to come and think. Looking around me, I lean over the edge of the building, gazing out over the city skyline while having a mouthful of my coffee. After a while, I sit down and lean against the barrier, closing my eyes. I feel like I need a day off to get my head around everything and maybe catch up on some sleep—not that I'd ever ask for it.

I sit there, just enjoying the silence for a moment, frowning when I hear the door open. I'm annoyed that my moment has been interrupted, but I probably should be getting back to work anyway. The handle turns, and I'm shocked to see Laura standing there. She steps out, stopping in her tracks when she sees me. Her grip on the door loosens until it slips out of her hands completely and slams shut. She jumps and flushes as she smiles at me.

"Sorry, I didn't know you were out here," she says.

"Obviously, or you wouldn't be here." I feel bad that she feels so uncomfortable around me still, even if it is amusing.

"I'm looking for Professor Lewin," she says, ignoring my comment. "Doctor Ballan needs a cardiac consult, and she said that I'd probably find him out here."

"Sorry to disappoint you," I say. "Just me."

She nods and turns around, yanking the door handle. She grabs it again, but nothing happens. She turns back to me, alarmed. I get the message and get to my feet, sauntering over to her. The handle turns freely in my hand. Too freely.

"It's broken."

I think back to the two other times I've been out here. Both times something was propping open the door. *Shit.* I wish I'd realized that earlier.

"Broken?" she repeats, alarm rising in her voice. "Well, can you *un* break it?"

"Not locked out here I can't."

I bang against the door, calling out, but my shouting goes unheard. Eventually, I give up and walk back over to the barrier and sit down.

"What are you doing?" she frowns.

"Nobody is going to hear us, so why waste the energy trying? We have to wait it out." I shrug. I'm not getting too worked up about it because someone will find us eventually.

"Where's your phone?" she asks.

I smirk. "In my locker. Right next to my pager. Where's yours?"

"Flat. And the first pager I was given kept going off randomly, so Ballan was going to chase up another one for me." She frowns at me. "Why are you even out here, anyway?"

"I'm having my dinner."

"There's a cafeteria for that, you know."

"So? I wanted some fresh air."

"Which is usually an indicator that something is wrong," she muses. "Are you coping okay with the workload? I hear it's a big change, moving into a fellowship program."

I look up at her and smirk. "I think I liked it better when you ignored me."

"Really? Well, that can be arranged," she retorts. She walks over and sits down next to me. "So... is everything okay?" she asks.

I sigh. She's not going to give up until I answer.

"Everything is fine. It's just adjusting to a new routine. New faces... I think the magnitude of what I'm doing is finally hitting me."

"Are you enjoying it?" she asks.

I glance at her. This is the most she's said to me the entire time I've known her. Well, with the exception of that first night, but I was the one asking the questions then.

"Hard. Especially when the patients are kids."

She nods. "Kids are always hard. So, why cardiac?"

I shrug. "I've always been fascinated with the heart, I guess. It seemed right that I focus on that as a specialty," I explain. "Besides, imagine all the pick-up lines I can use with that profession." She groans while I chuckle to myself. "So, what about you? Do you know what you plan to specialize in?"

"Fertility and reproductive science," she immediately replies. She glances at me, embarrassed.

"Really? That's impressive," I say, genuinely meaning it. "And very competitive. I'm assuming that's why you're here?"

She nods. "I thought it might be easier to get my foot into the fellowship program for next year if I was already working here. Only now that I'm here, I see that nearly everyone else apparently has the same idea," she says with a laugh.

"What is it about reproduction that interests you so much?" I ask. "Besides the obvious," I joke, winking at her. She glowers at me.

"Pretty much everything," she says. "Just being able to give people the chance to be parents that they might not have otherwise had..." She looks down at her hands and smiles. "It just feels pretty special to play God like that." She looks at me. "How long do you think we'll be out here?"

"Knowing how often Lewin goes through cigarettes, probably not that long."

She laughs at that.

"So, do you like it here? How does it compare to Orange...?" Her voice trails off at the mention of the hospital where we met. It's clearly sparked some bad memories because suddenly, she's closed off and glancing down at her hands again, but I pretend not to notice.

"I honestly like the fact that it's a smaller hospital. But, it's a completely different program which is much more intensive than I'm used to. And to be honest? Some of the surgeons here are real assholes."

"Only some?" she teases. "I can't think of a single one that doesn't intimidate me." She smiles and shakes her head.

"Everyone else is really nice, but I feel totally in over my head." She sighs and rubs her temples, before glancing my way again.

"Hey, can we start over? Like really start over? I'm sick of feeling like I want to pass out every time I see you."

"Sure. If we could do that, I'd love it," I say. I can't believe my luck. "I meant what I said about wanting us to be friends. Matt's right. We do have a lot in common, and I think if it wasn't for..." I pause. "If the dinner party was our first meeting, things would be different. I'd have totally asked you out."

"Really?" She looks over at me like she doesn't quite believe that.

"Are you kidding?" I laugh. "You're smart, intelligent, incredibly sexy... you're the whole package." I smile at her. "What happened isn't stopping me from asking you out. I don't care about that at all."

"Then what is it?"

"The fact that I'm pretty sure you'd say no," I admit. "Especially after I rocked up to your apartment like that."

"Which leads to my next question," she says. "What are your plans? I mean, don't take this the wrong way, but were you planning on finding somewhere to live or just move in with my brother permanently?"

I chuckle. "I have a lease on a place not far from yours. I just can't move in for another three weeks."

"Ah, that makes sense."

"Where did you go to college? Around here?" I ask her.

"Seattle. You?"

"I did both a business degree and then my pre-med at UCLA." I grin.

"Right, of course," she says with a laugh. "With Matt. I forgot about that." Her cheeks flush with color. "Are you from around here?" she asks.

I shake my head. "No, I'm originally from Manhattan, actually."

"Wow, that must be a big change, then. Living here?"

"Yes and no. It's more laid-back but just as busy."

"I've never been to New York," she says. "Aside from Seattle, I haven't really ventured too far from home at all. I've always wanted to travel, though."

"I spent a year in Europe," I offer. "It was great to get away from everything and just live."

She shakes her head. "As amazing as getting out there and seeing the world sounds, I don't think I could handle being away from my family for that long. That makes me a bit of a loser, doesn't it?"

"Not at all," I assure her. "A close family is a great thing to have and a valid reason not to travel."

Not that I would know what a close family is.

"I think I'd struggle to go overseas for a week, let alone a year..." She glances at me. "I'm sorry; I'm talking too much, aren't I?"

I laugh. "It's okay. I kind of like it. It sure beats when you won't talk to me."

She leans her head back against the bricks behind us and sighs.

"I'm really sorry about that. I was just so..." She shakes her head.

"There's no need to be embarrassed," I say softly. "Shit happens, you know."

"It's not even that I'm embarrassed about the incident itself. It's more that I can't stop thinking about the kind of person you must think I am when what you're thinking is probably so far from the truth."

"Well, let's test that out," I suggest. She stares at me, alarmed. I laugh. "I look at you and see a smart, incredibly sexy, woman, who's comfortable enough with herself to try new things."

"Whereas I feel like some awkward klutz who tries to be more than what she really is and gets stuck in a cycle of embarrassing situations."

I chuckle. "You're way too harsh on yourself."

She shrugs. "Maybe."

I glance at my watch again. Laura does too.

"I'm surprised we've been out here for this long without anyone looking for us," she mutters. "Have they even noticed that we're not there? I guess that says a lot about how much of an impact we're having if no one is even missing us."

"They probably think we just went home. It was so close to the end of the day," I reply. I'm sure Lewin probably thinks I just misunderstood what he was suggesting.

"Leaving without telling them is kind of unprofessional, isn't it?" She frowns. "I think I'd rather they don't think about me at all than think I'd do something like that."

I get up and walk over to the door again, trying to turn the handle, even though I know it's not going to open. I sigh and put my hands behind my head then wander over to the edge. I stare out over the skyline. Laura looks up at me, a wistful expression on her face. Her eyes dart to the sky, and she smiles.

"At least it's not raining."

"But now you've said that..." I tease.

She laughs until she puts her hands out in front of her. I close my eyes as I feel tiny drops of rain hitting me in the face.

"I blame you for this," I say.

"I'll accept that." She grins. "But really, who doesn't like standing in the rain, in the freezing cold, when you're locked out on a roof?"

I smile and watch her stare up at the sky, laughing as the drops of rain explode on her face. I have to admit, I like this happy, relaxed side of her.

Let's hope I see more of it.

CHAPTER SIX
LAURA

"SO MUCH FOR Lewin being out here every five minutes," I say, glancing at Luke. I shake my head as he winces.

"Yeah, I probably jinxed us when I said that too, huh?"

We've been sitting outside for close to two hours now, and not one person has come outside. If this is really the go-to place for all the smokers, then everyone on shift today must not smoke. My stomach grumbles loudly, reminding me that I missed breakfast again.

At least the rain has stopped.

The funny thing is I'm kind of glad to have been forced into a situation where I have to talk to Luke. He looks over at me, then offers me his half empty cup of coffee.

"It's probably cold, but it might settle your stomach for a little while," he offers.

I smile at him and take it, only because I have no idea how long we're going to be out here.

"You and Matt seem to get on well," he comments.

"We do. He's great, but you probably know that. So, you two went to college together?"

Luke nods. "Yeah. We were in the same dorm, before..." His voice trails off.

"Before what?" I ask tentatively, not sure whether what he was going to say is too personal.

"My father died suddenly during my senior year. I struggled and ended up taking a year off."

"Wow," I say, feeling a pang of sympathy for him. "That must've been hard.

"It was. I ended up traveling around the UK for the year just to try and put everything out of my mind, I guess."

"Did it work?"

"Avoiding reality?" He smiles. "Not really. It just delayed me having to face it, which I guess was all I really needed anyway."

I know that feeling well.

"I kind of went the opposite way when I lost my dad in my senior year of high school," I admit. "I didn't sleep for days at a time, and I put all of my energy and focus into studying. But it was the same sort of deal, I guess. That was my way of blocking everything out to avoid facing it. Matt handled it so much better. He was there for me and my mom."

"Then I guess your brother was right," he says softly. "We do have a lot in common."

"How old are you?" I ask him

"I'll be thirty next month. You?" he asks.

"Twenty-six. Almost twenty-seven."

"That's young to be doing your third-year residency," he observes.

I nod, a blush creeping across my cheeks.

"I did quite a few college credits in my final year of high school," I confess. "I wasn't lying when I said I put everything into studying."

"Impressive," he says with a small smile. "I lose someone, and I completely flake out. You lose someone and graduate college early."

I shrug. "It doesn't really mean anything other than that we cope with things differently. Did you have a good relationship with your father?" I ask.

He laughs. "God, no. Not at all. I think that's why it was so hard losing him because there was a lot of guilt and self-blame. Mainly because that's what my mother believed."

"I'm sure she wouldn't have really thought that," I say.

"Trust me. She wasn't shy about letting me know that she thought it was my fault," he says, his voice grim. "He was a lawyer. My whole entire family was lawyers, going back generations. His firm had been in the family for longer than anything else, and it ended with me."

"So, you becoming a doctor didn't go down too well, I'm guessing?"

"Didn't go down too well is an understatement." He chuckles. "They pretty much stopped talking to me once I began my pre-med."

I shake my head sadly. He smiles and nods.

"When my dad died, my mom told me not to bother coming to the funeral because I wouldn't be allowed inside. I thought she was bluffing until I arrived at the church and saw the muscle she'd hired. I guess that's what I get for going against my family's legacy." He pauses and reaches up to rub his eyes. "She said that I was selfish for choosing medicine and that I didn't appreciate all that they'd done for me."

"I can't imagine anyone not being proud of their kid for achieving what you need to achieve to be a successful doctor," I say with a frown.

He shrugs. "Families can be funny things. My point is, if you get on well with yours, then cherish that. Don't be ashamed of it."

ANOTHER HOUR PASSES and then another. Before long, it's dark, cold and I'm trying hard not to fall asleep. Luke motions for me to stop pacing and sit down again so I can snuggle closer to him. He shakes his head at my reaction, a smirk playing on his lips.

"I can promise you this is for warmth purposes only," he says. "You look like you're slowly freezing to death, and I thought preserving heat might be a better option than having you collapse on me from hypothermia." He smiles at me. "Not that I wouldn't enjoy giving you mouth-to-mouth."

I hide a smile as I glance down at my arms. I study the goose bumps that have sprung up and give in, even though the idea of mouth-to-mouth is pretty tempting. I sit down next to him, allowing him to wrap his arms around me. I'm still shivering, only now I'm not sure if it's having him so close to me or the fact that I'm so cold.

"I'm starting to think we might be out here all night."

He shakes his head. "No, security would have to check up here eventually."

I hope he's right. I glance up at him as he stares down at me. My heart races because his lips are so close to mine. Before I know what I'm doing, I'm inching myself forward, just enough so that his mouth is almost touching mine.

What the hell am I doing?

I jump back and look away. I'm embarrassed that I almost kissed him, but apparently, he's not. His fingers cradle my face as he gently turns me, so I'm facing him. My heart pounds as he stares into my eyes. I don't know what I want at this point because all I can focus on is his lips and how soft they look. I stretch my body out until my lips touch his.

As we kiss, the warmth of his mouth against mine sparks something inside me. My heart races as his fingers stroke my neck, just below my ear. I reach up and put my hand over his, holding it there, while his lips explore mine. He pulls away, his eyes staring into mine as he waits for me to react. For a moment, I don't know how I feel, but then, all the feelings of regret, begin to rush out.

I jump up and breath in deeply. I'm angry at myself for giving into some stupid moment that was only created because of the situation we're in. We never would've kissed if we weren't locked out here. If things felt messed up before, I'd just made them a whole lot messier.

"I'm sorry," I say. "That was my fault entirely. I shouldn't have done that."

Thankfully it's so dark that he can't see how red my face has gone.

"It was hardly all your fault," he says, getting to his feet. "I'm not sure if you noticed, but I was pretty into that kiss as well."

"Oh, I noticed," I say before I can stop myself.

He laughs, while my face goes even hotter. I reach up, inadvertently touching my lips which are still tingling from the feel of his mouth.

Before I can say anything else, the door springs open.

Sighing with relief, I brush past the surprised security guard, who is standing next to the door and I head down to the staffroom. Doctor Ballan has left for the day, so I send her a message, explaining what happened. Lucky for me, she's understanding and figured something had happened. She goes as far as blaming herself for not warning me about the door in the first place. Apparently, all the staff has been complaining about that door for a long time, and the response has always been to just not go out there.

As I stand outside the hospital, I don't know whether to risk going home or avoid it for as long as I can. What are the chances of me getting back there before him? I'm surprised that it's only eight o'clock, but I guess it's late enough that I can justify going to bed if I'm back first, considering the day I've had.

THE RELIEF I feel when I walk into my empty apartment is incredible. I quickly grab myself a drink and something to eat, bolting into my room when I hear the front door unlock. My heart pounds as I lean against the inside of my door, listening to the sound of him moving around inside the apartment. This is so childish. We're grown adults, and I'm hiding in my bedroom to avoid talking to him like a freaking adult? I shake my head then bang it softly against the wood. I feel so stupid. I shake my head and creep over to my bed and sprawl across it, then I reach for my phone to text Becca.

> *Me:* What are you up to?
> *Becca:* Not much. You?
> *Me:* Oh, you know, the usual. Hiding in my room to avoid talking to Luke—who, by the way, I just kissed.

Just as I expect, she calls me immediately. I smile as I answer because I feel like I'm fourteen again. Only I didn't even act like this when I was fourteen. My biggest crush back then was on one of my male nurses, Gabe.

"You kissed him?" I can tell by the tone of her voice she's smirking. "Hold up, did I miss the part where you were actually talking to him now?"

"It's a long story," I tell her. "We got locked outside on the roof together at work. I didn't have a choice but to talk to him. It turns out he's a nice guy."

"Fine, but kissing him?" Becca laughs. "And now you're hiding in your room like a twelve-year-old girl."

"No need to remind me of that. I know how childish I'm being." I huff.

"How about I come over?" she suggests. "Maybe having me there will ease the tension between you both? Have you eaten? I'll bring dinner if not."

"Okay, and yes, I've eaten," I agree. "See you soon."

I take a deep breath and then walk into the living room to wait for Becca like a grown-up. I push aside my anxieties when I see Luke sitting on the couch. He looks up from his spot on the couch just as I'm staring at those lips.

"Hey. I thought you must've gone to sleep early or something," he says.

He says "or something" like he knows I'm avoiding him.

"No, just calling my mom," I lie. *And now I feel bad that I haven't called Mom all week.* "I have a friend coming over," I add. Like I need his permission. He shrugs.

"Okay. If you want me to give you some space, I can go out somewhere."

My eyes widen. He thinks I'm inviting a guy over.

"No, not that kind of friend." I'm quick to correct him.

"The thought never entered my mind," he assures me.

"It's just Becca, the girl you met briefly at the hospital," I rush to explain.

I don't want to draw the conversation back to that night, but that's all having Becca here is going to do, anyway. Why did I think letting her come over was a good way to ease the tension? The only thing Becca is known for is making embarrassing situations worse. Becca causes tension; she doesn't ease it. Before I stress thinking about it anymore, she knocks on the door.

How much more awkward can she make this, anyway?

"Hey."

Becca flashes me a grin when I open the door. I cringe inwardly and brace myself for whatever is coming next. She walks in and waves Luke over. He looks amused as he stands up and saunters over to us.

"I think we just need to get all this out in the open." Becca looks back and forth between Luke and me. "You're embarrassed because of what happened, but you obviously like him, or you wouldn't have stuck your tongue down his throat. He likes you, too, or he wouldn't have let you." She shrugs. "There. Problem solved. Now, let's just all get over it, so you two can go and have dirty sex while I watch TV and pretend I can't hear the grunting."

I glare at Becca, ignoring Luke's soft chuckles. I can't even look at him as I grab her arm and steer her into the kitchen.

"What the hell was that?" I hiss.

"What? You invited me over here to ease the tension—"

"No, you invited yourself over here," I correct her. I shake my head and laugh.

"Okay, so that may be true, but I started thinking about how all I'm doing is enabling your avoidant behavior by not helping you address it. Is that really helping you? Am I being a real friend by doing that?"

"Now is not the time for you to go all psychiatrist on me," I growl at her. "You might as well just leave now because being alone with him can't be any worse than that."

"Okay."

She shrugs, her eyes sparkling as she hugs me and then walks out the door, while I gape after her. I walk back into the living room, feeling dazed by the whirlwind that is Becca. Luke frowns at me, confused.

"Hey, where's your friend?"

"She left," I say.

He steps closer to me, a smile creeping onto his face.

"So, is what she said true? That you like me?"

He studies my face as I nod.

"I'm surprised," he says. "The way you panicked after what happened on the roof..." He smiles at me and reaches for my hand. I don't pull away because his touch feels so good against mine. "I guess you asking Becca over here shows me that you're willing to face things head on and deal with them. I admire that."

"Yep, that was my plan all along." I nod, swallowing a laugh. "No point letting things get more awkward, right?"

"She seems like a good friend. You're lucky to have someone like her in your corner."

"Is she paying you to tell me that?" I grin. "No, she's great. I keep her around for a reason."

"So, where to from here, then?" he asks. He's so close to me that all I'd need to do is tilt forward and my mouth would be on his.

It's so very tempting...

"I guess we move on. There's no point complicating things, right?" I hear myself saying. "You're my brother's friend, and we work at the same hospital. Starting something with you would be silly."

The only thing silly is the stupid excuses that are coming out of my mouth. As if Matt would even care if we hooked up. He'd probably throw us a party.

"Very silly," he agrees, his eyes staring at my lips.

I swallow, my heart pounding then I laugh randomly like I do when I'm nervous. I run my hand through my hair, feeling hot all of a sudden.

"I've got an early start tomorrow." I can barely get the words out.

"Then I guess you'd better go to bed," he murmurs, his gaze rolling down my body.

I nod and back up, then I turn around and quickly rush off. I can feel his eyes on me as I all but run down the hallway to escape to my room. I close the door with a thud and slowly peel off my clothes. Climbing into bed, I stare at the ceiling. There's no way in hell I'm going to be able to sleep, but I close my eyes and at least try.

If only so I stop thinking about that kiss.

CHAPTER SEVEN
LUKE

SORRY, *I'm out again. Help yourself to whatever is in the fridge.*

Don't expect me home till late ;) L x

I frown as I reread the note she left for me on the kitchen counter. Even though she says she's not, I'm sure she's avoiding me. Matt said one of the things I'd like about living here is that she's very laid-back and a homebody. Only I see the opposite because she's never here. She's barely been home five minutes since I moved in. Don't get me wrong, I don't mind if she's out every night. Good for her, if that's what she wants. I just don't want to be the reason behind it. I meant it when I said I didn't want to upset her life.

I glance over at the door when someone knocks. I know it's Matt because he texted me a few minutes ago and said he was coming over. I open the door and nod at him, then walk back to the couch, throwing myself down. He follows me and falls into one of the armchairs, then we stare at the TV in silence. Around ten minutes later, he glances around.

"Hey, where's Laura?"

I laugh. He's just realized she's not here?

"She's gone out."

"Out?" Matt says with an incredulous snort.

"Out. I'm actually surprised you made it sound like she never leaves the house, considering she's been out nearly every night since I got here."

"Laura?" he says nearly choking on the word. "My sister? No fucking way. She's like allergic to fun and socializing. If she went any farther than next door, I'd be shocked."

"What's next door?" I ask suspiciously. Is there some hot guy living next door that I didn't know about? Why does that thought make me feel so tense?

"She's made it her mission to befriend her neighbor, who is like a hundred years old."

I smile because I can totally see her doing that.

"I think she's avoiding me," I finally say.

"Why would she do that?" Matt asks, confused. "Unless she's got a reason to want to avoid you." He smirks and nods at me.

I shake my head. "No, nothing like that. Want a drink?" I ask, pulling myself to my feet.

His phone buzzes before he can answer. He frowns and shakes his head as he examines it, then he gets up with a sigh.

"No, I have to go. Annie is freaking out about her parents

coming in, and apparently, me being over here, relaxing, isn't going down too well."

"Okay... so, did you come over for an actual reason?" I ask him with a chuckle, following him to the door.

He shakes his head as he walks out.

"I've got a nearly full-term, pregnant wife at home, stressing about the impending arrival of her parents, who she hates, and who are staying with us for the next three weeks. Is that not reason enough?"

Laughing, I shut the door. Point taken. A few seconds later, I hear Laura's laughter filter through the wall. Matt was right. So why did she make it sound like she was going out on some hot date? Was that just for my benefit? I lean against the door thoughtfully. What if me being here is making her feel so uncomfortable that she doesn't want to be home? Maybe I need to even the playing field somehow.

I smile because I know the perfect way to do it.

———

I GLANCE AT MY PHONE, an unfamiliar feeling of panic rising in my stomach. Half an hour ago, this was the best idea in the world. But now? Not so much. The doubts are beginning to creep in. This is never going to work. What I need to do is just sit down with her and have a real conversation. I nod to myself, all but decided to abandon this plan, but just as I'm getting up, the door swings open. I stand up, my eyes darting to the door in horror as Matt walks in.

"Hey, what the hell does this note on the door mean..."

He stops mid-sentence when he sees me standing there, ass naked and in full frontal glory. He laughs and throws his arms over his eyes to shield himself from the beauty that is me.

"Jesus, fuck, man. Put that thing away."

Shit.

My heart pounds as my hands shoot down to cover my manhood, while I try and cling to the shred of dignity I have left.

"What the hell are you doing here?" I snap, glaring at Matt.

"I forgot my phone," he says. He saunters over to the couch and rummages between the cushions my bare ass was covering only seconds earlier. He holds up his phone for me to see. "The question is what are you doing?" he asks, crossing his arms over his chest. "Would you like to explain why your standing naked in my sister's living room?"

I glare at him. This whole confrontation would be much more intimidating if he didn't have the biggest smirk on his face.

"I thought you were Laura," I mutter, shaking my head. Matt's eyes widen as he lets out a laugh. "Don't worry, there's nothing going on."

"Well, that kind of makes it worse, you know."

As if things couldn't get worse, I look up just as Laura walks through the door. She stops in her tracks, her eyes darting from Matt to me. She blinks, her expression confused.

"Uh, what the hell is going on?" Her gaze falls back to me. "Why are you naked?"

Matt chuckles to himself as he saunters over to the door.

"I think that's my cue to leave. Have fun," he calls out.

He closes the door behind him, then opens it long enough to slap the note back on the door. Laura stares at me, her arms firmly crossed over her chest. Her eyes unwillingly slide down to what my hands are covering. I laugh, because what else can I do? This isn't quite going like I expected.

"The plan was so much better in my head."

"What plan?" she says with a frown.

"I thought you were avoiding me because of what happened, so I figured I'd even things out and make it less awkward for you."

"What are you talking about?" she says, shaking her head.

"I've seen yours, so you see mine."

She stares at me for a moment and then begins to laugh, to the point where she's doubled over she's laughing so hard. She walks over to the door, snatches the note off it, then giggles some more.

"So, my brother just walked in on you, naked on my couch?" She giggles.

I nod sheepishly. She shakes her head as she walks slowly toward me.

"I haven't been ignoring you," she says softly. "I've just been so busy with work and everything and trying to work out how I feel about you..." She makes a face. "Well, I wasn't avoiding you because of that."

"You weren't?" I swallow. "Well, now I feel like an even bigger dick."

Her eyes dart downward, and she smirks. She stares at me so intently that I'm left feeling very vulnerable and exposed. Which is probably how she felt, lying there in the hospital with me—only hers was a thousand times worse because I don't have a dildo stuck up my ass.

She raises her eyebrows and shrugs as though she's waiting for something.

"What?" I ask, frowning at her.

"Well, to even things out, as you put it, you're going to have to move your hands."

I laugh and then slowly lift my hands, placing them behind my head. My eyes don't leave hers as I wait for her reaction. She smiles, raising her eyebrows ever so slightly. Then she lifts her gaze to meet mine. I'm not sure if she's impressed or under-whelmed.

"So?"

"So, what?" she asks.

"You can't just leave me hanging." I cringe at my choice of words.

She smiles at me. "I'm waiting for you to kiss me."

That's all the encouragement I need. I step forward and place my hands on either side of her face, guiding her mouth up to mine. My heart races as my lips massage hers because it's every bit as amazing as the first time. She smiles at me as I stroke the hair away from her eyes. I groan as her fingers trail down my thighs because for just a second, I'd forgotten that I was naked.

"I think we need to even this up a little more." I begin

tugging at her shirt.

"Really?" she raises her eyebrows. "Because I kind of like having this power over you. What is it that you want?" she asks as she toys with the top button on her shirt. "This undone?"

"Preferably on the floor, along with the rest of what you're wearing." I swallow as she opens it and moves onto the next but then reconsiders.

"No, I think you need to work for this a little more," she says, her blue eyes narrowing slightly.

I laugh. What the hell does that mean?

"And how am I supposed to work for it?" I ask.

She grins and sits down in the armchair behind her. I laugh as she makes herself comfortable and then nods at me.

"What exactly am I expected to do here?" I ask her.

"Dance," she orders.

I shake my head. She can't be serious!

"I don't recall any dancing occurring in that ER room," I remind her.

"Oh, I don't know, some of those orgasms had some pretty good hip movement to them," she jokes. "You should be grateful I'm not recording this and uploading it to YouTube."

I chuckle and place my hands behind my head, rocking my hips back and forth while she stifles a giggle. I edge closer to her, turning around so I can grind my ass against her lap when I'm close enough for contact.

"I hope you're enjoying this," I say with a smirk as I move back to the middle of the living room to continue my show for her. "Because this is the last time you're ever going to see me dance."

"Oh, come here, you pussy." She laughs.

She reaches out and takes my hand, pulling me onto her lap. I have to admit, straddling a woman as she sits in an armchair is as difficult and awkward as it sounds. I get to my feet. She laughs as I grab her by the hand and pull her into my arms.

"Are you done now?" I ask her.

She stares at me, her eyes filled with anticipation, then she slowly shakes her head.

"I haven't even gotten started yet," she whispers.

Growling, I lift her into my arms, cupping my hands firmly against her ass as I carry her down to her room. She laughs, holding onto me for dear life as I toss us both on the bed. I lie down and drag her over, so she's on top of me. She gasps as I rip open her shirt and roll it down her arms.

"That's for teasing me," I say.

She rocks against my erection, her hands rolling over my stomach. I shudder as she wraps her fingers firmly around my shaft, sliding her fist along my length.

"Holy fucking Christ," I bite out.

She smiles, her expression satisfied, like she's just realized she's in complete control—that is, until two seconds later when I roll her over. I cup her chin and press my mouth against hers, the taste of her lips incredible. I run my hand down over her body, bunching her skirt up around her waist. She jumps when my fingers creep over her lace panties. I pull back enough so I can study her face.

"So wet." I push aside the damp fabric and feel her inside. "And very fucking sweet."

She lifts her hips as I roll her panties down over her thighs and toss them aside. Then I settle myself between her legs, pushing her breasts out from the constraint of her bra. I suck hard on her nipple while she writhes beneath me, her hands clutching my head. She lifts my head, her mouth finding mine as my erection stabs at her thigh.

"You have no idea how much I've wanted this," I profess.

I'm so hard for her, I'm throbbing. It's taking all my resolve not to just thrust myself inside her, but not yet. She laughs as I kiss my way down her body. When I get to her skirt, I unzip the back and wrestle it off her.

"That was a workout in itself." I grin.

"Just be thankful I'm not in my jeans, or you'd have no hope," she retorts.

All she wears is a black bra that's made its way down to her waist. She looks down at it and smiles, then reaches behind her back.

"There," I say as she tosses it aside. "The playing field's even."

She pauses thoughtfully. "Well, there's one thing left to make it even," she says.

My eyes widen. "Just so we're clear, you're not penetrating me with anything," I respond, slithering my way back up to her face. She laughs as I snake my hand around the back of her neck and lift her to my lips. "Do you have a condom, by any chance?" I ask.

She reaches over to her nightstand and fumbles in the drawer. Her face goes red.

"You, uh, might want to check that it hasn't expired."

I laugh and check the package, then tear it open with my teeth, rolling it onto my cock. Then I kiss her, my mouth exploring hers as she wraps her legs around my waist.

"Let me know if I hurt you," I whisper, sliding myself inside her.

"You won't," she assures me. "I'm resilient, remember?"

She moans, lifting her hips off the bed, so they're pressed against me as I push myself inside her. My grip on her waist tightens as her movements push me deeper, her pussy clinging to me.

"Fuck, you feel good," I pant, growling the words out.

I kiss her neck, my lips savoring her soft skin as I slide my shaft in and out of her wetness, her thighs clenching around me.

"Oh, Luke," she yelps. I growl as she touches her breasts, tilting back her neck as I thrust into her tight, wet pussy. The sight of her playing with herself like that is driving me crazy, to the point where I can feel the throbbing in my cock begin to ache.

"Yes," I hiss. I pump inside her, faster and harder until I come. "I'm coming," I choke out, kissing her roughly on the mouth. She wraps her arms around my neck, her skin warm and sticky, as her lips explore mine.

Breathing heavy, I pull out, then roll onto my side, wrapping my arms around her. She smiles as I kiss her neck, both of us too exhausted to speak. Our hearts thud loudly, almost in sync, as we come down from our high. She turns to face me, her bright eyes shining as they study mine.

"Okay." She leans in for another kiss, this one soft and tender. "Now I think we're almost even."

"Almost?" I repeat with a chuckle.

She nods.

"I just need to hear one more time how it felt when my brother walked in on you."

CHAPTER EIGHT
LAURA

YAWNING, I roll over, smiling when I see Luke lying next to me. I watch him for a moment, my eyes traveling down to the way the sheet rises to accommodate his obvious erection. I smirk and reach over, running my finger gently over the outline of his cock. I bite my lip because the only thing better than waking up with him next to me, is waking up to him like this.

These last few days have been a whirlwind of work, mind-blowing sex, and one sneaky evening in the supply closet where we had mind-blowing sex at work. I have to pinch myself to make sure I'm not dreaming because this kind of thing doesn't happen to me. I squeal as he rolls me on top of him, his actions scaring the fuck out of me.

"You could have warned me you were awake."

"And where would be the fun in that?"

He smirks and cups my ass, pressing me against his erection. I push my hair out of the way as it falls over his face. He laughs and presses his mouth onto mine.

"So, do you always stroke people's cocks when they're sleeping?"

I flush. "Only when they're in bed next to me. Besides, you obviously weren't sleeping. Or complaining."

He grins and nudges my leg over, which lines his dick up with my entrance. I laugh because now I really feel bad, considering I'm already running late.

"I think I may have just started something I don't have time to finish." I giggle at the expression on his face. I do genuinely feel bad about it. "I'm sorry. I didn't realize it was so late," I apologize.

"Are you fucking kidding me?" I lose my breath as his hands grab hold of my ass. He pushes me forward and drives himself into me. "You're lucky I can work fast."

"I'm not sure that's anything to brag about."

I smile and lift myself off him. I ignore his protests and wrap my fingers around his cock, forming a tight fist. That shuts him up pretty fast. He watches me as I slowly rub my fingers along his shaft, then I crawl to the end of the mattress, my knees resting between his legs.

"Well this took an unexpected turn."

"Oh, before I forget," I say, stopping for a moment, "is dinner on Friday night at Matt's place okay?"

Luke glares at me. "For the love of God, you're asking me this now? It's fine, whatever, but text me this later, or something. Please."

"Right. Sorry," I reply.

I smirk as I take him in my mouth, running my tongue around the tip of his dick. He exhales and settles back onto the pillows, while I run my lips along his shaft. He's so big that I struggle to fit him all in, but I try my best, getting myself into a rhythm of rocking back and forth. I take his hand and put it on the back of my head, wrapping his fingers around my hair. He groans, taking the hint as he anchors down, pushing his cock hard my down my throat.

"Harder." He grunts as I slide my mouth from his tip to his balls, using one hand to massage them while my other hand grips his shaft.

"Look at me."

I slide my hand up and down his length and curl my tongue around his tip, staring him straight in the eyes as I do it. Knowing he's watching me is a huge turn-on, so I suck harder and faster, rolling my tongue along his thick cock. His grip on my hair tightens as he fucks my mouth harder. I control my gag reflex as he presses my face against him, his body convulsing as he releases. I whimper as his warm liquid coats my throat, but I swallow and keep sucking, and work his shaft with my fist until he physically pushes me away. Panting slightly, I smirk at him. He shakes his head, looking dazed.

"Come here," he beckons.

He grabs my hand, pulling me into his arms. He kisses me. The fact that he's not fazed that he can probably taste himself on me is turning me on something crazy. I kneel above him, one leg on either side and shake my head when he tries to pull me on top of him.

"I'd love to, but I'm *really* running late now."

As much as I'd love to lie in bed all day with him, I have to get to work. It's all fine for him; he doesn't start for another few hours.

"Okay," he relents with a shrug, the gleam in his eye unavoidable. "And here I was getting ready to repay the favor."

I swallow, my throat suddenly dry as he trails his finger along my pussy. I waiver, only for a second, because holy shit that feels good.

"Stop teasing me." I frown.

"So, what you're saying is, you can give it but not take it?" I groan, my legs buckling as he slides a finger inside me. "Though I have to admit, you're taking this quite nicely."

I swat his hand away, glaring at him. He laughs and takes hold of my hands, lowering me down onto his stomach so he can kiss me. I pry myself away while I can and climb off the bed. I stalk into the bathroom, ignoring both the sounds of his laughter and the aching between my legs.

"I told you I'd be quick," he calls out to me.

I CLOSE the door to the supply closet and lean my head against it, a smile on my face. I've been in the emergency department for most of my shift, and I love it. Working in here on a Saturday is such a rush. It's been nonstop since I started, and this is the first moment I've had to even think straight. I gather up the dressings I came into the supply closet for in the first place and then walk back to my patient.

"There you go. Just keep an eye on it and come back if you notice any swelling or redness," I say to the young woman when I've wrapped her arm up. The gaping wound had needed several stitches, but it had been nothing in comparison to the bus crash and building explosion we'd had to deal with today.

I walk over to wash my hands. I'm disappointed that my shift is almost over, but considering how exhausted I am, it's probably a good thing. As I dry my hands, my ears prick up when I hear Marina's name mentioned. I glance next to me where two doctors I recognize as residents, are talking. I catch enough of their conversation to figure out that my little session with Luke this morning caused me to miss out on a pretty major announcement. They walk over to the nurses' station, and I casually follow them, pretending to fill out some paperwork. I listen to them talk, trying to work up the courage to join in and find out more details.

"What research project?" I ask, jumping into the conversation.

The girl smiles at me. "Marina announced it this morning at the meeting. She's choosing a third-year resident to take part in some special fertility research project." She sighs, a dreamy expression on her face. "The winner gets to live in Switzerland for a few months. I'll change my specialty for that," she jokes.

A shiver of excitement passes through me. I don't care if the project is based in Switzerland or Antarctica, the idea of working with Marina on anything is incredible.

THE REST OF MY SHIFT, all I can think about is that project. I need to get my hands on one of those applications, but I'm not sure how to do that without admitting that I missed the meeting. I'm annoyed at myself for getting distracted with Luke, because even when I went down on him, I knew I was going to be late. *Typical.* The one time I'm late, of course, something like this would happen.

I finish the last of my paperwork and then walk back over to the staffroom. I go the long way, which conveniently takes me past Marina's office. I panic when I see her sitting in there, because I wasn't actually expecting to run into her. *What were you expecting?* I inwardly chastise myself and shake my head. I didn't know, but I've never seen her in her office and that first week, I made it a point to come this way all the time. She looks up and raises her eyebrows expectantly at me.

She must think I'm stupid, the way I'm just standing there, staring at her.

"Can I help you?"

Before I know it, I'm walking inside and closing the door behind me. I stand in front of my idol, twitching my thumbs like an idiot, unable to speak. What am I supposed to say? How every paper she's written, I've pored over until it was imprinted in my mind? Or how every study she's conducted, I followed the progress obsessively, to the point where I felt like I was right there with her?

Yeah. Make yourself totally sound like a stalker. Way to go, Loz.

Talk about making a bad impression. This is the first time I've spoken to her—because I'm yet to get a word out—and I'm making a fool of myself. I swallow and contemplate walking out, because this is such a bad idea.

"What can I help you with?" she gently presses.

"Right, I... I just wanted to find out how I apply for the research project you're offering." I squeak the words out as they stick in my throat.

"Are you a third year?" she asks. I nod. She frowns at me. "I don't think I've seen you before. Were you at the meeting this morning?"

"No," I reveal and close my eyes, realizing how weak this sounds. "Every single shift I've been here earlier than I needed to be. Except for today, when I slept through my alarm."

It's close enough to the truth. I'm not about to admit to the part where I spared enough time to suck Luke's cock. She stares at me for the longest moment of my life, while I curse myself for not inventing a family emergency or something.

"At least you're honest." She finally chuckles. "I admire that. Most people would have invented an emergency."

She reaches into her drawer and pulls out a form, handing it to me.

"It's all pretty straightforward. The thing I want you to

focus on the most is that last question. Convince me why I should choose you for this project."

I nod and stare down at the application, my heart racing. This could set me up. This kind of thing on my résumé would put me ahead of everyone else for that fellowship next year. But it's more than that. The idea of working alongside someone who has made such a difference in the world of fertility is just too incredible to believe.

"Thank you."

I turn around and start walking out, still staring at the papers in my hands.

"What did you say your name was?"

My heart skips a beat as I turn around. I smile at her.

"Laura."

"Well, good luck, Laura," she says.

I'M STILL THINKING about the project when I leave the hospital. I walk out to my car and unlock the door, sliding into the seat. My heart races as I reach into my bag and pull out the application. I read through, right to that last question. It's a thousand-word, essay question, asking why I want to specialize in fertility.

Wow, that is such an open-ended question.

I stare at the words, not sure how to approach it. I could keep my response professional, or I could try and entice an emotional reaction from her, by going into the more personal reasons as to why I want this. But I want to win this because she thinks I deserve it, not because she feels sorry for me.

I put the application back in my bag and click in my seatbelt. Just as I'm turning the key, my phone rings. It's Becca.

"Yo. Remember me?"

"Becs, I'm sorry." I wince, because there's no denying it. I've been a bad friend. "Work has been flat out and then—"

"When you're done with that, you've been flat out under Luke?"

I can't help but laugh with her as she chuckles at her own joke.

"God, I'm hilarious. What are you doing tonight? Want to catch up over dinner?"

"Would tomorrow night work for you instead?"

Tonight is one of the few nights where both Luke and I are going to be home at a respectable hour, so I wanted to make the most of it—especially being that it's a Saturday.

"Sure. Come over here if you like. I finish at four, so any time after that."

"Great, I'll see you then."

I hang up and text Luke. A smile creeps onto my face at the idea of spending time with him.

> **Me:** *What time are you finishing?*
>
> **Luke:** *Seven. Why?*
>
> **Me:** *I figured it it's about time you took me out on a date. You know, impressed me, that kind of thing. Make me put out.*

> **Luke:** *It's a little late for that isn't it? But seriously, I don't impress you? Is there an emoji for a broken heart? I'll fix this. Leave it with me. Be ready at eight. I'm going all out, baby. I'll text you when I want you to come downstairs.*

I bite my lip and smile. He amazes me every day, and I'm pretty sure he knew it. I was just sick of our relationship being sex and smiling at each other at work. I know it comes with the territory of having the kind of jobs we have, but I still want more. I want everything.

I head home, driving past Matt and Annie's on the way. When I see their car, I pull in behind it and get out. Annie waddles to the door when I knock. She smiles and waves me inside.

"Oh, thank God. Get in here and take my mind off this monster," she complains. "And I don't mean the child. Your brother..." she shakes her head and sighs. "You can settle the argument."

"What argument?" I giggle, walking inside.

"Down the hall, in the nursery. Go. You'll see. He says I'm insensitive, but tell me that thing isn't hideous."

"That thing I spent the last three weeks creating as a surprise for you," Matt hollers from the nursery.

"Yeah, well you shouldn't have," she roars back.

I walk into the nursery, not sure what I'm going to find. I stop in my tracks and stare at the wooden crib that Matt is proudly standing in front of. Although crib is a generous term for this thing.

"See? Go and tell Annie how great this is. Tell her that she should be happy that she has a husband who actually wants to do shit around the house," he rebukes, loudly.

"I would be, if that husband could actually do shit," she calls back.

I cover my hand over my face and stifle a giggle. Matt looks hurt.

"Seriously? You're on her side?"

"I'm, uh, just worried this might be violating a dozen or so safety regulations, that's all. You know, they have that kind of thing for newborns," I point out. "They try and keep them alive these days."

I step forward and touch the side rail, jumping back when it crashes to the ground. I giggle, trying not to lose my shit in front of poor Matt, but it's no use. I dissolve into a fit of laughter that is so intense I'm at risk of wetting myself.

"Well, it's obviously not finished yet," Matt grumbles. "I thought it would be really cool to make the crib. Remember our crib? Dad made that. There was no worrying about safety regulations then and we survived," he gripes. "And it lasted a long time, too."

"That's true, but maybe Dad had slightly better handyman skills than you do?" I suggest gently.

Annie wanders into the room. She wraps her arms around Matt's neck and smiles at him while she strokes the back of his head. "You know I love you, but there's no way in hell my child is going near that death trap," she says in her sweetest voice.

"Fine," he sighs, giving up. "We will go and buy one tomorrow, then."

He tosses his hammer on the floor and stalks out. Annie rolls her eyes at me as we follow him down to the living room. I sit down, while Matt makes coffee.

"Decaf?" he calls out.

"Are you kidding me? What's the point if you take the caffeine out?" I retort. "It's like sugar-free chocolate. It defeats the purpose," I protest.

"Okay, well you're the one who's going to be awake all night."

"I'm up all night anyway," I say. "At least now I'll have a reason."

"So, how are things with Luke?" Annie asks with a smile. She sits down next to me.

"Good, actually," I say, smiling. "He's taking me out tonight."

"Well, that explains it."

"What do you mean?" I ask Matt. I don't understand his cryptic comment.

"Oh, nothing." He smiles, making sure I know it is, in fact, something.

"Matt," I say in my sternest voice.

"No." He shakes his head adamantly. "I refuse to ruin Luke's surprise. You'll find out."

I shake my head. Sometimes I hate my brother.

I GO home and have a quick shower and then get ready. I choose a short black dress with lace trim that hugs my waist. I style my hair, but let it hang down, because I know Luke likes it like that. I glance at my watch and frown. I thought it was seven when I left Matt's, but it must have been six. Which means I've got more time up my sleeve than I thought, so I head next door to check on Iris.

"Hello?" I call out, banging on her door.

"Hold on, to your panties. I'm going as fast as I can."

I smile and listen to her ranting. The door opens. Iris frowns at me as she looks me up and down.

"And why are you all tarted up?"

I shake my head and laugh. "No reason, I'm just going out with a friend."

"A friend huh?" She narrows her eyes. "Male or female?"

"Male, thanks, Grandma," I tease her as I follow her into the living room. I sit down, keeping an eye on my phone so I don't miss Luke's text.

"Tea?" she asks. I shake my head.

"No, it's okay. I don't have that long. I just wanted to see how you are."

"You mean you wanted to make sure I wasn't decomposing on the floor?" she replies, frowning at me. I laugh and shake my head, because that wasn't how I would've phrased it, but I couldn't deny there was an element of that.

"Not at all, but it's good to see that you're still breathing."

No sooner than Iris turns on her TV, Luke texts me.

> **Luke:** *Okay, come downstairs when you're
> ready.*

"I've got to go," I say apologetically as I stand up. "I'll try and come over tomorrow, okay? You stay there, I'll see myself out."

"All right. Well, have fun, I guess," she says. "If the night ends up with you crying in the bathroom, you're always welcome back here to watch the bachelor with me," she calls out.

"Thanks," I say.

As tempting as that sounds, I'm confident Luke can handle this.

I EXAMINE my reflection in the mirrored wall of the elevator and then walk out onto the ground floor. I walk outside the complex to find Luke standing on the sidewalk, dressed up in a tuxedo. I smile at him, my heart pounding. He looks hot.

"Hey." He smiles at me as I walk closer to him.

"Hey," I reply, taking him by the hand. I suddenly feel all shy. "I feel underdressed," I joke.

He shakes his head. "No, you look absolutely stunning," he compliments.

"You do scrub up pretty well."

I laugh. Is that Matt?

Luke chuckles and steps aside to reveal a pedicab, being chauffeured by none other than Matt. He looks less than impressed in his shorts and collared shirt, complete with a bow tie. I crack up laughing. He scowls at me.

"What the hell are you doing?" I say, giggling.

"Apparently this is payback for a bet I lost nearly eight years ago," he whines. He glares at Luke, who can't wipe the smile off his face. "Just get in and let's get this over with."

I'm still laughing as Luke helps me up into the cart. I don't even want to know what the bet was. Luke leans forward and slaps Matt across the ass. Matt turns around and glares at him. I shake my head, because this is gold.

"Speed up a bit, please. We don't have all night."

DINNER TURNS out to be picnic in the park, complete with all my favorite foods.

"How did you know I like this?" I say picking up a little tub of olive and mint dip that I've only ever found in one grocers all the way over on the other side of the city.

"How do you reckon he knew?" Matt calls out from his perch across the way.

He has stationed himself on the other side of the park, leaning up against his pedicab. I giggle and shake my head, nearly losing it all over again. I glance at Luke, who looks pretty impressed with himself.

"This is great," I say. "Thank you." I lean back against him, but not before grabbing another handful of strawberries to dip in the chocolate sauce.

"Are you sure it's fancy enough?" he teases.

"I didn't want fancy, I just wanted something more than sex. As amazing as that is."

"Gross."

"Matt, stop listening," I yell back at him. "Shouldn't you be going home to look after your heavily pregnant wife, or something? What if she goes into labor and you're not there to help her?"

That sends him into panic mode. I feel bad as I watch him jump up. He grabs his phone and tries to call her, but there's no answer.

"Just go and check on her," Luke urges him.

"Okay, if you're sure you guys are all right?" He frowns at the pedicab. "What about this thing?"

"We'll handle it," Luke assures him.

He nods and walks off.

I rest my head in Luke's lap again. He smiles down at me, gently tickling along my collarbone.

"So, tell me about some of the things you got up to while you were traveling?" I say

He makes a face. "Honestly, some of it's probably better left unsaid. There was one time I drank too much and passed out on the train. I was headed to Germany, but I ended up in the middle of some village in Bosnia at two in the morning."

"No way," I say, laughing.

He nods. "Yeah. I wasn't in the greatest mindset when I

went over there, so I did plenty of things that my mother wouldn't be proud of."

"Do you regret not fixing things with your dad before he died?"

He thinks about that for a second.

"I let go of the guilt I felt over that a long time ago. I think what I regret most is that he didn't understand me. I did everything I could for him. I bent over backward to try and get them to understand that this was my life, but they never got it. They never wanted to get it." He looks at me. "How about you?"

I shake my head, a wistful smile on my face.

"Not guilt, just sadness, I guess. I see or I do things that remind me of Dad and I wonder how he would react. Even situations, like graduating or becoming a doctor, or meeting boyfriends..."

"Boyfriends?" he says, smirking at me.

"Well, one in particular."

He leans down, gently grazing his lips over mine.

"You're pretty special, you know that?"

"Yeah, I hear that from all my boyfriends," I joke. I glance at my watch my eyes widening. It's after midnight. "And I've got to get up for work in six hours," I complain.

"Then we'd better get sleeping beauty home and into bed."

He gets to his feet and quickly packs up the picnic, placing it in the back of the cart. Then he gets on the bike and motions for me to get in the cart.

"I'd help you up there, but that would probably end with both of us in the ER with bike crush injuries."

"I think I can manage," I say, giggling.

I can't stop laughing the entire ride home. It's got to be hard work, pushing that thing around, but Luke doesn't seem to even break out in a sweat.

"So, where are we parking this thing?" I giggle.

He shakes his head and laughs. "I have no idea."

Somehow, we get it inside and convince the doorman to let us leave it in the foyer so Luke can call the company to collect it in the morning. We head upstairs. I can barely keep my eyes open as we walk inside. I yawn and glance at my phone to see that it's just ticked over to one in the morning.

"Let's get you into bed," Luke says, lifting me into his arms.

I SPEND every spare minute the next day at work, filling in my application. I'm in the ER again, and while I was run off my feet yesterday, today there is nothing to do. I guess people don't get hurt on Sundays. I figure this counts as paperwork though, so I don't feel bad about using time on the clock to get it done.

By the time my shift is over, I've filled in everything, but the million-dollar question, because I'm still not sure how to approach it. I think I'm worried that once it's out there, I can't take it back. I know it's not hot gossip, but what if Luke stumbled across my application and discovered what I was keeping from him before I told him myself?

AFTER WORK, I drive straight to Becs apartment, which is only a few streets away from the hospital, and hunt for a parking spot. When I finally find one, I go inside, via the liquor store two doors down from her building. She opens the door before I even have a chance to knock, her eyes lighting up as she reaches for the bottle tucked under my arm. She's been sending me the most random text messages all day, and I can tell she's bursting to tell me something.

"It's like you read my mind. I totally couldn't be bothered walking down to get some."

"It's literally right downstairs." I giggle.

"Yes, I'm that lazy." She grins at me as I follow her inside.

"What's with all the messages you've been bombarding me with? Did you work today?" I ask, taking off my jacket. I toss it over the chair and sit down on the couch, tucking my feet up under me.

She nods. "Sunday rates, and you'll never guess who I met," she gushes, leaning against the kitchen counter. Her eyes light up excitedly as she waits for me to answer.

"So, tell me then."

"Channing Tatum."

She stares at me expectantly, barely able to contain her smile. I shake my head. From her reaction, I feel like I should know who this is, but I've got nothing.

"Um, yay for you?"

Her eyes widen in shock as her smile turns into a gape.

"Are you fucking kidding me?"

"Um... no?" I laugh, not sure what the big deal is. It's not like she had any idea who Marina Holden was when I'd gushed about her. "Stop looking at me like that." I giggle. "Between studying and this little thing called a residency, I haven't exactly been overloaded with spare time."

"That's still no excuse," she says. She walks over and slaps me on the arm.

I laugh. "What are you, twelve?"

She shakes her head. "No, I'm disappointed," she grumbles. She continues to shake her head and walks back into the kitchen, pacing back and forth like she's trying to solve some huge problem that she's just been faced with.

"Are you all right?" I tease her.

"I will be. When we fix this."

"Fix what?"

She marches back into the living room and grabs the TV remote, navigating to the MovieFlix app.

"You own me four ninety-nine," she says as she clicks on the Magic Mike double.

"If I'm missing out on that much then why don't you own it?" I tease as she glowers at me.

Before I can protest, I'm being forced to sit through four hours of Magic Mike. It turns out not to be the worst punishment in the world, but still, I came over to catch up, not watch movies. Every time I try and speak to Becs, she holds her hand up to silence me and points at the TV. I laugh glance at my phone to check the time, protesting shock when it's snatched out of my hands.

"Hey."

"You'll get it back later."

It's nearly midnight when I finally regain my phone privileges. When I think about how early I have to get up in the morning, and the fact that we didn't even eat dinner or catch up, all I can do is laugh.

"Thanks for the catch-up, but maybe next time we can do this without Channing Tatum."

"Said no one ever." Her expression softens as she winces. "Okay, so maybe I got a little carried away. We didn't even have dinner."

"Oh, I know." I smile at her and shake my head. "It's fine, really. I'll have some toast or something at home."

"So, how are things going?" She frowns at me. "Have you spoken to him yet?"

"Assuming you mean Luke and not Channing, no." I lean against the door and frown at her. "I know that I need to, but I just can't seem to find the right time to bring it up. That, and it feels way too early to be having that kind of conversation in the first place."

"It's never too early," Becca argues. "I'm just looking out for you. This is the kind of conversation you need to have with someone *before* you start falling for them."

"You think I'm falling for him?" I laugh.

"Yes. And you need to tell him for his sake as much as your own," she adds. "Think about how hard it will be for you to start this conversation, and then imagine how hard it will be for him to hear it."

I hadn't thought about it like that. I smile at Becca and give her a hug.

"I'll tell him. Soon. I promise."

Because she's right. This conversation needs to happen, and it needs to happen soon.

CHAPTER NINE
LUKE

I'M VAGUELY aware of Laura as she leans over and kisses me roughly on the mouth. When her thigh grazes my cock, I stiffen in a matter of seconds. I smile because waking up next to her never gets old. I chuckle and run my hands up over her curves, disappointed when I see she's already dressed for work.

"What time is it?" I ask, yawning.

"It's almost six. Sorry I woke you. I just couldn't resist kissing you, the way you were lying there, looking all sexy like that."

"The only thing you need to be sorry for is leaving me to attend to this for myself." I grin and glance down at the tent covering my cock. "Well, that, and that you have to start work so early."

"I bet you're sorry." She narrows her eyes at me and then stands up, shrugging on her jacket. "Don't forget dinner tonight at Matt's place—with Mom."

"Looking forward to it." I grin. My eyes widen.

Wait, what?

I stare at her, open-mouthed. She frowns back at me, looking confused by my reaction.

"Your mom?"

"Yes. I told you that." She almost sounds defensive.

"No, you said Matt and Annie," I correct. "There was never any mention of your mom being there. Ever. Trust me. I'd have remembered that."

She frowns at me and crosses her arms over her chest.

"If I didn't tell you, then I'm sorry. It wasn't intentional." She pauses. "It's not really that big a deal, is it?"

Not a big deal? Jesus, is she kidding me?

I take a deep breath and force a smile.

"It's fine. I'll meet you there, okay? I'm not sure how late I'll finish, but I'll get there as soon as I can."

She frowns at me for a moment before leaning over for another kiss, her lips lingering against mine.

"Okay." She turns around and walks out.

I lie back, my heart pumping in my chest. I'm sure as fuck wide-awake now, and I definitely won't be going back to sleep anytime soon after that bombshell. I didn't want to make a big deal out of it, because it obviously wasn't one to her, but shit... meeting Mom?

Why do I feel like we've skipped a dozen steps somewhere in between getting together and this? Maybe it's just me, and I'm making this out to be worse than it is. It's probably not helping that my own relationship with my mom is so bad. I wouldn't even think about introducing a girl to my mother until maybe my wedding day, though there was a solid chance that even if I did end up inviting her, she wouldn't come.

I guess it's not that crazy that I'm meeting her mother so early in the relationship, considering she's so close to her mom and Matt.

For her, this is probably nothing more than a Friday night dinner. Her mom has probably met all of her boyfriends. I frown, hating the thought of her with anyone other than me.

Having nothing else to do, I throw back the covers and get out of bed, walking naked across the hallway to the bathroom. I have a long shower, since I have time to fill in, enjoying the feeling of the scalding hot water as it nearly penetrates into my back.

Aside from me freaking out about meeting her mother, things with Laura are really great. Actually, great isn't the right word. They're fucking fantastic. But it's not just Laura—everything is going well. I love my job and the relationship I'm forming with Lewin and that feeling of being overwhelmed and completely out of my depth is slowly beginning to fade.

Being forced to live and work together could have made things really awkward for Laura and me, but it hasn't. I've always lived alone, but it's a nice change not having to come home to an empty apartment. And if anything, living together has strengthened our relationship. I'd be lying if I didn't admit I was a little nervous about how our dynamic was going to change next week when I moved out.

What if this is only going so well because we've been forced into each other's pockets?

"Fancy running into you here."

I glance over and see Laura sitting in the corner of the staffroom. I smirk at her and glance around, making sure we're alone before I walk over there to kiss her. There's nothing to say we can't fraternize at work, but I'm pretty sure it's looked down upon.

I've just finished my shift, and I'm pretty sure she finished a couple of hours ago.

"Checking up on me, making sure I'm not inventing overtime?"

I'm mostly joking, but her eyes narrow as she picks up on the small part of me that isn't. The thought had crossed my mind, and if she wasn't standing in front of me right now, it might still be crossing my mind

"No." She holds up some papers. "I thought it would be easier to get this done here."

"What's that?" I lean closer with interest.

"My application for a research position Marina is looking to fill with a third year."

"Really? Nice." I'm genuinely impressed. That kind of thing always looks good on a résumé. "Mind if I read?"

I don't expect her to say no, so I'm kind of surprised when she moves it out of my reach. Her cheeks flush pink as she avoids eye contact.

"Sorry. I'd rather let you read it when I know for sure if I've got it or not. It's one of those long winded, why am I so much better than everyone else, essay questions."

I shrug, pretending it doesn't bother me. I walk back over to my locker and get changed, then we walk out to my car. "Take my car? I can drive you tomorrow."

"Sure."

She glances at me as we walk through the parking lot.

"I'm sorry if I sprung this dinner with Mom on you. I didn't even think that meeting her might freak you out. Now I've gone and made things all awkward."

"You haven't," I assure her. I take her hands and wrap them around my waist, tilting her face up so I can kiss her. "And I'm looking forward to meeting your mom. If she's anything like you and Matt, I'm sure I'll love her..."

"But?" she presses.

I sigh because I want to be honest with her about how I'm feeling, but I also have a habit of things coming out wrong when I'm nervous.

"I like you a lot, and I know we've only been seeing each other for a couple of weeks..."

The way she's staring at me, I know it's the wrong time to pause, but I need to think about how I phrase this. How do I explain myself without coming across as an asshole?

"From my perspective, based on the relationship I have with my mother, you'll be lucky to meet her on our wedding day," I finally say. "So, meeting your mom is kind of scaring the fuck out of me."

She laughs as we get into the car.

"Wedding day, huh? Now who's rushing things?" she teases.

"I just meant if you're lucky enough to be the woman walking up that aisle toward me, that's when you'd meet my mother." I glance at her, getting serious. "Of course, I want marriage and kids. I want it all, but I don't want to rush into anything, either. Does that make sense?"

She smiles. "Of course, it does."

The whole drive over to Matt's, she barely says a word. I steal a look in her direction as we pull up outside their house, watching her as she stares out the window, lost in her own thoughts. I'm sure I've said something to offend her, but the problem is, I can't figure out what. Surely, it's not the fact that I'm not ready for kids and marriage yet? She can't be thinking about that kind of thing already, can she?

The moment we walk inside, I relax. Laura walks over and hugs her mom. I'm relieved Laura didn't make a big deal out of my anxieties. She doesn't even mention how nervous I was driving over here. Annie's parents are there too, so I don't feel like all the attention is on me anyway—mainly because they're really loud. But even if they weren't here, I doubt I'd feel any pressure because Laura and Matt's mom is really laid-back.

"And this is Luke," she says, smiling at me. She places her hand in mine and gives it a squeeze

"Lovely to meet you, Mrs. Black," I say, putting my hand out. She shakes her head and motions for me to step closer, throwing her arms around me instead.

"And call me Kelly," she says. "Mrs. Black makes me sound too old." She shakes her head. "I can't believe I'm finally meeting you. I've been hearing good things about you from Laura and not so good things about you from my son. I wasn't sure who to believe."

"Hey," Matt protests, poking his head out from around the kitchen and glares at Kelly. "What have I said about him?" He nods at me. "You wanna give me a hand in here?"

"Sure."

I walk into the kitchen and rub my hands together and then look at Matt expectantly.

"I don't really need help, I just thought you might want to escape the wrath of my mother," he says. "My in-laws are staying here. Trust me, I know the hell you're going through."

I laugh. "Your mom is great," I say. "If you want pain, go visit my mom."

Matt shudders. "God, no. I still have nightmares about that night she accosted you in our dorm room."

I smile, a twinge of sadness hitting me. That night was the last time I saw her before my father died. I lean against the counter and watch Matt slice carrots. Would things be any different now? It had been nine years since I saw her last. If I turned up on her doorstep, would she send me away?

"I'm glad things with you and Laura are going well," Matt says out of nowhere.

"Me too," I say.

"Are you hiding him in here so I don't ask him too many questions?"

I look over and see Kelly standing there. I laugh as Matt rolls his eyes. She raises her eyebrows at me.

"Or are you avoiding me so you don't have to answer them?" she asks, narrowing her eyes.

"Me? No way. I'm an open book," I say with a chuckle.

I take the beer Matt hands me and follow Kelly back out into the living room. Everyone is now sitting at the table, so I sit down next to Laura, while her mom sits on my other side.

"So, tell me about yourself, Luke. You're a doctor too, I hear?" Kelly asks.

I nod. "I'm doing my surgical fellowship in cardiac."

"Impressive," she says, nodding. "And you went to college with Matt? Why is this the first time I'm meeting you?" she asks suspiciously.

"I was on a scholarship, which meant I had to work my ass off while I studied. It was hard, so vacations weren't something I had very many of," I admit.

"Your parents didn't help out?" she asks.

"My parents were not very... supportive of my career choice," I say.

I smile at her confused expression. She was no doubt wondering how any parent could not be happy with their child becoming a doctor.

"I come from generations of lawyers."

"Ah," she says. "Well then, you've done exceptionally well for yourself, especially on your own." She nods at Laura. "Keep a hold on this one."

Laura smiles at me. "I didn't realize you were on a

scholarship."

"Yep. A lot of hard work," I say with a grin. "But it was worth it."

THROUGHOUT THE REST of the evening, I keep catching Laura sneaking looks at me, so I reach under the table and run my hand down over her thigh. She jumps so high that she slams her knee into the table, which gets everyone's attention.

"Sorry," she mumbles, her cheeks red. I stifle a laugh, which earns me a glare. "We had better get going," she adds, placing her napkin down in front of her. "We've both got early starts tomorrow..."

Matt nods. "Thanks again for coming, guys."

We say our goodbyes, and I promise to catch up with Kelly again soon, then we walk outside. I reach for her hand as we walk down the driveway. She lets me take it, but the tension in her body is obvious.

"Are you okay?"

"I'm fine." She eases her hand back and rubs her forehead. "I've had a really bad headache for most of the day and it's gotten worse since we left. I just don't want to risk getting Annie sick if I'm coming down with something."

"Okay." I'm not sure whether I believe her or not, but I'm not about to call her out on it. "Your mom is great."

"She is." She smiles at that. "I never realized how lucky I am to have her. I can't imagine not having a relationship with her. Do you miss speaking to your mom?"

"You can't mourn something you never really had in the first place," I finally say.

She glances at me. "When you told me you didn't get on with your parents, it didn't really sink in until tonight how much you did on your own. Putting yourself through college, getting where you are today, even dealing with your father's death." She smiles at me. "I'm not your mother, but for what it's worth, I'm proud of you."

"And that means more than anything to me," I say softly.

We drive home in silence, with Laura resting her head against the window and staring out for most of the way. When I pull up outside her apartment, her eyes are closed, but I'm not convinced she's asleep. I can't figure out if I've said something wrong, or if she really is just feeling unwell. I nudge her leg. She stirs and smiles at me, her eyes half closed.

Maybe she was asleep.

Once we're inside her apartment, she smiles and takes my hand, before reaching up to peck me on the lips. I sigh and slide my fingers around her neck, my mouth finding hers. I press my lips against hers, parting them enough to slide my tongue around hers. She puts her hand over mine and gently strokes my fingers, then she pulls away, her eyes still closed from losing herself in that kiss.

"Do you mind if I sleep alone tonight?" She curls her fingers around mine. "I'm not a very good patient when I'm sick."

"Of course. Are you sure you're okay?" I frown at her, concerned. "Can I get you something? Tylenol?"

She shakes her head and kisses me again.

"I'm fine. Thanks though."

She disappears down the hallway and into her room, quietly closing the door behind her. I sit down on the couch and rub my head. I'm feeling anxious, because meeting Kelly triggered feelings about my own mother that I hadn't felt in a long time.

A lot can change in nine years. People can change. The thought of reaching out to her, putting myself on the line like that, I'm not sure is something I can do. Can I forgive her for everything she did? Not letting me into my own father's funeral. Not being there for me when I needed her most. I shake my head, because I don't think I can. The funny thing was, even if I could forgive her, it was unlikely that she'd forgive me.

"Luke?"

I roll over and force my eyes open, a blurred Laura finally coming into view.

"What time is it?" I'm pretty sure I form the words.

I rub my head and struggle to sit up, then look around. I'm slumped on the couch at an odd angle, which at least explains the sore neck.

"It's eight o'clock. I wasn't sure what time you started, and I didn't want you to be late..."

"Thanks, but I'm off today." I release a yawn and rest my hands behind my head and rub it.

"Shit, I'm sorry," she says, covering her mouth with her hands.

"Don't be." I look at her and shrug. "I'd rather you wake me to be sure than not and have me turn up three hours late." I glance at her short nightgown, my cock starting to harden. "What time do you start?"

"I've got the day off. I'm still not feeling that great, so I called in sick."

I reach out and grab her hand, pulling her onto my lap.

"Well in that case, since you've woken me up..." I let my voice trail as I push aside her hair and kiss along her neck. She giggles, the color racing back into her cheeks.

"Did you miss the part where I said I was feeling sick?"

"You don't look too sick to me." I creep my hand up under her nightgown and stroke between her legs. Her breath catches as she squirms in my arms. "And you definitely don't feel very sick..." I smirk at her. "Although, maybe I better take a closer look. I am a doctor, after all." She squeals as I drag her completely into my arms, resting one leg on either side of me. I grunt as my cock begs to enter her, pressing against her thigh. She tries to hide her smirk as I reach down and grip my shaft, lining it up against her wet pussy.

"You might want to hold on." My words just a breath in her ear. She braces herself, laughing as I thrust into her, bouncing her on my cock. "And I should probably confirm you're taking contraception of some kind."

"You're lucky I don't get motion sickness," she jokes, wrapping her arms around my neck. "And yes, I'm on the pill."

I respond by cupping her jaw and exploring her mouth, sliding my tongue in against hers. She breathes out, her back reacting when I drag my nails down over her curves. She takes my hand and palms at her breasts, guiding her nipple into my mouth. Her eyes bore into mine as she watches me suck, getting off on the feel of me biting down. She arches her neck back and rides me harder, sliding her tight pussy all over my cock. I can hardly contain the sounds emanating from me, my shaft throbbing as I pump into her.

"God, you make me wanna explode the moment I touch you."

She smiles and kisses me. When she sucks on my tongue, that's it. I'm done. She keeps sucking, while her pussy works my dick until the feel of her is too much for me to handle. I grunt, my body shuddering as I come. I spray hard inside her.

"Well fuck me." I shake my head. "Sick, you say?"

I gently ease myself out of her, but keep her on my lap, because I don't want her going anywhere just yet. She laughs, her eyes sparkling.

"Yes, sick." She gives me a side-eye. "You're lucky that I'm so accommodating, even when I'm not feeling that well."

I smile, raising my eyebrows at her.

"I've always thought that about you. The very first time I saw you I thought to myself, now that is one very accommodating woman."

She slaps my arm, then wraps her arms around my neck and kisses me.

"You're an asshole. You know that?"

"I do now," I murmur.

She lifts herself off me and walks into the kitchen. My eyes follow her because I literally can't get enough of that perfect ass. She's just so stunning that she demands my attention whenever she's around me. I stare at her, the way her hair falls over her shoulders in a sexy, tangled mess. And that look in her eyes that perfectly complements the tiny smirk on her lips. I shake my head because I can see myself with her. I can see us getting married and having kids. It's an odd time to have that kind of revelation, right after blowing my load inside of her, but I feel like I've hit a turning point in our relationship.

When she walks back around to me, I pull her back into my arms. She laughs but doesn't fight me when I press my mouth to hers. She moves across me, lying down on the couch, so her head rests in my arms.

"What's up?"

I shake my head.

"Nothing."

The last thing I want to do is scare her off with all the random thoughts that are flying through my head. Then I decide what the fuck.

I smile at her. "We should do something today."

"Like what?" She eyes me suspiciously.

"I don't know." I laugh. "We've both got the day off, so why not spend the day together? Get out of the house. Go somewhere."

"That does sound good," she admits.

WE WALK around the city eating ice creams and then walk through the park, hand in hand, just enjoying each other's company. We even feed a little family of ducks down by the lake, which is kind of cute. Getting to know one another in such a casual, laid-back environment feels great. I love seeing her so open and happy like this, without the stress of work or trying to impress each other.

We sit down on a seat in the middle of the park, opposite her apartment. I watch as she twists her coffee cup in her hands and stares off into the distance. It's the first time all day where I've caught her lost in thought.

"What are you thinking about?" I ask her.

She looks up as if surprised that I noticed her tuning out. She shrugs.

"Just how a month ago I had no idea that you existed." She looks down at her cup. "I just find that freaky, considering how much I..."

"How much you what?" I smile because I'm pretty sure she was about to admit she likes me.

"How much I like you."

"I like you too." I reach for her hand and sit back, a thought hitting me.

"Ever think about the number of times we could've almost

crossed path before now?" I smile. "I was at his graduation, you know. I'm pretty sure I saw you there."

"You were?" she says, surprised. "Huh. I guess it's not surprising that I wouldn't remember you. I thought you were overseas?"

"I was, but I had just gotten back. I'm not really that memorable," I tease.

"No, that's not what I meant..." She narrows her eyes when she realizes I'm baiting her and shakes her head. "I wonder how many other times there were where we could've met."

"It's like fate wanted us together," I say. "Even if you didn't come into my ER, we would have met through Matt. Dinner party or not, I'm sure this would've happened eventually."

She smiles, like my words comfort her, then rests her head on my shoulder.

"Do you really believe in fate?" she asks.

I glance at her. "I guess I don't really? I'm a doctor. Doesn't medicine kind of go against the idea that whatever's going to happen will happen?"

"I guess," she says. "Or maybe you're not really changing anything at all. You just think you are."

"So, our jobs are pointless?" I smirk at her, knowing I'm winding her up.

"No. I just mean... things like your dad dying and my dad... do you think things like that happen for a reason?" I glance at her and shrug, because I don't know. "Why do bad things happen to good people?" she asks, frowning.

"Does it matter?" I ask gently. "All those things, good and

bad, just shape who you are as a person. You wouldn't be the same without that balance."

"I guess," she murmurs.

"Shall we go home?" I suggest.

She nods, and I take her hand in mine as we walk through the park toward her apartment.

While she has a shower, I order some Chinese food. After dinner, we sit on the couch watching TV. She curls up in my arms, relaxed and happy. She looks up at me and grins.

"Slouch on the couch night reinvented," she says with a giggle.

I groan. "I wish I had no idea what you were talking about, but unfortunately, I'm a victim."

She straightens up, her eyes widening as she stares at me.

"No way." She gasps and then shoves me. I chuckle and nod. "When?"

"One night last year," I say. "Is it strange that I feel like I'm opening up to you about a date rape experience?" I'm only half joking, too. "I felt so dirty after that night. Being forced to sit on that couch with Matt and Annie and watch some Zac Effron movie... I pause and shudder. "It was torture," I whisper in a shaky voice.

She laughs, her blue eyes sparkling.

"I don't know whether I find this hysterical or whether I feel betrayed. I feel like Matt and Annie cheated on me."

She snuggles back up against me. It's funny when I see the way she and Matt are together, and it makes me jealous. Being an only child, I never got to have that kind of relationship with a sibling. I feel like I missed out on something that I'd never want my own kids to miss out on.

"I wish I had a brother or sister."

"That's a random thought." She glances at me. "I get it, though. I'd be lost without Matt."

"I hated being an only child," I admit. "I still do." She smiles up at me. I smile back and stroke her cheek. "That's why I want at least three kids," I continue.

"Three?" she repeats. She grins at me, her brow creasing. "Why three?"

"Well, you don't know if the first two are going to get along or not, so always have a backup."

"A backup?" She giggles like she can't believe I just said that. "I'm sure number three would love to know that they're the backup."

"Oh, come on. Get off your high horse." I love teasing her like this. "Don't pretend you don't think the same thing and it's just as applicable for when we get old. Three is a good number in case we hate the first two..." I pause. "Or they hate us. We can guilt number three into caring for us. It's either that or end up in a retirement home."

"And what if three hates you too?"

"Good point. Four kids it is."

She shakes her head and laughs. "Maybe you shouldn't be having kids at all."

"I love that we can talk about shit like this so easily." I lean in and kiss her softly on the lips.

"ME TOO," she murmurs. Her face conveys her contentment, but I catch the flash of sadness hiding in her eyes. "And you know what else I love?" She smiles at me.

"What?" I smirk at her. I hope this is headed where I think it's headed.

"Sleeping." She giggles at my crestfallen expression.

Apparently not.

She leans up and kisses my lips, pressing her mouth to mine. Her hands cradle my face as she stares into my eyes.

"Thank you for today. It was fantastic. I think it was just what I needed."

"Anytime," I say.

I bring her to my lips again, my mouth exploring hers, while I gently stroke her cheek. The feel of her lips on mine is enough to make my already-hard cock harder. She bites the edge of her lip as she glances down.

"Well, good night then," she says.

Her eyes sparkle as she gazes up at me. She walks toward her room, while I stand there, feeling both disappointed and extremely aroused. She turns back to me and smiles when she reaches her door.

"I kind of thought you might join me..."

I smile, already on my way to her.

"I thought you'd never ask."

CHAPTER TEN
LAURA

"I THOUGHT I heard you come in."

I giggle as he wraps his arms around me and plants wet kisses all over my neck, while I try and struggle free from his grasp.

"At least let me put my things down first," I beg. I lean over to the hall table and dump my bag and my keys down. "Now, where were we?" I ask, turning around so I'm facing him.

I frown, because he smells way too fresh to have finished his shift. Which meant...

"I'm running late," he murmurs, kissing me. "They're short staffed again tonight, so Lewin asked me to cover half a shift. On the plus side, it's four hours, and then I'll be home." He gives me a devilish look. "The things I plan to do to you..."

"Okay, go already," I grumble. "I guess I'll take that cold shower alone, then." I push him out the door, rolling my eyes as he laughs at me.

I walk over to the couch and flop down, exhausted. With everything I've got going on at work and applying for this research project, the extra pressure of being in a relationship isn't helping with my focus. I'm worried that my feelings for Luke are taking the edge off my drive when it comes to getting where I want to be. Like making sure I get this research project.

Putting my career ahead of everything else used to be a no-brainer, but that was before my feelings started getting in the way. The thought of not putting work first is as scary as hell. I've put everything into getting where I am, because it was something that was mine. It was something that I wasn't at risk of losing.

I lost so much, growing up. First, most of my childhood, and then my ability to have children. Losing my father was the final straw. I needed something that I could invest everything into and know it would still be there when I needed it. How do I know that Luke and I aren't going to be over in six months? I guess that's the thing. I can't know that. All that time and effort is irrelevant if I mess things up because of Luke. But the thing about life is that nothing is ever really forever. It's only forever until it's not.

———

JUST AS I'M about to have that shower, my phone rings. Figuring I should answer it, I stomp out of my room, down to the hall table and rummage through my bag.

"How soon can you get over here?" Matt asks when I answer. He sounds panicked.

"What's wrong?" I ask.

"Annie is having contractions," he says. He sounds stressed. I know my brother well enough to know he'd be driving Annie insane already.

"Okay, I'm on my way."

I end the call, a rush of excitement filling me. I laugh, because holy shit, it's finally happening. I scribble out a message for Luke, letting him know where I am and leave it on the counter, then I pack a few things in my bag, just in case I have to stay over.

It's nearly nine by the time I'm in my car, heading over to their place. At this time of day, the drive across town is an easy one, so I'm there within fifteen minutes, screeching to a stop out in front of their house. I jump out of the car and race inside, not even bothering to lock it. Anyone who steals my shitbox gets what they deserve.

Matt stands out the front, with the door wide open, waiting for me. I race past him and find Annie lying on the couch, her face red as she puffs in and out. The poor thing looks so tired and miserable already. I feel sorry for her because she's got a long way to go before this is over, and my brother clearly isn't being much help.

"Are you okay?" I ask, crouching down beside her. I quickly take her pulse while she clutches her stomach, groaning as another contraction hits her.

"Fuck, it hurts so much," she cries.

"Have you called the hospital?" I ask Matt.

He nods. "Yes, but the contractions are still too far apart. They said there's not much point in us coming in yet."

I nod. "How far apart?"

"Fifteen minutes."

"Yeah, if you went in now, they'd probably just send you back home." I squeeze Annie's hand and give her a smile. "Could be a little while yet." I glance around. "Where are your parents?"

"They took an overnight trip out to Vegas," she says, gritting her teeth. "To be honest with you, I'm as glad as fuck. I've got enough to deal with without adding them to the mix."

I giggle and get to my feet.

"Maybe run a bath?" I suggest to Matt. "Sometimes that can help move things along, or at the very least, ease the pain of the contractions a little."

Matt nods, looking relieved that he can be of some use. He disappears, so I sit with Annie, trying to take her mind off the pain.

"How are things with Luke?" she asks, hissing as she tries to maneuver onto her side.

"Good," I admit. "Really good, actually."

She smiles at me and takes my hand, giving it a squeeze.

"Great, I'm so happy for you. If anyone deserves to find someone, it's you. You're such an amazing person," she says, tears forming in her eyes. I giggle because Annie sure gets emotional when she's in pain.

"Thanks," I say.

"Matt and I wanted to ask you something." She glances at Matt, who has just walked back in the room. He raises his eyebrows, suddenly looking nervous.

"I thought we were doing this after the baby was born," he says.

"Well, I want to do it now," Annie growls. I laugh and shake my head at Matt. Never argue with a pregnant woman. "We want to ask you if you'd be our baby's godmother," Annie says as she takes Matt's hand and looks up at him with love.

"Really?" I ask. My eyes well with tears. "You've got no idea how much that means to me." I'm so happy, but I'm also feeling bittersweet. This could be the closest I ever come to becoming a parent myself, and it would take a tragedy happening to both of them. "Of course, I will," I say, my voice trembling.

Tears roll down my cheeks. I don't bother trying to hide the fact that I'm upset because let's face it, it would take a lot of effort to stop the waterworks at this point.

"Are you okay?" Annie frowns. She glances at Matt, worried. "I didn't know whether to ask you or not..." She shakes her head. "You hate the idea, don't you? Oh God, I'm the worst person in the world," she says, throwing her hands over her face. I kneel down in front of her and take hold of her hands.

"No, don't do that," I say, looking her in the eye. "You've got no idea how happy you've made me. I'm thrilled that you both trust me with something like this. Honestly, I'm just..." I shake my head. "Thank you."

She smiles, her own eyes glistening with tears. I hug them both, my stomach all churned up.

"Are you sure you're okay?" Matt asks me softly.

I do my best to glare at him.

"Don't you start. I'm fine. Have you called Mom?" I give him a look, knowing he probably hasn't. He hangs his head. "I'll go outside and do it now if you like. Which hospital is she going to?" I ask. "I'll tell Mom that I'll text her when we're on our way."

"St. John's," Matt says.

I disappear outside and lean against the railing, taking a moment to breathe. I could have just sent Mom a text inside, but I needed a second to myself. I close my eyes and breathe in again, shivering as the cool air hits my lungs.

"Hey. Are you okay?"

My eyes fly open. Luke stands in front of me, an amused smile on his face. I guess I'm quite the sight, standing there in the cold, eyes closed and breathing heavily. I'm a walking, talking phone sex commercial.

"I got your message, so I thought I'd come over and see if I could help out." He frowns at me, probably just noticing the tears and the blotchy red face. "Is something wrong? Is the baby okay? Is Annie okay? Is Matt—"

"Calm down." I take his hands because he looks like the one who needs to breathe now. "The baby is fine; everything is fine. I'm just a little overwhelmed, I guess."

"Overwhelmed or feeling a little clucky?" he teases.

"Trust me, I'm in no way clucky," I say with a smile.

If only he knew.

We walk back inside. I quickly text Mom when I remember that's what I went outside for in the first place. I vaguely listen to Luke chattering beside me about how much babies scare him.

"So, neonatal was a hard no, then?"

He shudders. "Definitely not. Can you imagine how many shitty diapers you'd have to change?"

"Or you could go the other way and go into geriatrics and probably change the same number," I joke.

He shakes his head and frowns at me.

"You say the most offensive things, sometimes," he comments.

"Oh, like you can talk," I retort, to which he laughs.

The contractions have eased off, which I know can happen, so I decide to stay the night, just in case I'm needed. That and it's nearing close to midnight anyway.

"I can stay too," Luke offers.

"You might as well go home and get a decent sleep," I say. "I'll just be sleeping on the couch."

"If you're sure," he says. I nod. "Then I'll sleep with my phone on. That way, if you need my help, you can call."

I nod and walk him outside. I wrap my arms around his waist, smiling as he cups my chin in his strong hands, lifting it up to his mouth.

"See you soon," he murmurs, his lips grazing over mine. I shiver, amazed that his kiss still delivers that same tingle I felt when we first kissed.

"Bye," I say. The words catch in my throat. He waves at me and disappears over to his car.

I walk back in and settle down on the couch, but I know getting myself to sleep is going to be hopeless. All I can think about is Luke. Becca was right. I am falling hard for him. And fast. I should've had the conversation with him a long time ago, and now I've backed myself into a corner that I'm not sure I can get out of.

What if he ends up hating me? I question myself.

He might not at first, but the last thing I want is to be the reason he can't be a father. He might say he's fine with it, but then end up resenting me in ten years. It would've been so much easier to walk away before all these feelings began to develop.

I'm so damn selfish.

I only considered my own feelings in all of this when I should have been thinking of his.

I GUESS at some point I fell asleep because I'm woken up by Matt furiously shaking my arm, screaming in my ear over and over again, "She's having the baby, she's having the baby." I sit up, taking a second to compose myself before I spring into action. I'm already dressed, so that's a bonus.

"Have you called an ambulance?" I ask him, remaining as calm as I can. I'm not convinced the baby will wait long enough for us to drive to the hospital.

He nods, shifting on his feet impatiently. Anyone would

think that he's the one who's going to be popping out a baby. I walk into the bedroom. Annie tries to smile at me. She winces in pain as I crouch down beside her.

"How are you doing?" I ask her. She shrugs, trying to smile. "Can you lift your legs up and tuck them close to you? I'm just going to have a bit of a look and see how dilated you are."

Her eyes widen. "You think you're sticking your hand *where*?" she yelps. "I'm sorry, but isn't that kind of overstepping the boundaries of family?"

"I'm a doctor."

I hide my smile. Maybe if I tell her my story, this won't seem as bad. She takes a deep breath and lifts her legs up, squeezing her eyes closed. She places her tightly clenched fists against her stomach.

"You need to relax," I say to her.

"Yeah? How many times have you had someone feeling around your cervix?" she mutters.

You'd be surprised, I answer her in my head.

"I can't check if you don't relax," I say. "Just breathe in and out. Let yourself relax as much as you can," I soothe her. She finally relaxes long enough for me to feel that she's five centimeters dilated.

"How's that?" she asks, puffing out the breath she's holding onto.

"Good. Okay, we need to get you to the hospital soon." I turn to Matt. "The contractions are only a few minutes apart. I'm worried the ambulance won't get here in time," I say, low enough for only him to hear.

"Okay, so what do you suggest?" he asks, frowning at me.

"Can you drive us to the hospital?"

"I can if you stop talking to me like I'm five," Matt whines.

I laugh. "I'm sorry; I'm just trying to keep you as calm as possible."

He sighs and runs his hand through his hair. "No, I'm the one who should be sorry. I do appreciate you being here," he mutters. "Yeah, I'm okay to drive. If you weren't here, I'd be freaking the fuck out, but right now I'm okay."

"Good. Let's get Annie ready to go," I instruct him.

We help Annie down to the car and carefully lie her down in the back. My plan was to sit next to her, but she's taking up the whole seat. Instead, I sit in the front with Matt. I turn around and face her the whole time, holding her hand and trying to keep her mind off the fact that this baby could pop out at any moment. I'm half expecting to be pulling over on the side of the freeway to have this baby at some point soon, but somehow, we manage to make it to the hospital.

Matt races inside to get an orderly, returning a few minutes later with one in tow. I stand back, my heart pumping as he helps her onto it. It feels weird to take a step back and let him do his job when I'm so used to getting in there and helping.

I follow them inside, but hang back in the waiting room, because this is their moment and I want them to enjoy it without feeling bad for me. I sit down, glancing around anxiously because now I've got nothing but time on my hands to think. I text Mom and Luke to let them both know what's going on, then I try to relax.

After fifteen minutes of waiting, I stand up. If anything, my anxieties have worsened, so when I look up and see Luke walking through the door, I'm relieved for all of two seconds—until I remember that we haven't had the conversation yet. I don't particularly want to have it now with screaming babies in the background either, but I'm not convinced that I'm not going to randomly burst into tears at some point soon.

"Hey," he says. He smiles at me and wraps his arms around me, kissing me on the forehead. "Any news?"

"Not yet. Matt was freaking out pretty hard," I say, chuckling. "I'd hate to see how this would have gone down if I wasn't there."

"I'd put my money on badly."

We wait in silence, neither of us saying much, which, given that it's four in the morning, isn't surprising. I'm too scared to say anything because I'm feeling pretty emotional all of a sudden. I'm not sure if it's the lack of sleep or because I know I still need to tell Luke. I just prefer for it not to be while my sister-in-law is having a baby. I close my eyes and rest my head on his shoulder. He wraps his arm around me and kisses me.

"Are you okay?" Luke asks as I try and block out the cries of tiny infants. "Sounds like someone's not happy," he jokes. "There's always one. I bet if we walked around there and peered into that nursery today and next week, it would be that same kid screaming out. It's like puppies. There's always one, sitting at the bars chewing on it and screaming to get out."

I stare at him in mock horror.

"Did you just compare my new niece or nephew to a screaming puppy?"

"No," he says defensively. "I compared someone else's child to a screaming puppy. So, are you excited?" he adds after a moment.

"I am."

And that's the truth. I'm really excited about meeting my little niece or nephew and holding that tiny bundle in my arms. Who am I kidding? I'm fucking terrified. I'm not sure what kind of emotions that's going to bring out. That's what scares me more than anything else because it's a situation I can't control.

And we all know how much I like control.

MATT BURSTS THROUGH THE DOORS. We're the only ones in the waiting room, which is a good thing, because he can't contain his excitement. He races over to me, a dazed expression on his face as he throws his arms around me.

"We've got a daughter," he chokes out. He shakes his head, tears rolling down his cheeks. "Holy shit. I've got a daughter. I'm a fucking dad."

Mom races in, looking out of breath and wide-eyed.

"Has it happened?" she asks while trying to catch her breath. Matt nods and falls into Mom's arms, sobbing like a baby.

"I've got a daughter. You're a grandma, Mom."

Mom cries and hugs Matt. They dance around the room

together, laughing and crying, while I stand back a little, feeling lost. The last thing I want to do is make this special moment about my problems. Matt glances over at me. He looks like he's about to say something, so I shake my head and mouth to him that I'm okay. He nods and glances at Luke.

He's probably wondering if I've told him.

"Want to meet her?" Matt asks.

"Hell yes," Mom and I say at the same time.

We walk into Annie's private room. She looks exhausted as she clutches the tiny bundle against her chest. I get close enough to the bed to peer down at that tiny little face, and I nearly lose my shit. She's so cute, wrinkles and all. That little squished up face is the sweetest thing I've ever seen. I wipe away tears. I'm emotional, but they're not sad tears. They're happy because this is one of the most incredible moments of my life. I'm not sure anything can top this.

"Do you want to hold her?" Annie asks

"I'd love to."

I ignore the concerned look on Mom's face as I ease the baby into my arms. She cries for about a second and then nestles against me. When she reaches out and clutches onto my finger, my heart breaks for everything I can never have. How can I feel so sad and so happy at the same time? It's like my emotions are fighting it out inside me, and I'm not sure who's going to win.

"Such a little sweetheart," I say, unable to draw my eyes away from her.

I'm exhausted, tired, emotional, and a complete mess, but I

cradle her for a little while longer before I pass her over to Luke. Watching him hold her breaks my heart all over again. The look in his eyes and the way he's gazing at her is almost too much for me to take. There's no way this is going to end well for me. He's made to be a father. I look away, blinking back tears, I walk over and give Matt a hug and kiss him on the cheek.

"Congratulations," I whisper. "She's perfect." I glance from him to Annie. "Do you guys have a name?"

Annie looks at Matt and smiles.

"Elina."

"I think that suits her perfectly," I say with a smile.

"Go home," Matt says kissing me on the forehead. "Get some sleep. God knows you deserve it."

I don't argue with him because I am pretty wrecked.

"Okay. I'll come in tomorrow after work," I say.

I walk over and give Mom a kiss, while Luke reluctantly hands Elina back to Annie. Mom lifts my face up, so she can study me. I hate it when she does that because she sees right through my façade.

"Are you okay?" she asks gently.

I smile at her, trying to keep the sadness out of my voice.

"Not really, but I will be."

CHAPTER ELEVEN

LUKE

FOR THE NEXT FEW DAYS, things are strained. I can't quite describe the feeling in the air at the moment, other than to say it's flat. Laura has taken on some extra shifts, and when she's not working, she's over helping Matt and Annie. With my own long hours and trying to get things ready for my new place, I haven't really seen much of her at all. I know it's only going to get harder to find the time to spend with each other when we're not living under the same roof.

Neither of us has bought up the fact that I'm moving out soon. Part of me thinks that we should be discussing it, because I could be very easily convinced to stay here. Sure, this relationship has moved fast, but neither of us can deny that we're serious about each other.

Well, I can't, at least.

Maybe what I need to do is show her how much she means to me.

If I do something romantic and spontaneous to assure her that things aren't going to change when I move out, it might help both of us feel more secure. I check her roster. She finishes work at six. I ask Lewin if I can finish at five, blaming a family emergency.

"I'll start earlier tomorrow to make up for it," I say.

The longer he frowns at me, the more I regret asking, until he nods.

"Okay, sure."

Relieved, I sigh and glance at my watch. It's four thirty now, so only half an hour to go. I check my list and see our next patient to review is Ben. I've been spending a lot of my spare time in with him, just trying to lift his mood and take his mind off how sick he is. I have spent more time playing video games in the last week, than I did my entire childhood.

We walk into his room and my heart pounds. His condition has clearly deteriorated because the usual happy, cheeky boy can barely even look at us today. He manages a weak smile for us, but his eyes are drawn, and his skin is so pale that he's almost white. I glance at Lewin as he picks up his folder and studies his latest test results.

"Ben. How are you feeling?" Lewin asks. He leans over and messes his hair.

"Tired," he admits.

"You look it. We're going to run a few more tests, okay? No more playing Xbox or anything like that, you hear me? You just relax and take it easy for a few days."

"Did he tell you to say that?" he asks, nodding at me. "I

think he's scared I'm gonna beat his score again." His eyes are half closed, but he has the tiniest smirk on his cracked lips

Lewin laughs and raises his eyebrows at me. I shrug, not sure why I feel embarrassed.

"Yes, you guessed it." He nods at Ben's mom, Marissa, to speak with us outside. She gets up and kisses Ben, and then follows us out of the room.

"It's not good news, is it?" she asks. She wraps her arms around herself and studies Lewin. He shakes his head.

"I'm not going to lie to you, Marissa. Things have gotten dramatically worse. We probably have forty-eight, maybe seventy-two hours to find Ben a new heart."

"And if we don't?" She whispers the words.

"Then we'll need to look at hooking him up to a mechanical heart, just to give his body a rest."

"Oh God," she whispers. She clasps her hand over her mouth, tears filling her eyes. "Please help him. He's such a special little boy. Please fix my baby."

"We'll do everything we can," Lewin promises her. "You just look after him and let us do our job, okay?" She nods and thanks us, then slips back into the room.

I follow Lewin down the corridor in silence, my stomach twisting into knots.

"Seventy-two hours?" I frown at him. "And how long will he last on a mechanical heart?"

Lewin shrugs. "A few weeks? A few months? It depends on a number of things."

"So, what do we do about it, then?"

Lewin sighs and stops in the middle of the corridor. He turns to me and shrugs.

"We're already doing everything, Luke. I can't magic up a heart for this boy. The fact is, without a hell of a lot of luck—and shit luck for someone else's kid—he probably won't see the end of the month."

I clench my hands into fists as my body tenses. *This is affecting me a lot more than it really should.* I'm his doctor, not his friend. I look at someone like Lewin, who coasts in and out of here every day, like nothing bothers him. If I get this invested in every patient, I'll burn myself out.

Maybe I should be reconsidering my whole career path.

"Maybe I'm not cut out for this," I mutter.

"Because you've formed a friendship with a sick kid?" he asks. "You think that makes you a bad doctor?"

"Yes. I can't detach myself from feeling sorry for that little boy. What if that clouds my judgment? And then I look at you, who can just stand there and tell me he's probably going to die and not even flinch when you say it."

"You really believe that?" he asks. He shakes his head and laughs. "If you think I go through this without getting invested in my patients, then you're wrong. Hell, some of them, like that little boy back there, I actually like. Of course, I feel sorry for him. Hell, if he died, I'd probably even shed a few tears."

"Then how do you do it?" I press him. "You've been doing this for how long? How many kids have you lost? How do you put that aside and move onto the next one and pretend it doesn't matter?"

"Because for every ten kids that I lose, I might actually be able to save one." He stares at me, his eyes clouded with more emotion than I've ever seen from him. "*That's* what keeps me going. That's what makes me successful at what I do." He shrugs. "It's the only way you can look at it because the moment you start doubting yourself, you're done." He sighs and pats me on the back. "Go and fix your emergency, Luke. I'm going to organize some tests for Ben, and we'll take it one day at a time. I'll see you at eight a.m. tomorrow."

"But I said I'd start—"

"At eight. Now get out of here, before I change my mind." He pauses for a moment, before looking back at me. "You're a good doctor, Luke. You've got the passion and the drive to really make a difference, but you need to get it out of your head that being a cold, ruthless asshole is the only way you're going to be successful. Stop comparing yourself to everyone else, or you won't be helping anyone."

I THINK about what Lewin said the whole drive home. He's right about me needing to get out of my own head, but that's easier said than done. I rub the back of my neck and then rest my head back against the seat as I'm forced to stop for a red light. My plan of seducing Laura has taken a steep dive in motivation, because all I really want to do is go home and climb into bed

No. You're not going to waste the one chance you've had to

spend time with her all week because you're feeling sorry for yourself, I chastise myself.

I stop at the grocer's and get everything I need to cook her dinner. By the time I get into the kitchen and start my preparations, I'm feeling better. I'm pretty impressed with myself, actually, because my risotto smells delicious. Maybe I have taken the wrong career path, because if this risotto is anything to go by, I should've become a chef.

I set the table outside on the balcony, complete with candles, and rose petals, then I stand there with my arms crossed and survey my work. There's no denying I have talent. The front door opens, and I spring into action, quickly walking back inside.

"Hey, what are you doing home?" she asks, walking over to me. I kiss her, trying to block her view of outside. She narrows her eyes at me, my odd behavior tipping her off that I'm up to something. "I thought you had a late shift today?"

"I did, but I asked to finish early so that I could surprise you," I say.

She looks past me, her eyes widening when she sees the flickering candles outside.

"What have you done?" she asks with a grin. She walks over to the door and slides it open, smiling back at me, as her eyes shine. "You did this for me?"

I nod. "I decided to recreate our own personal little dinner party."

"Really?" She giggles and walks back over to me. "Does that mean you're going to insult me and make inappropriate comments all night?" I wrap my arms around her and narrow my eyes at her.

"I told you, that's how I get when I'm nervous." I smirk at her. "So probably. Yes."

She rolls her eyes. "You're lucky I forgive so easily."

I raise my eyebrows at her.

"Really? I would've thought you'd hold a grudge until the very end."

She giggles and kisses me on the lips. "You know me better than I thought you did."

I watch for her reaction as we walk outside. My heart races when her eyes light up as she takes in how much trouble I've gone to. I pull out her seat for her, then push it back in once she sits down. She shakes her head, a look of amazement on her face.

"You worked all day and then you came home and did this?" she shakes her head. "I struggle to find the energy to order a pizza after a shift."

"I wanted to do something nice for you," I explain. I smile at her. "Be right back. I hope you're hungry."

I disappear back inside and over to the kitchen. I load our plates with risotto and then carry them out to the table. She smiles when I place hers down in front of her.

"That smells amazing," she says.

She plays with her fork, eyeing her plate. I laugh.

"Go on."

She sighs after her first mouthful and closes her eyes.

"God, it's even better than it smells," she mutters as she goes back for more. "Are you going to eat, or just stare at me?"

"Is that a legitimate option?" I chuckle and reach for my fork. "I'm sorry, but I can't help it. You're gorgeous."

"This is perfect," she says, smiling at me. "Thank you."

"The key is to cook the rice just right."

She laughs. "Not the food. Everything, you idiot."

I slide my hand across the table and place it over hers.

"I'm glad you like it. I hope you saved room for dessert?"

"There's always room for that." She smothers a laugh. "Sorry, I was just picturing you on the couch when Matt walked in. The only thing missing was whipped cream."

I raise my eyebrows at her. "How do you know there wasn't any? You were late to the party, remember?"

"Oh, gross," she cries. She stares at me, horrified. "Are you suggesting that my brother—"

"Okay, I didn't think that comment through," I admit with a laugh. "Maybe I should just go and get that dessert."

"Yes," she says, biting her lip. "Good idea."

She sighs and leans back in her chair, pushing away her half-eaten cheesecake as she rubs her stomach. My mouth drops open in shock as I gape at her.

"I slaved for hours in the kitchen to prepare that, and you can't even finish it?" I accuse her.

Total bullshit. I saw the cheesecake in the deli of the

grocer's and thought I could get away with throwing a few berries on top and calling it my own. It worked, too.

"I'm sorry, but dinner was *so* good... if I eat this, there will be no sex for days because I won't be able to move."

I accept her answer by taking the cheesecake and finishing it myself. She laughs as she shakes her head.

"You're a dick."

I shrug. "Maybe, but I'm a dick who's getting sex." I wink at her.

"I'll clean up," she says.

Still laughing, she stands up and starts clearing the plates. I reach over and take her arm, pulling her down onto my lap.

"No, you won't." I nibble on her ear as I wrap my arms around her. "The only thing you'll be cleaning up is yourself— after I have my way with you."

I smirk as she dissolves into laughter and wipe away the tears from her eyes.

Smooth, Luke. Very smooth.

"Tell me that sounded better in your head." She chokes the words out.

"Much better in my head," I admit. "Granted, it wasn't the most flattering line, but it's all I had, so I went with it."

She shakes her head, smiling as I gently kiss her on the lips. She stands up and turns around, straddling me on the chair with her arms loosely draped around my neck. My heart pounds as my fingers creep underneath her shirt. She sighs as I touch her skin, running my hands up to her breasts. I reach behind her back to unclasp her bra, removing both that and her shirt. She groans as I close my mouth over her nipple.

"Oh God," she mumbles, closing her eyes.

I kiss her neck as my fingernails trail softly along her arched back.

"That feels so good," she mumbles. She cracks open an eye and smirks at me. "But if you really want to impress me, a massage would be amazing..."

I chuckle. "What do you think this is?"

She stands up and faces me.

I stand up, too, lifting her into my arms. I carry her down to the second door on the balcony, which leads into her bedroom. I roughly press my mouth against hers and then throw her on the bed, lying down next to her.

"You sure you're not too tired for this?" I tease her as I massage her breasts.

She whimpers as I kiss her mouth, then her neck. I unbutton her skirt and ease it down her thighs, then I roll her lacey panties off, her sweet scent hitting me out of nowhere.

"I'm sure." Her eyes flash as I smirk at her.

She stares at me with anticipation, watching me as I stand up and undress. I lie back down and roll her on top of me. She hovers above my length, one leg on either side of me, teasing my cock as she just barely makes contact.

My hands firmly on her hips, I thrust into her, sliding her down over my shaft. She groans, clutching my arms as I rock her back and forth.

"You feel fucking amazing," I grunt. "There's no better feeling than being buried deep in your pussy."

She reaches down, running her own fingers over her clit, while my cock invades her. I groan because the site of her touching herself like that is incredible. She knows it turns me on, and she's playing it up for me. She's trying to drive me crazy. I groan and bounce her harder and faster on my cock.

"I'm gonna come," I growl, clutching tightly onto her hips, ramming myself deep inside her as I release. "Shit." I chuckle. "That all happened a bit faster than I was expecting."

She laughs as she leans down to kiss me. I roll off her onto my side, pressing my mouth against hers. Just because I'm done, it doesn't mean she is. She exhales loudly as I slide my finger inside her and draw circles around her clit. As I kiss her, she presses her legs together, her hands clutching at my wrist, begging me to go deeper and begging me to stop at the same time.

"Fuck."

She whimpers and tilts her head and arches her back, as I close my mouth over her nipple. I suck hard as her fingers entwine in my hair. She gasps, her body convulsing as she comes.

"Holy crap," she moans, squirming beneath me. "Stop. Get away," she pants, pushing me away from her.

I chuckle, but oblige, because the last thing I want to do is torture her. I'll save that for another day. I kiss her again, this time letting my lips glide roughly against hers, the salty taste of her sweat turning me on.

"You're an amazing woman, Laura."

I mutter the words, as my tongue circles her earlobe. She smiles and curls up into my arms. Then she rolls over so I can spoon her. I wrap my arm around her waist and kiss her softly on the neck, pulling her against me.

"Have you heard anything about the research project?" I ask her. She shakes her head.

"Not yet. I've applied, probably along with every other person in the group."

"I'm sure you'll get it."

She smiles at me. "I wish I was as confident as you. I really want it, but so does everyone else, and unfortunately for me, everyone else is just as qualified as I am."

"Maybe, but they don't have one thing that you do."

"And what's that?" She stares at me, waiting for my answer. "You?"

I smirk at her response.

"No. I mean passion and the drive to succeed. I see it whenever you talk about your specialty and what you want to do. I see the need and determination in your eyes, and I know you'll achieve whatever you set your mind to." God, I sound more like Lewin every day. "That's what will make the difference. Trust me."

She still doesn't look convinced as she leans over and turns off the lamp. She kisses me, then rolls over, cuddling into my arms. I kiss the back of her head and wrap my arms around her.

She'll get it. I know she will.

I'м up early the next morning for my eight a.m. start and somehow even manage to get ready without waking Laura. As much as I want to kiss those sweet lips goodbye—especially with the way she's draped herself so sexily with that sheet—I resist because I want to let her sleep for as long as possible. She hasn't been sleeping well. She doesn't think I notice when she sneaks out of bed in the middle of the night, but I do, and I'm worried about her. There is something on her mind, but I don't know how to get her to open up to me. I just wish she felt she could talk to me about it.

HALFWAY THROUGH MY SHIFT, Lewin sends me down to the emergency room for a cardiac consult. I'm not even sure if that's allowed, but I go with it, because I'm flattered that he trusts me that much. He's been flat out planning the surgery for Ben's mechanical heart, so I'm happy to do whatever is needed to take some of that pressure off him.

The ER is busier than I've ever seen it, thanks to a multi-car collision and being short staffed. After my consult, things get even more chaotic, so I hang around to help out until things are back under control.

Nearly two hours later, it's returned to normal levels of chaos. I quickly scribble down my notes on my last patient so I can go back up to Lewin and find out how Ben is doing. My shift is almost over, but I want to make sure he's okay before I leave. I walk over to the elevator, stopping when someone calls my name. I sigh, convinced I'm about to be asked to stay down here longer.

"What can I do for you?" I say to the nurse.

"There's a lady asking for you in cubicle two."

"Okay, sure," I say.

I'm surprised, because in three years of residency and now this fellowship, I've never been requested by anyone. I walk over to cubicle two and push back the privacy curtain that is wrapped around it.

"Hello, I'm Doctor..."

I stop in my tracks and stare at the woman in front of me. She smiles, but there's uncertainty in her eyes, like she's scared of how I'm going to react. *Holy shit.*

"Abbey?"

She smiles weakly. "Hey. I wasn't sure if you'd remember me."

"Remember you? Of course, I remember you," I murmur.

I haven't seen Abbey in years, but I'd recognize her anywhere. There is no mistaking her because when I look in those eyes, all I see is Maya. I met Maya and her sister, Abbey, at a hostel when I was in London. The three of us hit it off and we hung out into the early hours of the morning. We stayed up all night, drinking too much and talking about my life in the states and their life in Germany. After Abbey went to bed, things between Maya and I heated up. That night, she ended up sucking me off in the bathroom, then I took her back to my bottom bunk bed of the eight-bed dorm I was in. Romantic, huh?

For the next three weeks after that night, Maya and I were inseparable. Until I went back to face the life I'd been trying so hard to forget. Seeing Abbey brings back a lot of memories, both good and bad.

Abbey steps forward to hug me, her movements awkward and forced. I hug her back and then step away, shaking my head. I still can't believe it's her. I want to ask her about Maya, but I can't force the words out.

"How did you find me?" I ask. "How did you know I worked here?"

"Trust me, that took a lot of effort," she says with a laugh.

I glance briefly at the little girl sitting on the examination bed. She smiles shyly at me as I crouch down next to her.

"Hello. What's your name?" I ask, smiling at her.

"Allie," she says quietly.

I glance at Abby and smile. "She looks just like you."

She smiles and then hunches forward. I frown and stand up, stepping forward to help balance her.

"Are you okay?" I frown at her. She lets go of my hands and nods. "I assumed Allie was the patient because she's lying down, but you look like the one who's about to pass out."

"Well, that's funny, because I feel like it." She forces a laugh and rubs the back of her neck, looking queasy. "Can we, uh, talk outside for a moment?"

"Sure. If you're sure you're okay."

"I think the fresh air will help," she says.

I lead her out through the side door, into the small sitting area near the garden. I'm not exactly sure what's going on, but I'm determined to find out. I start to say something, but she stops me.

"Please. Let me get this out." She takes a deep breath, not looking at me. "There's no easy way to say this," she mumbles.

She runs a hand through her long, blond curls, which remind me so much of Maya's. When she looks up at me the tears in her eyes make me nervous. I'm sure this is bad news about Maya. My heart pounds as I wait for her to speak

"Maya died."

Maya is dead?

My romance with Maya was a short and wild whirlwind that lasted all of a few weeks, but it still meant a lot to me. I was at a point in my life where everything felt helpless. I'd left college and gone overseas, because I couldn't get over the death of my father. Maya was what saved me. I knew our relationship wasn't based on love, but those few weeks with her were the turning point in my life.

"Wow." I shake my head, in shock. "How? When?"

"Six months ago." She pauses and stares down at her hands. "I've been trying to find you for the last four months. I thought you'd want to know, and I..." She shakes her head and wipes away tears.

"What happened?" I ask, still trying to get my head around the fact that Maya is gone.

"Car accident. She was killed instantly. A drunk driver

veered onto the wrong side of the road and smashed into her car."

"I'm so sorry. That must've been terrible for you." I don't know what else to say. I shake my head.

"There's more." She breathes out and seems to gather her strength, sitting forward to rest her arms against her thighs. I frown because sometime is really bothering her.

"What is it, Abbey?"

She looks up and meets my eyes, my heart pounding when I see the fear hiding in them.

"Allie is your daughter."

For a brief moment, my whole world stops.

I shake my head in shock, convinced I heard her wrong. I glance at her, half expecting her to break into a smile and tell me she's joking, but she doesn't. Holy fuck. No way. That can't be right. How could I have a child that I had no idea existed?

I shake my head. I just can't believe it.

Maya would've told me. Wouldn't she? I think.

"What do you mean she's my daughter?"

My voice is low and doesn't sound like my own. I frown at her, waiting for her to say something—*anything*, at this point because none of this is making any fucking sense.

"How is it even possible?" I add, my voice rising. I stand up and shake my head, the shock slowly giving way to anger. "How long has it been? Nine years and someone finally decides to tell me I have a child? How could she not have told me something so important?" I growl. I shake my head and glare at Abbey. I know this isn't her fault, but she's here, and I need to take this out on someone. "How did this happen?" I ask. "We were only together for three weeks, for God's sake."

"It doesn't take three weeks to make a baby," Abby points out.

"Thanks for pointing out the obvious," I snap. I take a deep breath. It's Maya I'm really angry at. "She had my e-mail," I say calmly. "She should have told me. If she wanted to, she could have told me. You know that as well as I do."

"She knew what you were going through with your dad and college..." She stops, realizing her excuses are just that —excuses.

"That was my decision to make, not hers," I say, spitting out the words.

"She thought she was doing what was best for Allie." Abbey swipes away a fresh round of tears. I shove my hand in my pocket and retrieve a tissue, handing it to her. "Allie has been well-loved and cared for. Maya had my help, and our parents, while they were still alive. She was a happy, well-adjusted kid, until... until this happened."

"Your parents?" I frown.

She nods. "They were in the car too."

That poor kid.

"So why are you here? Why now?" I ask. I frown at her, my fingers tightly clasped into fists at my sides. She shakes her head and shrugs hopelessly.

"I've been asking myself the same thing," she admits. "I want to do what's right for Allie. I wasn't going to find you at all, and then I realized how selfish that was. Not only to her but to you. That little girl in there is amazing. You've missed out on so much, Luke. And she's been through so much..." Her voice trails off as she fights back the tears. "She deserves to know her father, and you deserve to know her."

I shake my head and sit back down. I feel numb. I don't know what to think or what to say, so I don't say anything. I repeat the words over and over in my head.

She's my daughter.

My daughter.

I have a child.

I've had a child for more than eight years and I never even knew it.

"I'm sorry," I whisper as I glance at her. "I'm not being rude; I just don't know how to deal with this. I don't know what to say or how I'm supposed to respond to this."

"It's okay. It's a huge shock, I understand that. If you need time to digest all of this, that's fine."

She pulls out a scrap of paper and a pen and then scribbles something down on it. She passes it to me, her hands shaking.

"That's my number and where I'm staying. We'll be here for as long as you need to come to terms with this." I nod and stare at her number. "Give me a call when you're ready to hear more about your daughter."

She stands up and walks back inside, leaving me sitting out there, lost in my thoughts. I hold my head in my hands, at a loss at what to think. How am I supposed to process this? My heart aches for Maya. Raising a kid—our kid—alone must have been so hard for her, but then I'm so angry at her for keeping this from me.

Poor Allie.

She doesn't deserve any of this. What do I say to her? She must hate me. I shake my head because it's all too much.

I can't deal with this now.

I jump when my phone vibrates in my pocket. My heart races when I pull it out because I know it's going to be Laura.

Laura: *Looking forward to seeing you later for dinner. I love you.*

I laugh as frustration, anger, pain, and a fuck load of other emotions fight to control me. It's the first time she's said she loves me. Now I have to go home and tell her I have a child? How fucked-up is that? This whole situation is a mess. One I have no idea how to fix. Before anything else, I need to speak to Laura, because I don't want to hide something like this from her.

How the fuck am I going to tell her about this?

CHAPTER TWELVE
LAURA

IT'S after ten when I finally drag myself out of bed. I'm shocked that I slept so late, because I was half expecting to wake up when Luke went to work in the early hours of the morning. I don't know why I can't just let him sleep. Probably because every time I see him lying there, I can't resist kissing or touching him.

My stomach churns as I force down a coffee. I can't even think about food, because I've decided that I'm telling him today. Now that the decision has been made, I grab my phone to text Luke to arrange dinner before I can talk myself out of it.

> **Me:** *Dinner tonight?*
> **Luke:** *Sure. I should finish about six. Anything wrong?*
> **Me:** *No, I just want to talk. Have a good shift.*

I rummage through the freezer to see if I can avoid going shopping. Unless I plan to serve him out of date chicken and yogurt that is growing its own yogurt, I can't. I frown and look around the kitchen. *Maybe I should just order takeout,* I say to myself. Let's face it, my cooking sucks hardcore, anyway, and cooking under stress will just make things even worse. *Pizza makes the best "I can't have kids" discussion food anyway,* I continue my with my inner dialogue,

Throwing myself down on the couch, I text Becca to see what she's up to.

> **Me:** *What's up?*
> **Becca:** *Not much. I'm off for three days because I have a movie to be on set for next week.*
> **Me:** *Want to come over?*
> **Becca:** *Sure. Lunch? I can get subs from Marcos?*

Marcos is the place they use on set where she works for lunches and they're fucking awesome. They're also hideously expensive, so it's something we only have once in a while.

> **Me:** *Perfect. My treat.*

It's only eleven and I'm already feeling anxious. If I don't find something to distract myself with, I'm going to drive myself crazy. I glance around, embarrassed at how messy my apartment is. Tidying should probably be my priority, but any motivation I had for cleaning went out the window when I slept in. Who am I kidding? The motivation was never there to begin with, because I hated cleaning with a passion.

I can spend the day cleaning, or I can go and visit Iris.

Iris wins, but too bad for me, she's not home.

I shake my head, because she's always home. I vaguely remember her complaining about a lady from a community outreach program who's been trying to get her out of the house to do her shopping. I trudge back to my apartment, slowly coming to terms with the fact that it's clean or sit around and stress out.

The thing with cleaning is that once I start, I can't stop. I guess that's the power of distraction. It's like I'm possessed. I even rearrange the living room, moving the couch and the TV over to the other side of the room to take advantage of the beautiful views I have.

By the time Becca turns up just after twelve, I'm wrecked. I open the door, accept the sub she hands me, and start devouring it before we've even sat down.

"Thanks," I say, in between mouthfuls. I should have asked for two.

She stops in her tracks when she sees the living room.

"Been busy, I see." She smirks. "You hate cleaning with a passion. The only time you do it is when you're trying to avoid thinking about something." She smiles at me. "Or someone."

"How would you know if I hated cleaning?" I grumble.

She's right, but I hate that she knows me so well.

"Ha, because I saw some of the things that crawled out of your bedroom when we were kids? Dude, I was scared to sleep in your room for fear I wouldn't wake up."

"Overreact much." I sniff, lifting my head.

"Oh, come on. You got away with it, because you were always sick." She giggles.

We walk outside onto the balcony and sit down to eat. Well, *Becca* eats, because I've pretty much finished mine. I sit with my back against the wall and close my eyes, feeling as relaxed as I've felt all day, while Becca crosses her legs and carefully unwraps her sub.

"So, does this thing you're trying not to think about have anything to do with talking to Luke?" she asks.

"I'm telling him everything tonight," I admit. "And I'm scared out of my mind."

"Good." She smiles at me and reaches for my hand. "Well, not the bit where you're scared, but the telling him part. For what it's worth, I think you're overreacting. He's going to be fine. He likes you a lot. Sure, it's going to be a hurdle and probably a shock, but he'll get over it. You'll get over it together. I'm sure of it."

"I wish I was that confident," I say.

I glance at her, hoping for a subject change.

"How's work going?" she asks.

I sigh, relieved. I swear that girl can read my mind sometimes.

"Good. Did I tell you about the research project I've

applied for?" I ask. "If I get it, I'll spend six months in Switzerland, working on a fertility study."

"That's really cool," she says, sounding genuinely happy for
me. "But it's a long time to be away from your family... and
Luke," she adds, his name rolling off her tongue like an
afterthought.

"It's only six months," I protest. "Not to mention the fact
that this is my dream. It's what I've been waiting for."

"I know, but exactly how long have you spent away from
him since you guys got together?" I frown at her know it
all smirk.

"Well, that's hardly the same, considering we live together,"
I retort. "And the way our hours clash all the time, you'd be
surprised at how little time we actually do get to spend together."

Besides, he might not even be an issue then, I think to
myself.

"Hey, when's his place ready?" she asks.

"Any day now." I frown, not liking how that makes me feel.

"You don't look thrilled at the idea of him moving out."

"I guess because I'm not." I shrug. I like things the way they
are. "I hate the idea of him moving out, but I feel like I can't ask
him to stay until I've told him that I can't have kids." I pause.
That made more sense in my head.

Becca frowns at me. "What does him living here have to do
with having kids? Unless it's a requirement on your lease agree-
ment?" she teases. I glower at her.

"No, I just mean that asking him to stay is a big deal. It's pretty much asking him to move in with me. It means things are serious, and if they're that serious, then this conversation should have already happened."

"I guess there is some skewed logic in there somewhere." She shakes her head. "So just tell him, then ask him to stay?"

"That's my plan. But he might not want to stay after hearing what I have to say."

"If that happens, then you weren't meant to be together in the first place," she says softly. "I'm sorry, but if he can't look past this, then he's not the guy for you."

I know she has a point, but it's not always that simple.

"So, how are you *really* feeling?" Becca asks, as if reading my mind. "Not about Luke. I mean in general."

"I'm okay."

"I call bullshit," she replies. "Come on, Loz. I'm the one person that you can whine to without feeling bad about it. Take advantage of me. I'm all yours." She spreads her arms and nods at me.

"Fine. I'm pissed off and angry. Then when that subsides, I get upset, terrified and jealous and convinced I'm going to end up alone with a thousand cats. Happy?"

"Not really. I hate cats," she replies. She sighs and wads up her sub wrapper into a tight ball, tossing it at me. "Maybe that's what you need to tell Luke," she says softly. "Be honest, show him that you're hurting too. Don't take all of the emotion out of it and make this seem like nothing. You can't have kids. That sucks just as much for you, as it does for him."

"But I've had thirteen years to get used to the idea."

"And how's that worked out for you?" she asks. I frown at her, not answering. "Look, all you can do is be honest with him. The rest is up to him."

"I know." My heart races as I force the next sentence out. "I'm just terrified of losing him, Becs."

"I know you are."

She crawls over to me and gives me a hug, then she wipes away my tears.

"If he's not the guy, then I'll marry you and we can have two thousand cats." She pauses for a second, her brown eyes sparkling. "But just so we're clear, I draw the line at fingering you again."

I groan and push her away. "Are you ever going to let me live that down?"

"Nope. Probably not." She grins.

We move inside when the clouds threaten to pour down with rain, and for the rest of the afternoon, we laze on the couch, watching TV and talking. One of the things I love about Becca is that she can distract me from anything. And she has, because before I know it, Luke is due home.

"I better go," Becca says. "Unless you think me being here—"

"After last time?" I snort. "Go."

I smile as I walk her to the door. She gives me a hug and kisses me on the cheek.

"Call me if you need anything, okay?"

"Thanks, and thanks for coming over."

I shut the door and sit back down on the couch, tucking my legs up under me. I'm shaking, I'm so nervous. It's the not knowing how he's going to react that that gets me the most. I tap out a text, reminding him about dinner, signing it with I love you. I press send and then realize what I've done. I stare at the message and laugh, because it's the first time I've ever truly been honest about how I feel.

I love him.

I've hit that point, which means I definitely should've told him a long time ago.

Luke: *I'm looking forward to it too. Work is crazy, but I'll be home as soon as I can.*

THE MINUTES TICK by and six becomes seven, which turns into eight.

Before long, I'm sitting out on the balcony at nearly nine in the evening, staring off into the darkness. To be honest, I'm relieved that he got held up at work. I know I still have to tell him, but even avoiding the conversation for one more night sounds good to me right now. I don't even hear the balcony door slide open until he's standing there, in front of me. I glance up at him, my heart pounding, because I'm not prepared for this. I shiver uncontrollably, only just realizing how cold I am. He walks back inside, returning moments later with a blanket.

"What are you doing out here?" he asks. "You're freezing," he adds, wrapping it around my shoulders. "Are you okay?"

I nod, my heart racing as I build up the courage to tell him. He sits down next to me wrapping his arms around me.

"I need to tell you something."

I glance at him, because he took the words out of my mouth. The expression on his face scares me so much, that for a moment I forget about my own problems. Something is seriously wrong.

"What is it?" I ask, frowning at him. My heart races as I run through all the worst possible scenarios in my head.

"I don't even know how to tell you..." He shakes his head, looking down at the ground. "This whole thing is a mess."

"What is?" I ask. "What's wrong?"

I reach for his hand and wrap my fingers around his. He's so tense and he won't look at me. It's like he's in shock.

"I just found out... something." He takes a deep breath. "How am I supposed to tell you this?"

"Just tell me," I urge him. I'm not sure how much more I can take before I start trying to shake it out of him. *Something?* What the hell is *something?*

"I... I have a daughter."

With that one sentence, my heart stops beating.

My hand slips from his as I stare at him, my whole world stopping for one tiny moment. I hear nothing of the sounds around us, just the *beat, beat, beat* of my heart thumping wildly in my chest. I breathe in, forcing air into my lungs, because if I don't actively think about breathing, I'm going to forget and pass out.

He has a daughter?

A child.

I lift my gaze to his, but he still can't look at me. I shake my head, words completely abandoning me. He's a father. He has a daughter. I look at the ground, still unable to form a sentence or even think about what this really means.

"What..."

I cough, clearing my throat, and then I try again.

"How... What are you talking about? You have a daughter that you didn't know about?"

I string enough words together to qualify it as a sentence. He nods absently, as though he's trying to figure it out too. He stares down at his hands and shakes his head again.

"I had no idea she existed, until today."

"How?" I ask.

"It was after my dad died," he begins. "I met Maya in London. She was there from Germany, with her sister, Abbey. We spent three weeks together, which was apparently long enough for me to father a child." He laughs bitterly and leans his head back against the wall, staring up at the dark sky.

"And she never told you? How did you find out about her?" I ask. "That must make her, what, nine?"

"She's eight. Abbey came in to the hospital today. She'd been looking for me since..." He glances at me. "And yes, she never told me. Maya died in a car crash six months ago. Her parents were killed too. That poor kid has nobody other than her aunt."

"And you," I whisper.

"And me." He shakes his head and laughs bitterly. "God, I can't even fathom what she must think of me. She must hate me for not being there for her."

"I don't know what to say," I tell him, as my hand tightens around his. He glances at me and forces out a small smile.

"I'm so sorry to spring all of this on you. And like this? I didn't know whether to tell or not..." He closes his eyes and breathes out heavily. "At least until I had time to process it myself, but I didn't want to keep something so major from you."

"Thank you for telling me," I say. His words slice through my heart. "I can't imagine how hard this must be for you."

"The biggest struggle is feeling like I've failed her. All this time, she was there, and I never knew." He lets out a growl. "My first reaction was anger. I was so, so angry at Maya for keeping her from me. I mean, how messed up is that? How can I be angry at a dead woman?" He laughs.

"Do you know why she didn't tell you?" I ask softly.

He shrugs. "Abbey said something about Maya thought it would be easier that way. For everyone. But how was it easier for that little girl to think that her father didn't care about her? How was that easier for me?" He shakes his head and runs his hand through his hair. "I'm such a mess." He glances at me. "I'm sorry for ruining your night."

"It's fine," I say.

I wrap my arms around him and hug him, while trying to

process it all. We sit on the balcony, neither of us saying anything. At one point, I think I fall asleep, and then I wake up and remember... he has a child. This is such a nightmare. I can't let myself think about what this means for us, because if I do that, I'll lose my grip on everything.

"We should go inside." He stands up and extends his hand, helping me to my feet.

I sit down on the couch, hugging a cushion, while Luke disappears into the kitchen. He comes back a few minutes later with two beers.

"It was this or some funky looking yogurt you should probably think about throwing out."

I smile at that and take my beer, then flick on the TV. We both stare at it absently. I'm not watching it, and I don't think he is, but it's better than the silence that was dominating the room.

"Are you okay?" I ask him.

I feel like it's all I'm saying, but what else is there?

He nods and then shakes his head. "I don't know. I can't put into words what I'm feeling, because my thoughts are all over the place. I'm just..." He sighs and then covers his face with his hands. "I'm calm one second and then terrified out of my mind the next. I'm just... a mess."

He frowns at me.

"And I haven't even asked you how you're doing. I can't even imagine how this must be for you." He takes my hand and kisses it. "I'm so sorry, Laura. I've ruined everything," he mutters.

"It's okay," I whisper.

My heart races as he leans over and kisses me on the lips. His eyes plead with me, but I don't know what for. I can feel his pain and it's breaking my heart because I want to reassure him, but I can't.

"I might just go to bed. I think I just need to..."

He doesn't even finish the sentence. He just gets to his feet and walks out of the room, leaving me alone with my thoughts.

Switching off the TV, I sit there in the darkness with my head resting back and stare at the ceiling. I'm doing my best not to fall into a cycle of self-pity, and make this about me, but it's hard. Sometimes I just feel like it never ends, because it's one cruel twist after another.

I'm not sure how much more I can take.

CHAPTER THIRTEEN
LUKE

I LIE THERE AWAKE, staring into the darkness for the whole night, until dawn begins to break. At some point, Laura joins me, but I pretend to be asleep, until I hear the soft sounds of her snoring. When I'm sure she's sleeping, I sneak out of the bed and sit on the couch. It's cold, but I don't care. I'm too numb to care about anything. I feel like my whole life is a lie because I've had this huge part kept from me. Every time I close my eyes, I see Maya's face, which is strange, because I haven't thought about her in nine years. *Maybe that was the problem. If I'd kept in contact, then she might have told me about Allie,* I rationalize to myself.

I don't start work until eight, but I decide to go in early.

I thought the distraction would help, but all I end up doing is sitting in the staffroom, alone, waiting for my shift to begin. Ironically, exactly what I was doing at home, anyway.

I toss my phone from one hand to the other. I look down, startled, when it vibrates loudly. I unlock it and navigate to the new message waiting for me. It's the realtor, letting me know that my apartment is ready for me to move into. I frown at the message, because it's just another problem I'm in no condition to face today. Sighing, I shove my phone in my pocket and lean back against the chair. My head pounds from lack of sleep and the fourteen coffees I've had are making me jittery.

Maybe I should've just called in sick.

"You're here early."

I look up and see Lewin, leaning against the doorframe. He stares at me, his usual frown on his face. I stand up and nod at him. I hate him seeing me like this.

"I couldn't sleep."

"Great. Then you'll be in fine form to assist me in Ben's heart transplant."

My head shoots up. Did I hear him right?

"You mean his mechanical heart?" I clarify.

"No. A match just came in. He's getting his transplant today. A real heart."

I stare at him, my eyes wide. "Are you serious?"

Lewin frowns at me. "Am I the kind of guy to joke around?"

"That's true."

I laugh because I can't believe it. This is just what I need to get me through today.

"So, what do we need to do?" I ask.

"Well, *I* need to prepare Ben for a seven-hour open-heart

surgery."

"And me?" I wait anxiously.

"You need to go home and get some rest," he replies. He sighs as he looks me in the eye. "You're in no condition to help me out with this. You know that as well as I do."

"Are you kidding me?" I glare at him. "After everything I've done to help that kid, you're not going to let me assist?"

"If I did, you'd probably end up killing him. You want that on your conscience? Look at yourself. You're a mess, Luke. Be thankful that he's getting his heart and leave it at that. By all means, sit in the galley and watch, but I can't let you in there."

I curse under my breath and stalk past him. Out in the corridor, I run straight into Laura. She frowns at me, her smile faltering when I don't return it.

"Are you okay?" she asks. "You left early," she adds.

"Ben is getting a new heart."

"Isn't that good news?" she asks softly.

"Sure. Only Lewin doesn't think I'm fit to be in there, helping out." My voice is flat, which is ironically exactly how I feel. She frowns and glances down. I shake my head. "And you don't think I should be in there, either. Fucking great."

"Did you sleep at all last night?" she asks softly. "Put yourself in his position," she adds when I don't answer. "Would *you* want you in that surgery?"

"I have to get out of here," I mutter. "I'll see you later."

I push past her and race outside, stalking over to my car. I open the door, but just as I'm about to get in, a hand shoots out to stop me. I turn around to glare at the person and find Laura standing there.

"Can I show you something?" she asks.

I start to protest, but she slips under me and slides in behind the wheel. I give up and walk around, getting in the other side, because I don't have the energy to argue with her.

"Where are we going?" I ask her as she takes off.

"You'll see."

A few minutes later, we pull up outside a hotel. I shake my head. Is this some ploy to get me to sleep? It wouldn't matter where I was; here, at home, or my car. I wouldn't be able to sleep.

"This isn't going to work," I say. I'm frustrated, because all this is doing is wasting her time and money.

"Humor me."

She frowns at me until I give in and get out of my car. I follow her inside, standing back while she speaks to the receptionist. A few minutes later, she takes my hand and leads me to the elevator. We ride up to the tenth floor and then get out. I follow her down the hallway, not saying a word. She stops outside number one twenty-four, a satisfied smile on her face, then she unlocks the door. She walks in, with me following her. I stand there and stare at her as she sits down on the bed and studies my face.

"Do you know where we are?" she asks.

"A shitty hotel?"

"Not just a shitty hotel. This used to be the children's hospital before they built a new wing at Mercy. This very spot where I'm sitting is where I spent three weeks recovering from my first major surgery when I was thirteen. There used to be a hospital here before they built this hotel."

I stare at her. I had no idea she'd been through anything like that.

"What happened?"

"I was in and out of the hospital for a lot of my teen years, but what was wrong isn't the point. You think I cared who did that surgery? No. What made the difference to me was the intern who sat on my bed for two hours that morning, explaining to me what they were going to do. And the resident who used to let me beat him at poker every afternoon, just to take my mind off things. He spent his lunch break with me. *They're* the names I remember, because they made the difference to me."

"Why did you bring me here?" I ask, even though I already know the answer

"Because I see how much you care about patients, like Ben, and then you rip yourself apart because of it. I wanted to show you that those kind of doctor's matter too. That *you* matter." She pauses for a moment and looks up at me. "Ben doesn't care if you're in that operating room or not. He cares if you're there for him before and after."

"You're amazing. You know that?" I walk over and sit down next to her.

"I'm just pointing out what you already know," she says.

I lie back and rest my head in her lap. She gently strokes my hair as I close my eyes, then she leans over and kisses my fore-head. I sigh, remembering something else.

"I got a text from the realtor. My apartment is ready for me to move in."

"That's great," she says.

"Is it?" I gaze up into her eyes, trying to figure out if she really means that or not. "Yesterday, I was all ready to tell you that I didn't want to move out. Now I feel like after everything that's happened, staying wouldn't be fair to you."

I reach for her hand, because there is so much I want to tell her. Once I start opening up to her, it all wants to come tumbling out. And that's probably for the best. I need to get all of this out now. Even if it kills me.

"More than anything, I want you to be okay with Allie, but I know I have to respect that this is a big thing to accept and it's going to take time. I don't think it's fair to have Allie come over to your place while you're doing that. Maybe me moving out would be the best thing, at least until we know where we both stand."

I look at her, wishing she would say something, but she won't even meet my eyes. My heart pounds. All I want is to hear her say that everything is going to be fine.

"Now would be a great time for you to say something," I add anxiously.

"The problem is I don't know what to say." She takes a deep breath and forces herself to look me in the eye. "I wanted you to stay, more than anything..."

"And now?"

"I don't know." She looks like she's about to cry. "I don't want to be the reason you don't get to know your daughter. Maybe you should focus on your relationship with Allie, and then work out where we stand."

I open my mouth to argue, but then I don't. I haven't slept properly in days. Now isn't the time to be making major decisions that will affect the rest of my life. I stifle a yawn, fighting the urge to close my eyes, but I'm so tired.

I could so easily fall asleep...

I OPEN my eyes and look around, taking a moment for them to adjust to being awake. I'm still lying on the bed, with my head resting in her lap. I sit up and rub my eyes, stifling a yawn. I think I feel worse than before, if that's even possible.

"What time is it?" I yawn. "I can't believe I actually fell asleep." I shake my head, and then cringe when I remember what we were talking about.

"You've been asleep for nearly six hours." She smiles.

"Well, shit. I guess I needed it."

"We can go back to the hospital, so you can watch the surgery up in the galley, if you like?" she asks.

"That would be good," I say, gratefully. "Thanks for bringing me here and telling me about what happened to you." I glance around the room again and shake my head, smiling for the first time all day. "They really tore down a children's hospital to build this shitty hotel?"

She laughs and nods. "If it were a *good* hotel, I could kind of understand it, but this?" She shakes her head. "The first time I came here it felt so weird. Lying here in the dark now, all I could think about was how all those years ago I was in this very spot, feeling just as alone and scared."

"What was the surgery for?" I ask her.

She's quiet for a moment, then she speaks.

"I had a reproductive disorder that meant my body produced large cysts. Sometimes they just kept growing. When I was fourteen, one burst and became infected. It nearly killed me. I was in the hospital for weeks recovering, which led to more surgeries..."

"That must've been rough," I say, feeling for her. I had no idea she's been through so much.

She nods. "It was, but it could've been worse. I mean, I survived, right? I'm still here. Apparently, it could have easily gone either way."

She pauses and looks up at me, her eyes meeting mine.

"There's more," she mutters. "I have to tell—"

She stops when my phone interrupts her. I glance down as it vibrates madly in my hand, my heart stopping when I see the message. It's a page from Lewin, telling me to get back to the hospital ASAP.

"Shit," I mutter.

"What is it?"

"Lewin paged me. He wants me there now."

I stare at the alert, my heart pounding. This can't be good. Laura stares at me for a moment then she nods and gets to her feet.

"Let's go, then."

WE CHECK out of the hotel and race to the car. Laura insists on driving, and given how anxious and scared I'm feeling, it's probably not the worst idea. I stare out the window, annoyed that the traffic is stopping us from getting there faster.

"He must have died."

Laura glances at me. "You don't know that."

"Why else would Lewin page me?"

She doesn't answer. She reaches over and squeezes my hand, trying to reassure me.

We pull into the parking lot and I jump out while Laura finds a parking spot. I race inside, sprinting down to the other end of the hospital, toward the operating rooms. I stop at the board and search through the schedule for Ben's name, but I can't find it.

I'm too late, a voice inside my head says.

"Did you find him?" Laura asks. She pants, her cheeks flushed red, like she ran here. I shake my head, and then she grabs my arm. "Luke. Down there."

I look in the direction she's pointing and see Lewin waving at me. *Thank God.* I run down the corridor toward him. I try to read his expression, but he gives me nothing.

He nods through the window of the intensive care unit room he's standing in front of. Ben lies on the bed, surrounded by equipment, but he's alive.

"I thought you'd want to know," he says. "Sorry if I had you worried. These stupid pagers only allow for about three words. He's stable, and for now, his body is accepting the new heart. Things are going as well as we could have hoped."

"Thank fuck for that," I say, breathing out.

Lewin glances at me. "What's going on with you? I know you've been worried about Ben, but you're even more stressed out than usual."

"It's nothing," I mutter. "Just some personal issues I'm trying to work through."

"Okay. Well, go home and figure them out." He frowns at me "If you need to talk..."

I glance at him and choke back a laugh. I couldn't imagine opening up to Lewin about anything, but I appreciate he cares enough to offer.

"Thanks," I say.

"Go home and get some sleep, okay? You look like shit."

Laura wraps her hands around mine. I smile and kiss her on the lips. She hesitates for a second, and then pulls away as though she's embarrassed to show affection at work.

"Listen to Lewin and go home. Get some rest, okay?" she says.

"What about you?" I frown.

She shakes her head. She smiles, trying to hide the troubled look in her eyes.

"I'm fine. Don't wait up for me, okay?"

"Sure."

I watch her as she walks down the hallway, away from me. I have no idea what just happened, or what to do about it. Do I give her space or make her talk to me? That's the thing. I don't know. I have no idea where she's at with the whole Allie thing. We need to talk, but not here and not while I'm running on empty.

I WALK from my car into Laura's apartment, texting Abbey on the way to see if we can arrange for me to spend time with Allie tomorrow. I let myself inside and collapse on the couch. I'm exhausted and not even sure I can make it to the bedroom. I glance around, feeling bittersweet at the idea of moving out. I don't want to leave Laura, but maybe it is for the best. At least until Laura figures out whether Allie is a deal breaker for her. The last thing I want to do is put extra pressure on her and I think by staying here, that's what I'm doing.

I climb into bed and stare at the ceiling. I've got the gnawing feeling that I'm going to struggle to sleep again, only this time, it will be a number of things keeping me awake. Sighing, I reach for my phone to check for a reply from Abbey. I sit up when I see the little message icon.

> **Abbey:** *Sure. She would love to see you.*
> **Me:** *How about the park near the hospital? I take my lunch break at twelve. There's a playground and ducks there.*

I frown. Is eight too old for ducks and playgrounds? I shake my head. I guess I'll find out.

Abbey: *Sounds good. We'll see you then.*

I close my eyes and try to force myself to sleep, which turns out to be even more unsuccessful than every other technique I've tried. All I can think about is Laura. She's still not home, which makes me wonder if she is avoiding finishing our conversation. I know she started early, and while she could be doing a double, it was more likely that she went to stay with Matt, or Becca, rather than come back her. I'm trying so hard to do the best thing for both of us, but nothing feels right. I've got the sinking feeling that nothing is going to be able to save us.

BETWEEN THE FATIGUE, looking after Ben, and the nerves about spending time with Allie, it's been a killer of a day already, but the moment I see Allie, my mood begins to lift. I wave at them as they walk across the park and over to where I sit. It's still so surreal to look at her and think she's my daughter. I made her. How freaky is that?

"Hey," I say when they're close enough to hear me.

I smile at Allie, who shyly smiles back at me. She tucks a loose blond curl behind her ear, which makes me smile. All those honey blond curls and that bright grin... she's definitely going to be breaking hearts one day—which also means I'm going to be breaking some necks.

She stands so close to Abbey that she's almost using her as a shield. It's a cold day, much colder her than I was expecting, so

I suggest we sit around the other side of the park, inside the small café. Allie walks between us as we cross through the park in that direction. The burst of warmth that hits us when we walk inside, is a welcome change.

"Want a milkshake?" I ask, raising my eyebrows at her.

"Oh, yes, please." She nods

"Chocolate?" I guess.

"You mean there are other flavors?" she jokes with a laugh.

"And a coffee for you?" I say to Abbey.

"Cream, no sugar." She nods.

I order our drinks and then lean against the counter to watch Allie. She laughs at something Abbey says and I feel a stab of jealously. It comes so easily for them. I hate that she's so much more relaxed when I'm not around. I get why, but it still hurts to think that I'm her father and she's not comfortable around me. I know that she's known Abbey all her life and comparing myself to her is never going to end well, but I can't get doubts out of my mind. My own daughter can barely say a sentence to me. What if that never changes?

What if we never have a real relationship? I wonder.

We take our drinks back outside. It's warmer now the sun has come out. Allie feeds some birds her left over bread from breakfast, while Abbey and I talk. I keep my phone on, just in case Lewin needs me.

"How's she doing?" I ask.

"She's doing well, all things considered." She glances at me. "You, on the other hand, look really nervous."

"You think?" I shake my head. "Sorry, I'm just really tense. Not just about this, but about everything. Allie. Work..."

Laura.

"It must be really stressful, what you do," she sympathizes.

I shrug. "It is, and it isn't. A little boy I've been looking after got a new heart yesterday. He's about Allie's age."

"Wow, that must've been scary for his mom," she says with a frown.

"It was, but without it, his prognosis was very poor. It feels good to make a difference, you know?"

I watch Allie, a knot forming in my stomach. I felt so much for Ben. I couldn't even imagine if it were Allie in that situation. I don't know how Marissa handled it.

I turn to Abby. "What do you want out of this?"

"Pardon?" She stares at me, shocked by my question. "What do you mean?" she asks, frowning at me.

"I mean, why are you here? I know that you want what's best for Allie, but on some level, you must be hoping for a particular outcome." I pause for a second, because I'm not even sure what I'm getting at. "Do you want to leave her here with me? Take her back home? What do you want, Abbey?" I ask quietly.

"Leave her here..." Her voice trails off. She shakes her head, her eyes flashing with anger. "You think that's what this is? You think I want to abandon my niece in a country she's never been to, with a man she barely knows?"

"I'm sorry, but I don't know what to think. I'm just... this is the first time I've ever had this kind of thing dropped on me," I say.

I cringe when I think about what I just said to her. It came out completely not how I had intended it to. I hope she understands that I didn't mean it like that.

"I want to do what's right, but I can't figure out what that is," she says softly. "One thing I do know, is that rushing into anything is a bad idea. For the both of you. I'm not planning on leaving her here with you, if that's what you think. I don't know what the right thing is. Whether she eventually lives with you or whether she stays with me and my husband and you visit her every now... I don't know. I just don't know."

I nod, because neither do I.

"I didn't realize you were married," I say after a while.

She smiles. "Yes, Sam and I are going on six years now. He's why I moved to London. We've got a little girl. She's two."

"Allie must love that." I grin.

"She does. I think Jessie has really helped her heal after her loss. The last few months have been hell on that poor kid."

I watch Allie giggle as a duck chases her and smile.

"Hey, do you guys want to come to my place for dinner tonight?" I ask.

"Sure." Abbey smiles. "That sounds great."

"What's her favorite meal?" I ask, nodding at Allie.

"Well, that's an easy one. Spaghetti Bolognese."

"I'm pretty sure I can manage that." I chuckle.

I LEAVE Allie and Abby in the park and head back over to the hospital. I try calling Laura on the way, but there's no answer.

When I get back, the first thing I do is go to the ICU and sit with Ben for a while. He's still in an induced coma to give his body the best chance at accepting the heart, but I hate the thought of him being alone in there, hooked up to all those machines. I sit there for nearly an hour and talk about random things that would mean nothing to anyone who isn't an eight-year-old boy. I look up and see his mother standing there, smiling at me. I smile back, embarrassed that she caught me rambling to her son.

I stand up. "Sorry, I'll leave you alone."

"Don't be sorry and please don't feel like you have to go."

"No, I should've gone back to work a while ago, only he wouldn't shut up." I grin.

She laughs at my joke, then her expression turns serious.

"Thank you for sitting with him," she says. "I had to go and do some errands. It will mean a lot to him that you came to visit."

"I'm just glad he's doing okay," I say, touched by her words.

"He is, and it's all thanks to you and Professor Lewin. I can't thank you enough for everything you've done for us," she adds, her voice a whisper.

She steps forward and wraps her arms around me, hugging me. I respond awkwardly, caught off guard by her gesture, but then I relax. It feels good. It's like everything Laura said to me in that hotel room yesterday is validated by this reaction. The gratitude she feels toward me, makes it all worth it.

As I leave work that evening, I spot Laura outside. She has her phone in her hands, but she's too far away for me to yell out to, so I call her phone. She stares at the screen, and then ignores my call, placing the phone back in her pocket. My heart races. What was that? If I ever needed proof that she's avoiding me, there it was.

I WALK AROUND HER APARTMENT, feeling lost. It feels weird, leaving like this, but I think it's the best option. We didn't really resolve anything yesterday at the hotel, but I got the feeling that she needs space. Then, when she ignored my call... I need to give her the space to work all of this out, and maybe I need it too. I sit down at the kitchen counter to write her out a note. I intend on writing one or two sentences, but before I know it, I'm pouring my heart out. It feels good to just let it all out. I stand up and walk over to the door, where I pick up my suitcase. I take one last look around her apartment before I walk out.

I head toward my apartment, but then drive straight past it, because I need to speak to someone. Someone who understands what I'm going through. Someone who was there. Matt met Maya, and Laura is his sister. He's the only person that can really understand everything.

"Matt," I call out.

I bang on his door again, this time louder. I'm not sure what I'm going to say to him, mainly because I don't know what Laura has said. She might not have told him anything. The door swings open and an angry looking Matt stalks outside.

"Can you shut the fuck up," he hisses.

Fuck.

The baby.

"Shit, I'm sorry, I'm sorry, I forgot about Elina," I mumble, rubbing my head.

He stares at me and shakes his head, his anger turning into concern.

"What's wrong?"

"Uh, how about everything?" I shake my head and laugh.

"Sit down," he orders, guiding me down the porch.

I sit down on one of the seats leaning against the wall

"Okay, talk to me," he says.

I lower my head. "Jesus, where do I even start?" I mutter. "You know who turned up in the ER the other day?"

"Who?" he frowns.

"Abbey. As in Maya and Abbey."

Matt's eyes widen. "Are you kidding me? What did she want? Was Maya with her?"

"Nope, but her daughter was."

"Her daughter?" he asks.

I nod and look at him. "*My* daughter."

"Jesus fucking Christ."

"Yep."

"Maya died in a car accident six months ago, and Abbey has been trying to find me pretty much ever since."

"Holy fuck," he breathes. He shakes his head. "Man, you've got a kid. How old is she?"

"Your math that bad?" I smile. "She's eight."

"Fuck," he growls. "You and Maya..." He shakes his head, obviously in shock. "What did you do? What did you say to her?"

"What could I say? My mind is all over the place at the moment. Then, on top of all this, I'm pretty sure Laura is freaking out about it. I thought she was okay. I mean, I know it's a huge deal, but I thought she was okay. But I don't think she is." I look at him like he has all the answers. "I can't lose her, Matt. I love her."

Matt looks down at his hands, like he's avoiding meeting my eyes. I study him for a moment, convinced he's hiding something.

"What is it?" I frown at him, because he's holding back on something.

"Nothing. It's not my place to tell you."

"Matt, just spit it out," I say, my frustration growing.

"I thought she would've told you by now."

"Told me what?" I ask.

He looks over at me with what looks like sorrow in his eyes. He leans back, resting his head against the wall, like he's fighting himself on whether to say something or not.

"She'll kill me if I tell you."

"And I'll kill you if you don't," I growl. I'm one second away from punching him in the throat. "Matt, if you don't—"

"Laura can't have kids."

I stare at him, dumbfounded. I shake my head, trying to find the words to respond to what he just said.

"What do you mean?" I stare at him.

"She was sick when she was a kid. She had a bunch of surgeries, which meant removing everything needed to grow a kid. Uterus, ovaries, all of it. She's physically incapable of having a baby."

I bow my head and bury it in my hands. I feel sick, because all her odd behavior now makes sense. I think about all the stupid and ridiculous comments I've made over the past few weeks and I want to take it all back. No wonder she acted weird whenever I made a comment about getting married and having kids.

I cringe. "Jesus. I told her I wanted three kids, so that the last two could be backups," I mutter.

"What kind of asshole says that?" Matt gasps. "That's a really insensitive thing to say." He frowns at me.

"Well obviously. I didn't mean it. I was joking around."

"Look, the comments don't matter. None of that shit would worry Laura. Not even a little bit. Trust me, I've been putting my foot in it for the past God knows how many years. She's struggling with this because you have a daughter. You suddenly come with this instant family. You have the one thing that she can never give you, and you got it from someone else."

"Shit," I say. I rub my forehead. "I've really messed things up."

"No, you haven't. She should have told. Really, it was

selfish of her not to tell you everything the moment she started feeling anything for you."

"But how does she bring up something like that?" I defend her, because I'm not angry at her. I'm angry at myself for not being more sensitive.

"I've got to go," I mumble.

I have to figure out how to fix this.

CHAPTER FOURTEEN
LAURA

Laura,

I'm not sure if you're avoiding me, but I thought maybe it would be best if I gave us both some space to digest this news. We started the discussion on me moving out, but we never finished it. I'll be over there if you need me for anything.

Who am I kidding? The last thing I want is to leave. I want to stay here, with you and work through this, but I don't want to pressure you to accept this. I know it's a shock. I get it. I do. Things are so much more complicated now, but I'm not giving up. I'm not ready to lose you over this.

Call me or text me when you get this. Please.

I love you.

Luke.

I READ the note for the fifteenth time and then I carry it over to the couch and lie down to read it again. He's right. I have been avoiding him. I stayed at Becca's last night so that I wouldn't have to face him, but the funny thing is, I want to work through this as much as he does, but I'm struggling.

I can't stop my mind from going around in circles. Someone else has given him the one thing I'll never be able to, and then I feel awful for thinking that way about that poor woman. I wish there was some way I could fix everything, but I can't. I can't change the future and I can't change the past. I've only been away from him for a day and I'm already missing him. Becca had a point. How would I have gone six months without seeing him?

I lie there in the silence with my eyes closed. So many times, over the last week, I wanted to tell him to forget about his apartment and just stay here. Things were working so well. I was scared that him moving out would change things. And now what? He sleeps in with me, so his daughter can have the spare room? I laugh, because it's ridiculous. The kicker is that he still doesn't know that I can't have kids.

I remember the way he looked when he held Elina in his arms at the hospital. What if Allie makes him realize how much he's missed out on? I wouldn't blame him for wanting more kids. I know there are other options and maybe I'll want to explore them one day, but right now, I don't. My phone rings, interrupting my thoughts. I pick it up, frowning at the number, because I don't recognize it.

"Hello?"

"Hi. I'm looking for a Laura Black?"

"That's me." I sigh, rubbing my head.

"I'm Doctor Banks, I'm one of the registrars at UCLA hospital. An Iris Billingham has been admitted here and you're listed has her emergency contact."

"What?" I sit up, my heart pounding. "Iris? Is she okay?"

"She slipped and broke her hip. She's stable, but she's asking for you."

"I'm on my way now. Thanks."

I scramble to my feet and get dressed, then I grab my keys and sprint out the door. The hospital is literally a few hundred steps down the road. It would take longer for me to get my car out and drive there than it would to go on foot. So I run.

Two minutes later, I'm regretting it, but I work through the pain, ignoring the burning in my chest as I cross the road and head toward the emergency entrance. *I had no idea I was so unfit,* I mentally yell at myself and make an empty promise to start exercising again.

The guilt is killing me. I've been neglecting her. Every day, I've been meaning to go over there, but something always came up. *What if she was lying there for with a broken hip for days and I never knew?* I curse myself, because I'll never forgive myself if that happened. I was too caught up in my own problems.

I'm out of breath by the time I reach the information desk. I get her room details and then take the elevator up to her floor, before staggering into her room. I sink down into the chair next to the bed, panting and gasping for air as I try to gather my composure. Iris frowns at me.

"Should I get out of the bed so you can have it?"

I chuckle. "I'm sorry. I ran here," I say, my heart pounding.

"Why on earth would you do that? You've got a car. Use it."

I shake my head and laugh, because she can't be too sick with all these insults flying out at me.

"How are you feeling?" I finally ask.

"I'm fine, apart from this silly hip. That and they don't even have a TV in here," she grumbles. She *tsks* in disgust.

"They do. Up there," I say, nodding up to the small screen hanging from the ceiling.

"That tiny thing is smaller than my phone screen," she retorts. "I'd rather not watch anything."

I laugh, because I think the real problem is they don't have cable.

"Then hurry up and get better so you can go home and get back to your bachelor 2013," I tease her.

"What? They don't age," she says frowning at me. "It's like a fine wine."

"A fine *whine*, you mean. Have you heard half those women talk?" My joke goes right over her head.

"Where have you been, anyway?" she asks, nodding at me.

"I'm sorry. Work has been full-on—"

"It's that man I see disappearing into your apartment every day, isn't it?" she cuts in.

"He's my brother's friend." I laugh. God, she's nosy. "He's staying with me for a little while. Well, he was."

"Bull dust. I've seen the way he looks at you."

"What do you do, stand at your door and peer through the peephole?" She opens her mouth to protest, but then snaps it shut. "That's *exactly* what you do," I say with a laugh.

"Well, what else am I going to do with my time? I'm just looking out for you. I like to make sure you're being looked after. So, does he cook? Work?" she asks with a frown.

I giggle to myself. "Yes, he cooks and he's a doctor."

"Good, then. He's a keeper."

I cover my face with my hands, because all I can do is laugh.

"I better go and let you get some rest," I say. "I just wanted to make sure you were okay."

"I'm fine. I am worried about Milton, though."

"Don't worry, I'll look after him."

"Thanks, darling," she says as I lean over to kiss her. "He likes you more than he does me, you know."

"I know." I grin.

I USE IRIS' spare key to let myself into her apartment. Milton scrambles over to me, meowing wildly around my feet. I lean down to pet him. He purrs like a maniac and tries to jump into my arms.

"I can't leave you here," I tell him, feeling sorry for the poor little guy.

So, I pack up his things and take him back to my apartment.

After I set up an area for Milton, I go to bed, where I

quickly learn Milton thinks he's sleeping too. I relent and let him stay. It's too early to go sleep, but I lie down anyway, still fully clothed. I snuggle into the warmth of my bed while I listen to Milton purring. I wipe away tears as Milton meows around my face, trying to lick me. I giggle, because it's like he's trying to cheer me up.

Maybe a thousand cats wouldn't be such a bad thing after all...

The sound of the front door unlocking startles me. My heart races as I push back the covers and stand up. I walk into the living room, shocked to find Luke standing there.

"Hey," I say.

My heart pumps wildly in my chest. There are so many things I want to say to him, but I don't know where to start. I slowly edge closer to him.

"Sorry to walk in. I did knock..."

"It's fine," I say with a smile. Milton comes bounding into the room. Luke looks at him, confused. "Iris broke her hip. She's in the hospital."

"Shit, are you okay?" he asks.

I nod. "I'm fine." I wet my lips and look at him. "Why are you here?"

"I just came to get a few more of my things," he mumbles. "I'm not sure if you got my letter, but I thought it might be best to just go to my apartment and give you some space..."

I nod, blinking back tears. "I'll leave you to it, then."

I turn around and walk back into my room, cursing myself for not reaching out to him. I fight back tears as I fling myself on the mattress. Milton plants himself on my stomach, purring madly as I gently stroke his back. I'm such a coward. He wrote me a letter and I can't tell him the damn truth? I owe him that much. I've messed things up for good this time.

I hear a chuckle and open my eyes. Luke stands in the doorway, smiling at me. I smile back, through my tears. I so badly want to tell him everything, but every time I try to speak, I choke.

He smirks as he walks over to me.

"I've dreamed of this moment so many times, you know. Walking into your room and finding you on your bed, rubbing your pussy."

"Only it's not my pussy I'm rubbing," I fire back. "It's my eighty-year-old neighbors."

He winces. "And there's that fantasy crushed. Thanks for that."

I laugh and sit up as he climbs onto the bed next to me.

"You're not okay, are you? You're feeling bad you weren't there for her."

I've been neglecting her since..."

"Me?" he supplies. I smile. It's like he knows me. "This isn't your fault, Laura. And she's fine, right?"

"I know, but I still feel bad." My heart races. "I've missed you so much." I finally choke the words out. He wraps his arms around me while I lie back down, sobbing.

"I've missed you, too. More than anything."

He tilts my face up to his and kisses me. He hesitates for a moment, like there is more he needs to say. I frown, because I'm not sure what's next. If anything, I should be the one talking to him.

"Why didn't you tell me that you can't have kids?"

I stare at him, my heart aching. I feel like I've just been punched in the chest.

He knows. How the hell does he know?

Matt. I'm going to kill him. I sit up and move away, until my legs swing over the edge of the bed. I feel sick, like I'm not sure how to react. What do I say to him? I'm so angry at Matt, because it wasn't his place to say anything. I should have been the one to tell him. *But you didn't,* my conscience says to me. I had the chance to tell him, and I didn't.

"How much do you know?" I ask, turning back to face him.

He stares at me, concerned, as he reaches for my hand.

"Not much. He didn't go into detail. Why didn't you tell me?"

"Because I was scared?" I whisper. "I thought we'd be over the moment I did, and then I fell in love with you..."

"I'm so sorry," he murmurs. He wraps his arms around me and pulls me into his embrace. "You're such a strong, amazing woman. Watching Matt and Annie have Elina and now this thing with Allie? I'm so sorry you've had to deal with all of this on your own."

He shakes his head as he caresses my face, kissing me on the mouth. I can't believe how well he's taking all of this.

"I wish you could have told me. I think of all the things I've said to you, and I just cringe."

"You mean like having back up kids?" I tease. He glares at

me. "Come on. If I can laugh about it, you can too. I know I should've told you. I wouldn't blame you if you hated me, but when I started falling in love with you, the thought of losing you..."

"You'll never lose me," he says.

"But isn't that what's happening now?" I whisper. "How can you look at Allie and not want more kids?"

"That's irrelevant, because I look at you and I can't imagine my life without you," he growls. His voice is thick with emotion as he fights the tears from falling. "Honestly? If it came to the choice of having to choose between having you and having more kids, I'd choose you every time."

"You say that now, but how do you know that won't change? In ten years, you might wake up, hating me."

"I might do that anyway," he quips.

I laugh and wipe the tears from my eyes.

"The thing is, how do you know *anything*?" he asks. "You need to let go of this obsession you have with controlling every situation. You have to step back and live, because you don't have all the answers."

"But what—"

"There are not buts." He reaches behind me and cups my ass, his mouth lifting into a smirk. "Well, except for this one."

"Hey!" I laugh, pushing his hand away. His expression turns serious again.

"How do you know that in five or ten years, new techniques won't be available? The reality is, you don't know anything about the future."

"I guess you have a point," I agree.

"You know today, and you can try to predict tomorrow, but beyond that? Anything can happen."

My body shivers as his words sink in and hit something inside of me. He's right. I hold on to control so hard that I forget about everything else, but in the end, I'm just kidding myself.

"This is why you're so focused on fertility as your specialty?"

I nod. "Not just, but yes, it's a big part of it. On some level, I guess I think that if anyone has the determination to find a way for me to have a child, it will be me."

"There are other ways we can look into down the road, too," he murmurs. "Adoption, surrogacy... there are options, if that's what you want. We can make this work in whatever way you want it to." He pulls me into his arms, lying me on top of him. I straddle him, my hands resting either side of his head as I lean down and kiss him. "Please don't push me out again. Don't keep anything from me, okay?"

I nod, smiling as I press my lips against his. He gently eases his hand around the back of my neck and presses his mouth onto mine, his mouth is soft and warm against my own. I roll off of him and pull with me, so I'm under him, gasping as his fingers move under my shirt and over my bra.

"God, I've missed you," he mutters, kissing my neck as he rubs my breasts. I arch my back and with one hand, unclip my bra. He shrugs it off my breasts, then lifts my shirt up until his mouth finds my nipple.

"Oh, wow." I moan as he flicks his tongue against it until

it's stiff.

I run my fingers through his thick hair, while he gently reacts with subtle noises to my fingernails penetrating his scalp. He sits up and rips off his shirt, tossing it away, then shuffles out of his pants. I reach out and wrap my fingers around his cock, stroking him, while he stares at me, his eyes hungry.

"Let's get these off," he says, helping me out of my shirt. Then I unbutton my jeans while he roughly tries to tug them down over my thighs. I giggle when he curses, and help, until I'm lying there, wearing nothing but my underwear.

"I want nothing more than to bury my tongue deep in your pussy."

I shiver, his words driving me crazy. He loops his thumbs around the band of my panties and tugs them off, then he spreads my legs and lowers himself until his mouth covers my lips.

I gasp as his tongue curls around my clit with much more intensity than I'm expecting. He grabs me by the wrists and puts my hands firmly on his head as I sway my hips toward his face. I stare into his eyes as he slowly pushes me to the brink of orgasm.

"You taste so damn sweet," he murmurs. He licks and sucks his way around my pussy, while I clutch hold of his hair, my legs tensing when he thrusts his tongue deep inside me.

"Oh God, I can't..." My voice trails off as I come.

He swiftly moves back up over me so his face is against mine. His lips find my mouth and he thrusts his length inside me. I'm still throbbing from my orgasm, but the feel of his cock deep inside me is incredible. He wraps his arm around my waist and pushes me against him, pushing himself deeper into me. He grunts, kissing his way along my neck, then back to my lips, the smell of me on his breath making my heart race.

"Can you taste yourself?" he asks, reading my thoughts. "I could lick you out every day of the week, if it meant watching you taste yourself after. It makes me so fucking hard."

I take his hand and guide it down my body, forcing his fingers between my legs. He groans as I slide one inside me, rubbing it against my clit and his cock. I kiss him, my mouth exploring his, as I slowly bring his hand back up to my mouth. I lock my eyes on his and suck hard on his finger.

"Holy fuck," he strangles the words out.

He pumps harder inside me, watching me suck his finger, until he groans. His hips buck against mine as he releases inside me, his cock throbbing against my tightness. I take his hand out of my mouth and wrap my arms around his neck, my mouth engulfing his. He's breathing hard as he thrusts against me. He pulls out, rolling onto his side. He shakes his head and laughs.

"That was fucking incredible," he murmurs. "You have no idea what you do to me."

I smile and roll over, facing away from him. He wraps his arms around my waist, his warm body pressing against mine. I sigh as he kisses my back. I close my eyes and try to stay awake. Milton curls up next to me.

"Probably the only time I can ever joke about having two pussies to myself, huh?" Luke murmurs in my ear.

I giggle, and then drift off to sleep.

CHAPTER FIFTEEN
LUKE

"CAN I stay over with you tonight?" Allie asks.

I glance at Abbey in surprise, who shrugs and then smiles. Behind the smile, I can see the sadness there, hiding in her eyes. This must be hard for her, because as much as I feel sorry for Allie, Abbey has been through just as much, only she doesn't get to show how much she's hurting.

"So long as Luke is okay with it."

"Sure," I say with a grin. "I'll set up the spare room."

I pad down the hallway to the spare room, grabbing some bedding along the way. I'm feeling great, like everything is starting to feel like some sort of normal. I've been spending time with Allie nearly every day. It's been great getting to know her. I feel like every time we're together, she opens up a little more. She's such a good kid. It's hard to get my head around the fact that nearly three weeks ago, I had no idea she existed. My life has been turned upside down, but I wouldn't change a second of it.

It's NOT JUST Allie where things are progressing. My relationship with Laura is finding its feet again too. She hasn't met Allie yet and I haven't pushed it, because it is something she needs to decide on her own. At least, that's how I hope this will go down. I keep telling myself that by giving her space, she'll eventually come around to the idea of Allie being in our lives, but a small part of me worries about it.

What if she doesn't? I'm not sure what I'll do if I have to choose.

I settle Allie in her bed, then walk back down to Abbey. She smiles at me as I sit down. She's got something to say. I can tell by the way her eyes keep darting around the room.

"Whatever it is, just spit it out."

"I have to go back on Monday." She blurts the words out and then stares at me, her eyes wide. "Sorry, I didn't know how to tell you, since you and Allie are getting on so well, but I can't miss any more work, and I need to get back to my husband and child."

I nod. My stomach fills with anxiety at the thought of her going back home. I really do enjoy having her around.

"So, where do we go from here?" I ask.

"Well, that depends. What do you want, Luke?"

I sit back and think about that for a moment. So many things feel out of my control at the moment. I'd be lying if I didn't admit that I'm nervous how any relationship with Allie is going to affect my relationship with Laura. I don't want to lose her, but Allie is my kid. I can't ignore that. God, I don't want to ignore that. I look at her and my heart aches over what I've already missed out on. I'm not prepared to miss out on any more of her life.

But what does that mean?

The last thing I want to do is uproot her from her life and move her over here. She barely knows me, and a life here would be so different than what she has back home. *Home.* That's the thing. Home is over there, where she grew up, where all the memories of her mother are. And I'm over here. I sigh and shake my head.

I just wish I knew what the answer is.

"I'm going to go. Think about it, okay? This isn't just my decision."

After Abbey leaves, I get ready for bed. Just as I lie down, my phone vibrates. I pick it up, my heart racing when I see Laura's name. The last few nights have been amazing, and I'm not just talking about sex. She's been so happy and full of energy. It's like me knowing her secret and being okay with it has changed everything for her.

I click on the text and open it.

> ***Laura:*** *I miss you and I love you. I wish you here with me now.*

I press call, my heart aching to hear her voice.

"I miss you too," I say, my heart racing.

"I'm glad you called, I wanted to ask you something." She pauses. "Can I meet Allie?"

I'm elated, her words making my heart skip a beat.

"You really want to meet her? There's no rush. The last thing I want is to pressure you into anything."

"No, I really want to meet her," she says.

"Okay then. She's staying over here tonight. Want to come over in the morning, before work?"

"I'm off tomorrow, but that sounds perfect. I'll see you then. And Luke?"

"Yes?"

"I love you."

"I love you too."

I'm up early the next morning, because I thought kids got up early to watch cartoons and shit. Instead, I find myself sitting on the couch for nearly two hours, before Allie shows her bleary-eyed face. I smirk at her, because it's nearly nine o'clock.

"Not a morning person, I see?"

She shrugs. "Not really. I hate getting up for school," she admits.

"What can I get you for breakfast?" I stand up and wander over to the kitchen. "Cereal, toast—"

"Coffee?" she interrupts, with a hopeful smile.

I laugh and shake my head. "Nice try, but I'm pretty sure that Abbey, or your mom, wouldn't let you drink coffee."

She smiles, sadness clouding her eyes. I curse myself for bringing up her mom.

"Sorry about your mom," I say.

Now that it's out there, I might as well acknowledge it. We haven't really spoken much about Maya, or why it's taken until now for us to meet.

"It's okay." She frowns at me. "How come you've never contacted me before?" she asks softly. I sit down on the couch next to her. She grabs a cushion and hugs it against her stomach. I sit forward and rest my hands against my legs. I know this is a conversation we need to have, but it's one I'm not looking forward to.

"I didn't know about you," I admit. "The first thing I ever learned about you was three weeks ago when you turned up at the hospital."

"Why would Mom not tell you about me? Was she ashamed of me?"

"God no. Don't you ever think that," I say, growling the words at her. "She would've been so proud of you. I can tell by the way your aunt talks." How do I explain this to an eight-year-old? "She didn't know what to do. I lived over here and she was in Germany. She thought she was doing the best thing for everyone by not telling me."

"Did you think that too?"

"No, not for a second. I wish she'd told me the moment she

found out, because I've missed so much of your life. I wish I could go back and be there for everything."

"I'm glad I met you," she says softly.

"Me too."

I reach out my hand. She looks at it for a moment and then creeps her fingers closer to mine.

"So. Who is Laura?" I laugh, because her question is so out of the blue. "I heard you on the phone with her when I got up to go to the bathroom. Is she your girlfriend?"

I chuckle at her, because you really can't hide anything from kids.

"Yes," I finally say. "She's my girlfriend."

"Am I going to meet her?"

"She's on her way over here now for breakfast, actually," I say. "If that's okay with you?"

She nods and smiles, her eyes lighting up when someone knocks on the door. I raise my eyebrows.

"That's probably her now."

I get up and walk over to the door and open it. Laura stands there, holding two coffees and a bag of doughnuts. Allie stands beside me, smiling shyly at Laura.

"Hey," Laura says. She hands me the coffees and crouches down. "You must be Allie."

"Yup. Are those for me?" she asks, eyeing the donuts.

Laura laughs and glances at me. "You better ask your dad."

"Fine, just don't tell your aunt."

Allie cheers and takes the bag over to the couch, where she sprawls out and watches TV. I follow Laura over to the table and sit down, taking a sip of my coffee. I watch Allie, a bitter-sweet feeling stirring inside me.

"That's the first time anyone has referred to me as her dad," I admit.

"Sorry, I hope I didn't put my foot in it," Laura says.

I shake my head. "No, I liked it. If anything, it reminded me again of what I've missed out on." I turn back to Laura, just in time to see the guilt flash through her eyes. I reach for her hand and shake my head firmly.

"Don't do that," I murmur.

"I'm trying not to, trust me," she says with a soft laugh. "So, how are things going?"

"Good. No, great, actually. I'm enjoying getting to know her. We've got a long way to go, but..." My voice trails off as I meet Laura's eyes and smile. I stare at her hand in mine and run my finger over hers. "She's going back on Monday with Abbey."

"How do you feel about that?" Laura asks.

I shrug. "Okay, I guess? I'm still processing everything. The guilt is amazing," I admit.

"Why are you feeling guilty?" She frowns.

"Because I wasn't there for her. I just feel like I should've known. She must have thought I'd abandoned her."

"But it's not your fault. How could you have known if Maya didn't tell you?"

"I didn't say it was rational." I laugh.

"What matters is that you're there for her now, right?"

I nod and swallow the lump in my throat, then tighten my

grip around her hand. The only problem with that is how do I do that when we're thousands of miles apart?

"You matter too," I say gruffly.

"I'm not going to come between you and her," she says.

I glare at her. "What does that mean? After the last few nights, I thought—"

"I'm not ending things with you, Luke. I'm just giving you the option of having an out, if you want it."

"Well, I don't. I love you," I say.

I reach up and wipe the tears from her eyes, wishing I could also take the fear hiding in them.

"What if I can't do this?" she whispers. "I don't want to make things harder for you."

"Then we deal with it. But right now? I can't let you walk away from me. I won't let you."

She opens her mouth to respond, when her phone rings. She glances down, her expression changing.

"It's Marina. She wants to see me." Her eyes meet mine. "I better go."

"Congratulations," I say. I take the opportunity to lean over and kiss her while Allie is still mesmerized by the TV.

Laura shakes her head. "Don't jinx me."

"Call me and let me know, okay?"

•She nods and breathes out.

"I will."

CHAPTER SIXTEEN
LAURA

"THANKS FOR COMING IN."

I sit in Marina's office my hands fidgeting in my lap. I don't think I've ever felt so nervous in my life.

"I'll start by saying congratulations." She smiles at me from across the desk. "I've chosen you to participate in the research project with me."

"Really?" I squeal. I can't believe what I'm hearing. "Thank you so much." I sit there dumbfounded, because this is so surreal. "I don't know what to say," I add.

"Then I'll do the talking. Your essay is what got me. I asked you to convince me as to why you wanted this and stand yourself out. You did that. Your response was head and shoulders, above the rest. Even without factoring in what you've been through, everything you wrote resonated with me. That, combined with your outstanding college results is what sealed this for you."

"Thank you," I whisper.

"Don't thank me, just prove me right." She smiles at me. "I think that with the right support, you'll be a leader in this field. I'm looking forward to seeing what you can achieve."

She hands me a stack of information so thick, it makes my stomach flip.

"This looks overwhelming, but it's really not. Most of it is just basic information on the project and what I expect from you. It also covers housing arrangements, things like that, and how this research will lead into your fellowship next year."

"My fellowship?" I ask her. My eyes widen. She nods and looks at me strangely.

"That was mentioned at the meeting... which you didn't attend," she smiles. "The purpose of this research project was always to prepare the candidate for the fellowship within my department for next year. If you're interested, of course."

"Interested? Of course, I am," I say. My voice shakes as I try to control my emotions. This is amazing. "Thank you. Thank you *so* much. You won't regret choosing me, I promise."

"I'm sure I won't. You do need to understand this is going to be a lot of work for very little reward in the short term? It's going to be very taxing on you and your life. Just make sure this level of commitment is what you want, before you agree to it."

I nod and thank her again, before walking out. My heart races. I can't believe this is happening. It's what I've dreamed of my entire life.

It's all I've ever wanted... isn't it?

I walk through the park across the road from the hospital, clutching the information to my chest. I'm not sure what to do or how to feel. This is what I've worked so hard for. It's everything. If I give this up, I'd never forgive myself. I shake my head, shocked that it's even entered my head not to accept this. What the hell is wrong with me? But I know exactly what the problem is.

Or who the problem is.

Luke.

It's only six months, but so much can happen in that time. We have enough to still work through without adding this into the mix. What if the pressure of a long-distance relationship is too much? I frown, my heart racing. Just the thought of leaving him makes me feel sick. If I leave and our relationship suffers, I'll never forgive myself. But if I stay and miss out on this opportunity, I won't forgive myself either. The cool breeze is like a slap in the face, reminding me that this is a huge, life changing decision.

I lift my hand to knock on his door, but I stop when my phone vibrates in my hand. I glance down and smile, because it's him. I shove my phone back in my pocket and pound on the door. I'm still not sure what I'm going to say to him. The door swings open. He studies my expression, as though he's trying to figure out whether it's good or bad news.

"I just tried calling you," he grins.

"I know."

"Ignoring me again?"

"What do you mean?" I frown, confused.

"Nothing. The other day, I saw you, but you were too far away. I called you and you ignored me."

"Because my pager went off at the same time. I had to get back inside."

"Well now I feel silly." He studies my face and frowns. "You didn't get it, did you?"

He wraps his arms around me and leads me inside, not giving me the chance to correct him.

"It's okay, they're will be other opportunities like this," he soothes me.

I look around. "Where is Allie?"

"Abby's taken her out for the day. She wanted to give me time to think."

"And?" I ask him.

He shrugs. We walk over to the couch and sit down. I fall into his arms, loving the feel of him holding me. I rest my head against his chest and close my eyes, the sound of his heartbeat comforting me.

"I don't know what the right thing to do is," he admits. "Abby is happy for her to live over there with her and maybe that's best. For now, at least, until she gets to know me better? It would be such a huge change to uproot her from her life and move over here..." He shakes his head. "As much as I want her here with me, I can't do that to her."

He rubs his forehead and sighs.

"You could move over there and get to know her?" I suggest. He frowns down at me. "But you won't do that because of me," I say, answering my own suggestion.

He wraps his arms around me again, holding me against him.

"You want to hear something funny? I was so sure you'd gotten that project, nearly the whole time you were gone, I was here, fantasizing about moving over to London for the six months. I figured it all out. I could visit you on weekends and get to know my daughter through the week. It would've worked out perfectly."

I pull away and look him in the eyes, a smile slowly creeping across my face. He looks at me strangely, but then he catches on.

"You got it, didn't you?" He kisses me. "Why didn't you tell me? You could've saved me a whole lot of stress."

"I was trying to figure out how we could make this work. How was I supposed to know that you had it all planned out?" I take his hand in mine. For the first time, I let myself really feel excited about everything.

This could really work.

"So, let me get this straight."

Matt stares at me and then turns his attention to Luke.

"You're *both* moving?"

He frowns, while Mom shakes her head, tears in her eyes. Poor Becca stands in front of them, looking like she might pass out. We're at Matt and Annie's place, after inviting everyone over here for a last minute, Friday night drink to share our news. So far, the reactions have been less excited and more stunned than I'd been hoping for. I know they're all probably just in shock, but as I look around the room at the stunned faces, I'm becoming more and more unsure about this decision.

"Guys, it's six months. Quit acting like you're never going to see us again."

Becca steps forward. She beams at me and throws her arms around me. I smile, because that is exactly what I needed.

"What am I going to do without you for six freaking months?" she wails. I laugh and hug her back. "You'll keep yourself busy. You can borrow Iris if you like," I tease.

"I might just do that," she mutters. "Can I borrow your apartment too?" she asks hopefully. She laughs as I swat her across the arm. "But seriously, you guys. I'm so happy for you."

"Thanks." I grin.

"I'm happy too, but I only just got you back after college," Mom protests. "Sorry if I'm not *thrilled* that you're moving away again."

"It's only for six months," I say, my voice weak. "You all could always come visit."

"On a plane?" Matt gapes at me. "With this thing?" he nods at Elina, who as if on cue, starts wailing. I walk over, scooping her up in my arms, which makes her abruptly stop crying. "I had you down for babysitting duties every Saturday night for the next six months," he jokes.

"I'm pretty sure you'll manage," I tease.

"Have you met me?" Matt mutters. He glares at Luke. "And you're going to live in London?"

"Yes."

Matt shakes his head, like he's having a hard time working all of this out.

"With Allie?"

"No, with the queen. Of course, with Allie. I'll get my own place, but the idea is to get to know my daughter and hopefully, one day she might even want to move over here."

Matt breaks into a grin as everything clicks into place. He steps forward and pulls us both into a firm hug. Annie steps into rescue Elina from me, before she's crushed by Matt's enthusiasm.

"Good for you guys," Annie says. "This is fantastic news. I'm so happy you worked things out and how perfect is this?" She shakes her head. "I've got plenty of friends over there if you need somewhere to stay," she adds.

"Thanks, I'll keep that in mind." Luke smiles at me and wraps his hand around mine. "I guess we better get back, considering how much we need to do before we fly out."

"I guess we should." I nod, suddenly feeling overwhelmed.

"When are you leaving?" Matt asks.

"Next week," I say, my heart racing. "I'll go to London with Luke for two weeks, then fly to Bern."

"Jesus, so soon?" Becca frowns. She hugs me again, which makes me tear up. "Really though, I'm so happy for you guys. I knew you'd work it all out."

"Dinner here Sunday night." Matt's voice is firm. "If you think this is your farewell, you're in for a shock."

"Fine." I grin. "I wouldn't expect anything less."

WE SAY goodbye to everyone and then head back to my place. I walk inside, and I reach over and take his hand and squeeze it, his warmth calming me down. I let go of his hand to slip out of my jacket and leave it hanging over the chair, then I turn to Luke and put my arms around his waist, kissing him. He grins at me. I smile back and then take a deep breath out.

We're really doing this.

"You're not having second thoughts, are you?" he asks.

I shake my head. "Hell no. I'm nervous, excited and a bunch of other things, but not doing this hasn't even entered my mind."

"Good," he grins. "If it makes you feel better, I'm shitting myself too."

"Have you told Allie yet?" I ask.

He shakes his head. "I'm going to surprise her. Just rock up at school next week to pick her up."

I love the way his face lights up when he talks about her.

"She's going to love having you around," I say.

"I'm going to love it too," he admits. "What I'm not looking forward to is not seeing your beautiful face every day. I guess we will just have to make the most of the time we have together."

"Oh really?" I smile. "What did you have in mind?"

He places his hand beneath my chin, lifting my lips up to his. I smile as he kisses me, brushing his mouth against mine. I shiver as he takes my hands and leads me down to my room.

"I'm going to miss this too," I murmur.

"There are ways around that. We can skype. Phone sex." His eyes sparkle. "I hear there are some great sex toys on the market you might want to test out."

"You did not just say that," I growl at him.

He laughs and attempts to shield himself from my attack, then he pulls me into his arms and kisses me.

"You're wasting time. You know that, right? The things I could be doing to you right now..."

"Fine."

I glower at him, and then relent, putting my hands up in defeat. I laugh as he scoops me into his arms and carries me down to the bedroom.

"But you've got some serious making up to do for that comment..."

EPILOGUE

LAURA

Two years later

"OH GOD, WHAT AM I DOING?"

I pace back and forth inside my penthouse luxury hotel suite in Santa Monica, where I'll be marrying Luke tomorrow afternoon. Marrying Luke. I run my hands through my hair and hunch forward, my stomach twisting into knots. *I'm getting married tomorrow*. It's not the married part that's scaring me—I would have eloped the day after he proposed, if I could've talked him into it. It's the wedding and thinking about all the things that can go wrong.

The last few months had been non-stop stress, trying to get this wedding together. Everything that *could* have gone wrong, had—from our first choice of venue burning down, to our celebrant double booking the day. I have no fucking idea how it's all come together so nicely in the end. I'm getting ahead of myself now, because there was still plenty of time for shit to go wrong.

I'm going to be sick.

Becca launches herself off the couch and grabs hold of my shoulders, shaking them as she gives me a stern look. I stare back at her, breathing heavily as the panic slowly begins to lessen. Becs. God knows that I'd do without her in my corner. I nod and breathe in deeply, but then a fresh wave of panic hits me. Becca glares at me.

"Pull your shit together, woman."

"Yeah," Allie pipes up, getting to her feet. "Get your shit together."

Becca turns around and glares at her. "Hey. You're ten. You don't get to swear."

"Oh, but it's fine for you?"

She sticks her chest out as she stares Becca down with all the pre-teen angst she can muster. The problem with that is she's underestimating Becca's ability to act like a thirteen year old.

"Double standard much?" Allie mutters, backing down. She pouts and looks at me for support.

"The world is full of double standards so get used to it," Becca grumbles.

"She's right. No swearing," I say, shrugging at her.

"What was the point of you adopting me if I you're not going to stand up for me?" She sighs. "Sorry, I didn't mean that."

"I'm glad to hear that I didn't adopt you so you could use

me to win arguments." I cross my arms over my chest. I stare at her and raise my eyebrows. "Now, considering how early we have to get up tomorrow, I think it's your bed time," I add.

"But what about the stripper?" she protests.

Annie snorts as I turn around and glare at Becca, who puts her hands up defensively. I rub my head, because I can't deal with this right now.

"There is no stripper."

"But I heard Becca on the phone—"

"Seriously?" I huff, glaring at Becca. "A stripper when you *knew* Allie was staying with us? That was the condition of you staying with me tonight. That you go to bed when I tell you to."

"No, I—"

I Hold my hand up at her. I'll deal with her later.

"You. Bed." I raise an eyebrow at Allie, who releases a loud sigh and hunches her shoulders forward.

"Fine," she grumbles. "You're worse than Dad," she adds.

She stalks off to her room while I sit down. I'm still shaking, but feeling more in control of myself. Allie walks back out a few seconds later, holding up a package.

"I almost forgot. This is from Dad. He said to give it to you when you made me go to bed."

She practically throws it at me, before stalking back to her room. I nearly laugh when she reappears a few seconds later and throws her arms around me.

"I'm so happy you and Dad are getting married," she says.

I kiss her on the cheek and smile sweetly at her.

"You're still going to bed."

"Seriously?" she says.

She shakes her head, before stalking off to her room in a huff for the third time in five minutes. I groan and shake my head, burying my face in my hands.

"And she's not even a teenager yet," I mutter. Becca giggles, which reminds me I'm still annoyed at her. "A stripper?"

"What she heard was me organizing an escort for the wedding," Becca mumbles. Her face reddens.

"An escort?" I want to laugh, but she looks kind of serious.

She nods. "Well, not the kind that you have sex with. I just wanted someone to dance with and sit next to. All the shit you guys take for granted," she adds, looking from Annie to me. "I didn't want to be standing at your wedding, wishing I was in relationship," she grumbles.

"Oh Becs," I say. I wrap my arms around her. "I'm sorry if I've been making you feel left out."

"No, it's not you at all," she protests. "It's just..." she shrugs. "Well, I officially hate being single. But, enough about me. Let's focus on you. And that rat of a kid," she adds.

I laugh, because I know how much Becca adores Allie.

The truth is, the day I adopted Allie was the happiest of my life. After Luke and I returned from overseas, Allie came out to visit us every school break, until just over a year ago, when she told us she wanted to live with us permanently. We were thrilled, because Luke had just proposed, and Allie moving over to live with us was the icing on the cake. Luke and I had talked about adopting, but we'd decided that, for now at least, having Allie in our life was enough. I'd just completed my fellowship and was looking forward to continuing to work in Mercy's fertility program and Luke was doing a specialist degree in children's cardiology, so extending our family wasn't something that was possible in the short-term future. As much as I loved our life and Allie, there was still something missing.

But all that changed the day she asked me to adopt her.

It was three months ago on the morning of my birthday. She presented me with a card she'd made herself and inside, she'd written a lovely message, asking me to adopt her. I was shocked, and Luke was too, because he had no idea she was even thinking about it. For her to want me to take on that role meant everything to me. I swallow, my eyes tearing up just thinking about it. I shake off everything else and focus on the package in front of me.

I start with the card attached to the gift, carefully unsealing it and sliding it out. I smile at image of two oldies on the front, hugging. I flip it open and read the message. And then I read it again, this time with a smile on my face.

Just in case you start freaking out (if I know you at all, it's what you're doing right now), open this to remind yourself how much I love you. I'll see you tomorrow when you make me the happiest guy in the world by becoming my wife.

Love you,

Luke xx

I take a moment to reflect on how lucky I am, until Becca shoves me impatiently in the arm. I laugh and glare at her, rubbing the still stinging spot that she poked.

249

"Are you right?"

"I will be if you open the damn gift," Becca says as she impatiently peers over my shoulder. "Isn't it enough that you're always so kissy kissy with each other? Now he's gone one step closer into perfect man territory by buying you gifts?"

"At least you're not bitter about it," I joke with a smirk.

Her eyes widen as she claps her hand over her mouth.

"Oh god, I'm that person now, aren't I?"

SHE WALKS AROUND to the couch and flops down , while Annie and I laugh at her dramatics. I turn my attention back to my gift, carefully peeling away the paper, which reveals a small box, tightly wrapped in brown paper. Becca starts to laugh. I shake my head and smile as I tear into the paper. I open the box, expecting to find something I'd be glad I didn't open in front of my mother, but instead I find...

I frown and pick it up. He got me a tee shirt? Could he be anymore random? I shake my head, not getting it—and then I turn it around and see the words that are scrawled across it.

The Girl in Cubicle Nine

I start laughing.

"Seriously, if you don't marry him, he's all mine." Becca sputters, clutching her stomach as she laughs. "I love him, Loz. I legit *love* the guy."

"What the heck is that supposed to be?" Annie frowns, nodding at the shirt. "Cubicle Nine? It sounds like a name of a really bad American sitcom."

That makes us laugh even harder, because I can so see James Van der Beek starring in that. Annie looks like she's going to blow her lid, as she would put it. I try to calm myself down enough to tell her the story, but it's hopeless.

"Do one of you want to fill me in before I leave in a huff?" She speaks in her best, no nonsense, British accent.

"I hear Laura's great at filling things in," Becca falls on the floor, wheezing, she's laughing so hard. "One Energizer and she'll keep going *all* night. She's a real bunny—"

"Oh, shut up," I say, laughing.

"Okay, if someone doesn't tell me what the bloody hell is going on..."

I look at Becca and motion for her to tell Annie, because I'm laughing too hard to speak. She nods and tries to compose herself. Her third attempt, she manages to get something out.

"Okay. So, you think that Laura and Luke met at your dinner party, right?"

Annie nods, looking even more confused.

"Well, that was their *second* meeting. Their first meeting was actually in the ER where Luke was working at the time."

"What happened?" she asked, bewildered.

"Laura got a sex toy stuck up her clacker."

"*Clacker?*" I repeat, giggling at her. "Vagina, Becs. Don't be afraid of it. And there was a lot more to it than that—"

"You mean how you made me try and dig it out of your *vagina?*"

"It's what a friend would do," I protest, while poor Annie stares at us, both shocked and confused.

"I guess you Americans have a different idea of friendship, than us," she mutters.

"Becca got me a voucher for an online sex toy shop. I picked the most innocent looking thing I could find. Long story short, it got stuck. So, I drove—"

"Last time I checked, I drove you there after you called me in a fit," Becca cuts in.

"Sorry," I say. "Becca drove me to an ER far enough away that nobody would know me."

"And Luke was the doctor who saw to you," Annie finishes.

I nod. She starts to giggle, until she's clutching her stomach, doubled over nearly on the floor she's laughing so hard. She shakes her head as tears roll down her cheeks.

"Oh my God, it just hit me how awful it must have been for you at that dinner party, walking in and seeing him sitting there." She wipes her eyes. "Matt and I couldn't for the life of us work out why you hated Luke so much when we thought he'd be perfect for you."

"So, it was a set up?" I accuse her.

She rolls her eyes. "Of course, it was."

I glare at her, my eyes narrowed, but I can't be angry.

"The worst part was when Matt turned up on my doorstep, begging me to take Luke in, and made some offhanded comment about *the girl in cubicle nine*," I say.

"Oh, he didn't," Annie says, laughing. "I would've died."

"Trust me, I wanted to."

I shake my head and stare at the shirt. This did exactly what he wanted it to. The panic is gone and all that's left is excitement about marrying such an amazing man. I'm not sure if it's the laughing or just remembering how much we've been through together, but I can't wait for tomorrow.

I get up and lean over, kissing Annie and then Becca.

"Thanks for staying with me tonight."

"Thank your Mom for babysitting," Annie says, holding up her glass. "I'll do just about anything these days for a night off."

"Now I feel extra special." I grin.

"And you know nothing would stop me being here," Becca says. She gets to her feet, throwing her arms around my neck. When she starts to sob onto my shoulder, I groan.

"Yep, you've definitely drank too much."

THE MORNING PASSES in a blur as we frantically rush to get ready. I thought getting up at five would give me plenty of time, but even that was pushing it. Wait, who was I kidding? I didn't sleep at all. I sat on the couch for most of the night, thinking about Luke and how amazing he is.

I'm doing my best not to freak out about the fact that I'm about to walk down the aisle and marry the man of my dreams, but it's hard. For so long, this was beyond anything I could have even let myself dream. A family inevitably leads to kids, which wasn't in my future. But I guess it's all about perspective. I have an amazing daughter, and after today, the three of us will finally be a family. I know this day means as much to Luke and Allie, as it does to me.

Allie walks out, wearing her beautiful dusky pink, raw silk bridesmaids dress.

"Maybe go and change into something that isn't going to matter when it's covered in makeup and hair product, rather than your five-hundred-dollar dress?" I grumble, pushing her back down to the bedroom.

"Sorry," she says, rolling her eyes, like I'm being overdramatic. "You're a real treat when you're stressed, you know that?" she adds as she stalks inside and shuts the door.

"Laura, hair!"

Shit. I race back up to the front of the hotel suite, where the hairdresser is waiting for me. Mom walks over to me and kisses me on the cheek, then she leans down to hug me.

"You look stressed," she smiles. "Just relax and enjoy this."

"Thanks," I say. Even my voice is shaking. "I just want it to be perfect, you know?"

"I know. And it will be. And you know what? All the little imperfections that do happen are what's going to make it *your* day."

I nod, because that's a great way to look at it, but it's unfortunately not making me stress any less.

"I'm going to head down to the chapel. I'll see you down there in that beautiful dress of yours soon."

She kisses me again, then smiles at Annie, who appears, looking stunning in her dress, her hair and makeup already done.

Becca's laughter rips through my thoughts. I glance up, my eyes widening when I see Allie standing there. She changed, like I told her to, into a pair of sweatpants and a tee shirt...with *Girl in Cubicle Nine* scrawled across it. Oh shit. I jump up, not sure what to do. If I make a big deal of it then she's going to want to know what's going on. Allie frowns as she examines the front of the shirt, then looks at me.

"What is this?" she sneers. "Some crappy band from the seventies that Dad likes?"

"Yes."

Becca nods, without missing a beat. It's like she's rehearsed this, or something. She walks over to us and winks at me. I give her a warning look, which she ignores. I know Becca, so I also know this isn't going to go well.

"A very small, one-woman band. She only did the one show, but boy could she strum that instrument. There was a lot of screaming too, apparently."

Allie frowns and furrows her brow, then shakes her head and stalks off to get her hair done.

"Weirdo's"

I glare at Becca and Annie, who are both nearly in tears.

"Thanks," I hiss to Becca.

"What?" she frowns. "I totally saved us from that disaster."

WITH MY HAIR and makeup done, I close my eyes and step into my dress, shivering as I pull it up over my body. I hold my breath as Becca zips me up, the bodice almost forming a second skin against my own. So long as I don't want to breathe today,

I'll be fine. I turn around, my heart stopping when I see my reflection in the mirror.

Holy shit, is that me?

Becca stands behind me, her eyes teary.

"Why are you the one crying?" I tease her.

"Because you're my best friend and I'm just really happy for you. I love you so much, Loz. You deserve all the great things."

She wraps her arms around me, careful not to crush my dress. Then she takes a deep breath and fans her face, while I giggle. I thought I'd be the one falling apart, not her.

"We have to go." Annie sticks her head in the door, looking panicked. "Matt said they're starting to freak out down there because the celebrant is on a time crunch."

"Okay." I nod and take one last look at myself in the mirror, then I walk out.

I STAND outside the small chapel and watch as Allie disappears inside, followed by Becca and then Annie. I'm shaking, I'm so nervous, and doing everything I can to remember to breathe so I don't pass out halfway down.

"You look nervous." I jump at the sound of Matt's voice and turn to him and laugh. Nervous is an understatement. "You'll be fine," he adds, linking his arm through mine. "You can't do any better than Luke." He pauses for a moment. "Which could be taken as a good thing, or an insult."

I shift anxiously on my feet, waiting to be given our cue. I peer through the door, freaking out a little bit when I see everyone.

"Laura, are you ready?"

I look back and see the coordinator nodding at me. I smile at her and nod, then squeeze Matt's hand. Lifting the hem of my dress so I don't trip, I make my way down the aisle, with Matt by my side. Dad would've loved this. I hate that he couldn't be here to walk me down that aisle, but if it had to be anyone else, I'm glad it's Matt. I swallow back tears, because I miss Dad so much. Only I can't cry, because once I start, I won't be able to stop.

Lifting my head, I smile when I see Luke standing at the end of the aisle, waiting for me. My whole body shakes. I don't think I can do this. Then I lift my head and my eyes meet his. In that one, tiny moment, everything is perfect.

Nothing else matters, so long as I have him. Every step leads me closer to the one thing I'm certain of, my love for Luke. I stand next to him, my heart pounding when he wraps his hands around mine. Tiny shockwaves race up my arm, the same way they did that very first time he touched me—although that could have been the small, buzzing device I'd managed to lodge inside me. Either way, a tingle is a tingle. I look up into his eyes and smile.

"You look stunning," he whispers, his eyes twinkling. "Did you get my present?"

I nod slightly. "Or at least, your daughter did."

"What?" he asks, confused.

"She was wearing the shirt this morning," I mutter. "She

thought it was one of your shitty bands." I bow my head and stifle a giggle.

"Oh no." The color drains from his face. "How did you explain that?"

"With great difficulty, thanks to Becca," I admit.

"Typical Becca." He chuckles. "I got my own shock today too, and it's sitting in the front row."

I turn my head slightly, my eyes widening when I see the very proper looking woman who is sitting next to Matt.

"Your mom?" I ask softly. He nods, but I can't work out whether this is a good thing, or not. "Holy shit."

The celebrant clears his throat and raises his eyebrows at us, looking very unimpressed.

Matt makes a face as our guests chuckle.

"I think that was a subtle hint that we should probably stop talking now and get married."

I nod and smile.

"Okay, but only so I get to kiss you."

Luke

"WHAT?" she asks, smiling at me.

"Nothing."

I wrap her arms around me and gaze down at her. She shakes

her head, her cheeks flush with color as she stares back up at me. It's such a cliché thing to think, but I've never seen her look as beautiful as she does right now—today—on our wedding day.

"Then why do you keep staring at me?"

"Isn't that a right of mine, now I'm your husband and everything? I think you'll find that I'm allowed to stare at you while you cook and clean for me—*ouch*. Hey. Spousal abuse already?" I chuckle as she whacks me on the arm again, this time even harder. Never mind the fact that we're in the middle of our wedding dance and all eyes are on us.

"You deserved that. Besides, you've tasted my cooking," she retorts. "Is that really something that you want to do to yourself?"

She has a point, I suppose.

I spin her around into my arms and kiss then her. I don't care that everyone is staring at us, because she is the only person in the room that matters. She shakes her head as I tilt her lips to mine, ignoring the cat calls and cheers, and what I'm pretty sure is Matt, trying to spark up a Mexican wave.

"Everyone's watching," she whispers in a hushed voice as she tries to squirm away from me.

"So, let them watch," I say.

The song finally ends so I take her hand and lead her off the floor. She glances over at the table on the other side of the room, where my mother sits. My body tenses as I try hard not to react, but I can't help myself.

"Have you spoken to her?" Laura asks softly.

I shake my head. "I've said maybe two words to her," I admit.

I had decided to invite her at the last minute after Laura had said something that made me realize I might regret it down the road if I didn't. Inviting her was easy, because I didn't expect her to actually come. When I was standing out the front of the chapel, and I saw her walk up, it was like my whole world was imploding. She didn't look any different, and yet, at the same time, I almost didn't recognize her. How does that make any sense?

Laura and I walk around, mingling with our guests for a while. My face is sore from smiling, but I guess that goes with the territory of getting married. Everyone is here. Laura's old neighbor, Iris and her daughter—which is apparently a big deal, according to Laura, because their relationship has never been great. People from work are here. Even Lewin came, which is impressive, since he was on call. As great as it is to see everyone, I can't wait until this part is over so we can get on with the good stuff.

I would have eloped in a second if I thought I could've talked Laura into it.

It's been such a whirlwind of a day that all I want to do is curl up in bed with her in my arms. I watch her fondly as she chats to Becca, then I squeeze her hand and then leave them alone to talk. I make my way over to the bar and sit down, surveying the room. My heart races when I see my mother. Our eyes meet for a brief moment until I turn away.

I wave over the barman.

"Scotch, please. Straight up," I mutter.

I never drink scotch, but I think this can be the exception to that rule.

"You act like you don't want me here, so I'm wondering why you invited me in the first place."

I turn around to see my mother standing there.

"That's funny because I was wondering why you came," I reply.

I have a sip of my drink and try to read her expression, but I can't. I pretend not to be nervous about seeing her, but inside, I'm a wreck. She smiles at my drink.

"Reminds me of your father," she says wistfully.

"Which is enough of a reason for me not to drink it," I say in a dry voice.

I run my hand through my hair and shake my head.

"Does it really surprise you that I came? It's your wedding, after all."

"You kept me out of my own father's funeral," I remind her.

"I owe you an apology for that," she says. "I'm not proud of that. In fact, I think about it every day."

"So do I," I say softly.

I shake my head, the anger I'm feeling unwelcome on a day when I should be feeling happy. All inviting her has done is dampen my mood.

"It's good to see you," I say.

I lean forward and kiss her with the same intimacy I have every other person I've thanked today because that's all she is. Another guest at our wedding. I walk back over to Laura, forcing myself to breathe. I link my arm in hers, and she instantly eases my mood. She glances at me a concerned look on her face.

"What's wrong?"

"Nothing," I say. All talking about my mother is going to do is spoil both our moods.

"It doesn't look like 'nothing,'" she says, shaking her head.

"I'm just looking forward to getting you back to our room," I mumble. She smiles and slips her arms around my neck. "Want to get out of here?"

"Leave our own wedding?" she laughs.

"Why not? It's nearly over. People will understand."

She narrows her eyes at me. "People will think you just want to have your way with me."

I cock my head to the side and grin. "And they'd be wrong, how?"

"Now, *this* is what I've been looking forward to," I say.

Laura laughs as I lead her into our room, my hands roaming all over her body while she laughs and swats my fingers away. I try to tug down the zipper at the back of her dress, but she spins around and glares at me.

"What?" I say innocently. "I'm just helping you out of that big, heavy dress."

"Oh, and that's the only reason, huh?" she says.

"Okay, so maybe my real goal is to get you out of this, so I can get into you." She snorts with laughter, while I nod. "Tell me that wasn't smooth." I grin, wrapping my arms around her waist.

"You crack me up, you know that?" she giggles.

I use her being distracted to successfully lower the zipper on that dress. She gasps and glances at the open door.

"Anyone could walk past," she protests.

As if on cue, Iris is wheeled past by her daughter. She waves, and I wave back, while Laura laughs into my arm and tries to cover herself.

"Make sure you give her a good banging," Iris calls out.

Her daughter gasps and whispers something to her mother. Laura laughs and clutches onto me. I shake my head because that was definitely an erection killer.

"Okay, you win," I groan, giving up. "I'll back off." I hold up my hands and walk over to the bed, throwing myself down. I shake my head as I bury my face into the pillow.

"Really?" she asks, laughing.

I roll onto my back and watch her as she closes the door, and then walks over to the bed, letting her dress fall down along the way. I groan at the sight of her in that transparent, lacy underwear and the way it clings to her curves.

"I'm not too sure about all these mixed signals you're sending me," I tease her. "One second you want me to back off, and when I do, you're all over me."

"What can I say? I like a challenge," she says with a smile.

"Well, so do I."

She climbs on the bed and crawls over to me, swinging her

hips along the way. I sigh as she straddles me and presses her lips against mine, while I run my hands over her smooth ass. She sits on my stomach and rocks herself against me, her lips exploring mine.

"Thank you," she whispers. "For everything."

"I should be thanking you," I mutter.

I reach behind her and unclasp her bra, pushing it off her breasts, then I close my mouth over her nipple and suck it until it's stiff. She moans, her hands fumbling to undo my zip. When she does, she reaches in and grasps my cock, rolling her fist around it. I grunt, barely able to contain myself. Just the feel of her touch almost has me exploding.

"Not yet," she says, her lips parting into a smile as she kisses me. "I want to feel you inside me first."

I shuffle off my pants with her assistance, then I roll her panties down over her thighs.

"Hold on," she says.

She takes my hand to steady herself and then stands up on the mattress to kick off her panties. With a shriek, she overbalances and almost topples forward. Not that I'd have complained too much if she landed on top of me. It's where she's going to end up anyway. I steady her and bring her back down to me. She places one leg either side of me, her back arching as she slides down on my length.

"Fuck, you feel good," I mutter, grabbing hold of her ass. I thrust myself deeply inside of her. "I've been wanting to do this all day."

"And give the celebrant another thing to be upset about?" she whispers in my ear as she rocks herself against me.

"Yeah, thanks for that."

"What? You're still hard," she giggles as she leans over to kiss me.

"In spite of that comment," I say with a grunt.

I bounce her against me, my grip on her ass tightening with every movement. My heart races as my climax begins to build. The fact that I'm fucking her as my wife feels surreal. I can't get over how amazing she is. She puts her palms against the wall as she rides me harder, rocking herself against my rhythm. She gasps and stretches her back as I thrust deep inside her.

"Oh god," she cries out and clenches her thighs against me.

Her pussy milks my cock as her body convulses.

"Fuck," I hiss as I come, harder than I have in a long time.

My cock throbs as she rocks against me, until she can't take anymore. Panting, she lowers herself onto me and kisses me, then she creeps into my arms and nestles against me.

"I guess now we're really married," she says, her grin is so wide that I can't help but return it. "We've sealed the deal, and all that."

"Actually, I'm pretty sure the ceremony sealed the deal," I chuckle, shifting her hair aside, so I can kiss her neck. She yawns and closes her eyes. "Oh, I'm boring you, am I?"

"No, it's been a long day. You didn't have to get up at five in the morning," she reminds me.

"We got married at one," I laugh. "What the fuck did you do for eight hours?"

"Such a guy," she teases, shaking her head. "But you're *my* guy."

"I don't doubt you'll still be saying that in fifty years, but for some reason, I think the tone will be different then."

"Probably," she grins, pressing her mouth against mine. "I suspect you're going to be one, annoying, grumpy old man."

I CRACK OPEN my eyes and look around, letting them adjust to the light filtering in through the room. It takes me a moment to remember where I am. When I do, I roll over and smile at my wife. *God, it feels good to say that.* She lies next to me, hogging the sheets, still fast asleep. I reach out and run my fingers down over her naked back, then I prop myself up on my pillows and just watch her. I could lie there for hours, studying that beautiful face, and I do until she finally wakes up. She frowns at me like she's trying to work out what I'm doing.

"Were you watching me sleep?" she asks. "Because that's kind of creepy."

"Don't sound so surprised. I do it all the time." I chuckle as her eyebrows shoot up. "I'm kidding. What am I, a creep?"

"Well, I do wonder..." She laughs as she leans over to kiss me.

"It's one of the best times to watch you," I admit. "When you're sleeping."

"You mean because I'm quiet and not saying anything?" she

quips. I reach over and tickle her. She squeals and tries to slither away from me.

"Stop putting words in my mouth," I growl at her.

She rolls back over to me and curls her arms around my neck, kissing me tenderly on the lips. We're already acting like we've been married for ten years, and I love it.

WE SPEND most of the morning together until it's time to meet some of our guests for lunch. We've only got about two hours before we need to be at the airport, but Annie and Matt insisted on seeing us first, before we embark on our honeymoon. Allie will stay with them for the two weeks we're gone. She acts like she's not happy about it, but I know how much she loves them.

I glance at Laura and take her hand in mine as we walk through the restaurant. She's looking as relaxed as I've ever seen her. Annie and Matt are already there, along with Becca, and Laura's mom. Allie smiles at me from where she sits on the floor, holding Elina.

"It's about time you two took a break from whatever it is people get up to on their wedding night," Becca jokes.

"You mean sleep? Because that's all we did," Matt cracks. He protests when Annie punches him in the chest. "Really? I swear, all you do is hit me."

I laugh and sit down, listening to everyone talk. I look around the table at our friends and family and feel happy. I think about Mom and feel a stab of regret. Maybe I should have tried harder to fix things between us, but it's too late now.

It's fun catching up with everyone, and all too quickly, we need to leave.

"This has been great, but we're going to miss our plane if we don't leave now," I say.

Even though we're only going away for two weeks, it's hard saying goodbye to everyone. It's a difficult feeling to describe. The person I'm going to miss the most is definitely Allie. I contemplated asking her to come along with us, but I guess it wouldn't be much of a honeymoon with an eleven-year-old in tow. That, and she's at the age where she wouldn't be caught dead on her parents' honeymoon anyway—not even for a free trip to paradise.

Annie picks up Elina and balances her on her hip. Then she, Matt and Allie follow us outside. Annie gives Matt a look, and then when he doesn't react, she nudges him hard in the side. I chuckle because the poor guy is getting punished today. I'm not sure what's going on, but it's kind of amusing to see Matt getting beaten up by his wife. Then again, maybe that's what I have to look forward to.

"Will you stop hurting me?" he snaps, frowning at her.

"I will, but *do* it already."

"Yeah, you're nailing subtle there, Annie," he mutters, shaking his head. He reaches into his shirt pocket and retrieves an envelope. "We weren't sure how to do this," he admits, glancing back at Annie. He breathes out as he glances up at Laura.

"What?" she asks, frowning at him.

He studies the envelope for a moment, before handing it to her. His fingers shake as he brings them back to his side and clenches them into fists. He's nervous about something. Laura rips open the envelope while I watch.

"Wait a second." Matt grabs her arm. Laura looks up, startled. "You don't have to say anything, okay? We just wanted you to know that it was an option."

Now, I'm even more confused, and I can tell Laura is too. I wrap my arm around her as she carefully opens the envelope. She reaches inside and pulls out a few leaflets for surrogacy.

"I don't understand," she mumbles, flicking through them. She looks up at Matt and Annie, who both look terrified.

"Please don't be offended," Annie says, taking Laura's hand. "That the last thing we want to do is upset you, but we've been speaking about it a lot, and we hate the idea of you guys not being...having..." Her voice trails off.

"God, maybe this was a bad idea," Matt mutters. He looks at Laura. "I just wanted you to know that it's always there if you decide that it's something you want to explore. We'd be honored to do that for you both."

"You'd really do that?" Laura whispers.

She stares down at the leaflets for a long time. When she looks up, there are tears in her eyes. She smiles through them as she stands up and throws her arms around Matt.

"Thank you," she whispers. "You have no idea how touched I am by this," she adds as she hugs Annie.

I extend my hand to Matt's, who shakes his head and wraps

269

his arms around me.

"We're practically bros, yo."

"Never say that again, but thank you," I say, my voice breaking as I kiss Annie and then hug her tightly. "And on that note, we really need to go," I say to Laura.

"Okay."

She nods, her eyes still wet with tears as she steps forward and kisses Allie.

"Be good," I warn, giving Allie a hug.

"Am I ever anything else?" she asks lightly.

Laura takes my hand as we walk over to our car, waving back at Matt and Annie along the way. I unlock the door and then pull her toward me, so she's facing me. That was a huge thing for them to offer, and I don't believe she's as okay as she says she is.

"Are you sure you're okay?" I ask her, stroking her cheek. "We can get a later flight."

She shakes her head and smiles at me.

"No, I promise I'm fine. Let's go have some fun."

I GLANCE OVER AT LAURA, who's been staring out the window of the plane since we boarded. She's barely said a word since we left the hotel and I'm worried about her. I reach over and touch her. She jumps and gives me a forced smile as she covers my hand with hers.

"I'm okay," she nods, to herself as much as me. "I'm just

thinking about Matt and Annie." She smiles, her eyes glistening. "I just can't believe that they'd even offer that."

"All can I say is that they're two amazing people, who've been there for both of us through a lot of shit, so it really doesn't surprise me that they'd be so selfless."

"I can't even get my head around how it would work," she says, shaking her head. "I guess it would be yours and Annie's..." Her voice trails off.

"No. It would be *yours* and *mine*," I say firmly. She nods but won't quite meet my eyes. "And Matt's right. This isn't something we even need to *think* about yet. Maybe sometime in the future, somewhere down the track, it might be something we want to consider."

She looks up at me, her expression terrified.

"But what if I do want it now?" she whispers, looking into my eyes.

"Really?" I stare at her, overwhelmed, because I was not expecting her to say that.

"I don't know," she admits. "I'm all confused about what I want."

"Then how about this. When we get back from our honeymoon, we'll sit down and talk about it, and then we can decide. Once we know what we want, we'll talk it over with them. How does that sound?"

She nods and curls her fingers around mine.

"That sounds good," she whispers. "I love you so much."

I lean over and kiss her softly on the mouth.

"I love you more."

BONUS EPILOGUE

LAURA

Fifteen months later

"Where is she?" I demand, racing up to Matt.

"She's in there but calm down. Everything is fine. She's six centimetres dilated, but both she and the baby are good."

I nod and run my hands through my hair as I try and calm myself down. I'm shaking with nerves, but I'm determined to get through this without breaking down.

Matt chuckles. "Hey, this is like the total opposite of last time, huh? Whoever thought *I'd* be the calm and collected one?"

"Not me," I snap. "And so long as I'm not overflowing the bath and flooding the house, then I'm one up on you."

He laughs and shakes his head at Luke, who has walked up behind me. I relax as his arm slides around my waist.

"I feel for you, man. She's got the anger issues of a heavily pregnant woman."

"Sympathy anger," Luke explains. I turn around to glare at him. He winces and holds up his hands in defence. "Hey. I'm sorry, but you're wild when someone else is pregnant with your kid."

"What an incredibly insensitive—" I stop mid-sentence and shake my head. Who am I kidding? I'm just as offensive as the both of them—probably worse. "Just shut up and go find out how she is, okay?" I say impatiently.

"Sure," Matt grins. He walks over to the doors and then stops. "Hey, why don't you go in?"

"Really?" I whisper.

"Sure. It's your kid, after all."

My heart races as I walk over to the door and push my way through. I've seen plenty of babies being born, but there's something so terrifying about another woman having your child. I bet that won't be the weirdest thing I say all day, either.

I walk into the room and edge closer to Annie, who is clutching her rounded stomach, legs up in the air, while the doctor examines her. I sit down next to her. She glares at me, her eyes flashing.

"Fucking *fuck*," she mutters. "This little shit better not steal toys from my kid."

I laugh, tears forming in my eyes. I've seen Elina sucker punch Matt in the balls over a lollypop. Nobody is stealing shit from that kid.

I jump when she cries out again. She grabs hold of her

stomach with one hand and my wrist with the other as she winces in pain.

"*Fuuuuck,*" she screams.

The doctor pops up from between her legs, a concerned expression on his face.

"The baby isn't engaging," he explains. "We've going to have to do a C-section."

"Surgery?" Annie says, her face pale.

I squeeze her hand, feeling terrible. This is my fault. She's doing this for me.

He nods. "It's nothing to be alarmed about. You'll be awake through the whole thing. We just need to get this baby out now, because her heartrate is up marginally. It's concerning, but still a common problem."

The doctor walks out of the room. I glance at Annie, who looks much calmer than I feel. My mind is running at full speed, thinking of all the ways this can go wrong. Then there's the fact that Annie has to have surgery, because of me.

"Don't you feel bad about this, okay?" Annie says. She nods for me to come closer, so I lean over and hug her. "We wanted to do this for you guys, and you heard the doctor. It's really common."

"But you'll have a scar," I whisper.

"But on the plus side, I won't have a tear from my vagina to my anus," she replies.

I laugh and take a deep breath. If she can be calm, then so can I.

"Okay. Look after my bubba for me."

"I will," she promises.

The doctor steps out of the room and returns moments later with an orderly. I step back when he starts wheeling the bed out of the room. I take a deep breath and release it slowly as I blink back tears. Then I walk toward the other door, which leads back out to where Luke and Matt are.

This whole giving birth thing is so emotional.

"Are you not joining us?"

I turn around to see the doctor staring at me as he holds open the door.

My eyes widen. "Really?"

He nods. "Unless we need to put her under a general, you're fine to be in there."

"She knows the rules. She's a bloody doctor," Annie mutters.

I don't need to be told twice.

I stand next to Annie in the OR, holding her hand, while the doctors prep her for surgery. My heart is racing at a million miles an hour. I feel sick, faint, anxious. Hell, I'm just a mess. And I'm about to meet my daughter. God, this is really happening. Annie smiles at me reassuringly.

"It will be fine," she soothes.

I groan and laugh. "You're the one about to be cut open. Why are you comforting me?"

"Good point," she says with a grimace.

"Okay, here we go. Just keep breathing and stay nice and

still," the doctor encourages. "Laura, do you want to come up here and see this?"

I nod and swallow the lump in my throat, prying my hand from Annie's. I'm not sure who is clinging to who, but at this point it doesn't matter. I'm shaking as I move down the bed. I reach her stomach, just as they're lifting her out. A sob escapes me as I watch my daughter enter the world. Tears stream down my cheeks as I shake uncontrollably.

Holy shit, she's beautiful.

Any doubts I had over whether I'd feel love for her are gone the moment I see that face, because I feel so much love for her already.

"Congratulations," the doctor smiles at me. "Would you like to hold your daughter?"

I nod furiously and wipe away tears, which only allows for more. He places her carefully into my arms. She cries one tiny cry, then she grasps hold of my finger, settling down into my arms. There is no way to explain how I feel, holding this tiny thing in my arms. I'm lost for words and completely in love with her.

My daughter.

I shake my head, because I never thought I'd be blessed with two beautiful little girls.

Annie looks at me quizzically when I laugh.

"I just realized that next month I'll be a mother to a newborn *and* a teenager," I say with a grin.

"God help you, but look at that little face," she swoons.

She gazes down at her, while I lean over the bed so she can get a better look. I'm careful to press down on her wound, because I can only imagine how painful it must be. I sit there on the edge of the bed for a while, keeping Annie company while she's in recovery, until I remember Luke is out there, probably panicking. *Shit.* I carefully bundle her in Annie's arms. She takes her, but gives me a confused look as I stand up.

"I better go tell her daddy that everything is okay."

Luke jumps to his feet the second he sees me and walks over to me. He hugs me, then pulls away to study my face, his expression riddled with anxiety. I smile and he sighs, then laughs, then hugs me.

"They're both fine. She's been moved back to her room now if you want to go and meet her?"

"Of course I do," he mutters. He slips his hand into mine and we walk over to her room. I glance back at Matt.

"Are you coming?"

"I thought you guys might want some privacy," he says.

"Without you and Annie, this wouldn't be possible," I say, my voice soft.

Annie looks up and smiles at us as we walk inside.

"Come meet your daughter," she says to Luke.

He laughs, not letting go of my hand as we walk over there.

"God, she's so little," he mutters, staring down at her.

I smile as he takes her from Annie and smother a laugh, because I've never seen anything so awkward as him trying to cradle a newborn.

"Holy shit, would you look at her," he marvels, shaking his head. "That tiny little mouth." He looks at me and laughs. I put my arm around him, then reach up to kiss him on the cheek. "This little thing is ours," he mutters to me.

The door opens look up and smile as Mom and Allie walk in.

"Oh my god," Allie gasps, racing over. She coos at her little sister, the most adorable expression on her face. "She's so cute."

"You want to hold her?" Luke asks.

Allie nods and positions herself on the edge of the bed, carefully taking the baby from him.

"Did we decide on a name?" she asks, not taking her eyes off her sister.

"We did." Luke glances at me. I nod, unable to speak through fear of crying. Mom wraps her arms around my waist and kisses me. "Amaya."

"Beautiful," Mom whispers, peering over Allie's shoulder at her new granddaughter. "Congratulations to you both. I'm so happy for you."

"Are you going to call your mother?" I ask Luke softly. He leans down and kisses me on the forehead.

"Not yet. I will, but not now."

I nod, and don't push it. If they're meant to reconnect, then it will happen.

The door opens again. I look up and see Becca this time.

"They said it was already overcrowded in here, so I might as well just go in," she says with a shrug. She keeps her distance, staying over near the wall. I chuckle, because she looks terrified.

"What are you doing?" I laugh at her.

"What? Babies scare the fuck out of me," she mutters. "Give me a dog any day of the week."

"*Becca,*" Mom frowns, nodding at Allie.

Becca winces. "I know, I'm sorry...."

Her voice trails off when the nurse walks in to check on Annie and the baby—the very hot, athletic nurse that Becca can't take her eyes off. He takes Annie and Amaya's vitals, notes them down and then walks back over to the door, obviously trying not to disturb us. As he's walking out, Becca unsuccessfully does everything she can to try and catch his attention. She scowls at me as I laugh.

"What? He's so hot. Hey, maybe I need to do a Laura and get myself injured and into the ER. I mean, look what *you* scored for yourself," she says, nodding at Luke, while she chuckles to herself.

Fuck. I'm going to kill her.

"What do you mean?" Mom says, her expression confused. She glances from me, to Becca, and over at Luke. "I thought you two met through Matt."

"So did I," Matt says suspiciously.

Annie smothers a giggle as she tries to be discreet, but Becca doesn't even bother hiding her amusement. She's nearly on the floor, she's laughing so hard.

"Oh fuck. I just put my foot in it, didn't I?" she gasps

through her laughter. Then she turns to my mother. My heart races as I recognize the look in her eyes.

She wouldn't fucking dare.

"Maybe it's time you asked your daughter about cubicle nine."

ABOUT COMFORT ZONE

Want more **Becca?**

Book #4, Comfort Zone
will feature Becca as the female lead.

Walking into Jake's bachelor party to see my professor motor-boating a stripper?

Talk about Awkward.

It wouldn't have been so bad if I wasn't completely hot for the guy. I had been since I first walked into that feline anatomy class and saw him performing chest compressions on a Persian cat named Andrew. All I could think about was how I wanted to be the next creature to slither under those strong, masculine hands.

It was every woman's dream, right? Finding a man who knew how to handle a pussy.

So, as I sat in that strip club and knocked back my third tequila, I started thinking... I should make a move on him.

When our eyes locked over the busty blonde stripper who was gyrating against me, and he smiled, it was all the encouragement I needed. I politely pushed her aside, stood up, and walked over to him and...

I've got no idea what happened next. I knew there was a reason I avoided drinking tequila.

Judging by the way he's smirking at me as I walk into his class on Monday?

I'm not sure I want to know...

Keep reading for a sneak peek!

COMFORT ZONE EXCERPT

BECCA

Amy: *Okay. Would you rather masturbate in*
public or lick Professor Sullivan's asshole?

I choke back a laugh and screw up my nose, not finding either
of those options particularly appealing. *Not that I'm going to*
tell Amy that. I glance up to make sure Professor Sullivan is still
talking before I type out my response.

Me: *Lick Professor Sullivan's asshole,*
preferably while stroking his cock. Then
again, I've always had a thing for
exhibitionism. Can I just say both? Or
maybe lick his ass in public, while getting
myself off?
Amy: *I knew you were a kinky bitch.*

I attempt to turn a burst of laughter into a cough, but I end up swallowing air the wrong way and spluttering so loudly that half the room turns around to look at me. I sink farther down into my seat and focus on my laptop, pretending I can't feel everyone staring. I shoot a glare at Amy, who sits three rows away, chuckling to herself.

"Is everything okay, Ms. Chambers?"

I freeze as I look up right into the intense blue eyes of Professor Sullivan. We stare at each other for a moment, until his lips lift into a grin. I flush, somehow managing to nod my head.

"As I was saying..."

Another message from Amy pings through, but I close it, not wanting to risk getting myself into more trouble. I last five minutes before my curiosity gets the better of me and I have to open it.

> **Amy:** *You're such a dick. Want to hang out tonight?*

Amy and I hit it off after we were paired up for a group project earlier in the year. Like most of my peers, she's a few years younger than me, though some of the shit I get myself into, you'd think *I* was the younger one.

> **Me:** *I can't. Jake's bachelor party, remember?*
> **Amy:** *I still think you should've gone with Sacked.*

I laugh softly, because I could just imagine the look on Jake's face if I'd arranged his party at the hot new gay strip club. Twenty guys standing around awkwardly, looking anywhere but at the cock swinging in their faces? It would have been pretty fucking funny. For me, at least.

I'd been looking forward to planning this since Jake got engaged. He's one of my best friends, and I'm determined to throw him a night he'll remember. It's not like anything I do will make his fiancée hate me any less, so what have I got to lose?

I've tried everything to get along with Brooke, but she just flat-out hates me. I'm not sure why, and I'm past the point of caring. I'd be lying if I didn't admit there were times I wished he would find someone else. That sounds awful, but Jake's my friend and I want to share everything with him, including his partners—in a totally nonsexual way, of course, because my fantasies are reserved for Professor Sullivan.

I'm kidding...sort of.

I fiddle with a loose thread on my shirt as anxiety shifts through my stomach. I never thought I'd be the kind of girl who had a crush on a teacher, but here I am, a twenty-seven-year-old college student, lusting after her professor. Yes, my life is that sad. I sneak a look in his direction, sucking in a mouthful of air when his eyes meet mine.

His lips twitch, highlighting his strong jawline and the undeniably sexy layer of stubble that covers it. He's definitely attractive, but beyond that? I have no idea. These feelings I've developed for him are definitely infatuation. For all I know, he might be a total asshole. Still, a little fantasizing never hurt anyone. And it's not like he'd ever find out about my crush, right?

The end of the lecture can't come soon enough. When it's over, I stand up and follow the crowd to the door, my mind preoccupied with everything I still have to do for tonight. Why do I leave shit till the last minute? You'd think I would eventually learn, but I never seem to. Just as I'm about to walk out of the hall, I hear my name. I freeze, because that voice...

Why is Professor Sullivan calling out my name?

I'd had this fantasy before, but we were both wearing much less clothing.

I turn around and clutch at the strap of my backpack so tightly that my knuckles turn white, and then I saunter over to his desk, ignoring the looks and giggles I'm getting from passing students. Amy mouths *good luck* to me. I roll my eyes, hoping to God I look calmer and more in control than I feel.

"You wanted to see me?" I say.

Professor Sullivan looks up, his expression giving nothing away. Then he nods and runs his hand through his thick, dark hair as he leans back in his chair. "I did."

He looks at me in such a way that I feel dirty—or maybe that's the naughty thoughts that smirk is putting into my head?

Focus, Becca. Now is not the time to be fantasizing about him.

"I wanted to speak with you for a moment about the internal instant messaging service you love to abuse so much."

My heart thumps in my chest as I force myself to swallow.

"What about it?" I finally manage to ask.

He smiles at me, those electric blue eyes burning through me. My skin goes hot as I shuffle on my feet, waiting for him to tell me what the hell this is all about. A horrible thought hits me. *I hope he's not cutting me off.* I shudder at the thought.

"I'm an administrator, Becca. That means every single text sent within that system pops up on my screen. Most of them I ignore, but every now and then one captures my attention." His eyes twinkle as he stares at me. "Oddly enough, the ones that stand out are nearly always yours."

I stare at him, my eyes wide. Is he fucking kidding me?

"Is that even legal?" I ask, my voice coming out a strangled growl. "Surely that's an invasion of my privacy."

"No, not when you signed a disclaimer on the first day of class," he reminds me.

He stands up and walks around to the front of his desk, parking his ass right in front of me. He's within my reach, which means there's a fifty-fifty chance of me doing something stupid, like reaching out to touch him. I cross my arms over my chest, just in case, because if today has established anything, it's that I'm stupid enough to unconsciously stroke his cock through his pants or something.

"On that first day, I went through the terms of use in extreme detail because I wanted everyone to be aware those messages are filtered through my system. I said it twice, but you obviously weren't listening." He turns around and grabs a file, flicking through it until he reaches a certain page. "Your signature?" he asks, holding it up.

My heart pounds as I nod. *How did I miss that?* I was probably too busy messaging Amy. I drop my gaze, beyond embarrassed. It's a strange feeling, because I'm usually the *cause* of this kind of humiliation. All I can think about are the hundreds of embarrassing, inappropriate, and often downright weird messages that I'd sent Amy during his class. I close my eyes and swallow, my heart pounding, because I fail to see how this can get any worse.

"Look, I'm not telling you to stop messaging your friends—I just wanted you to be aware that I could see them." He pauses, the tiniest smile visible on his lips. "Since so many of them involve me."

"Is that all?" I whisper.

I don't want to stand here making small talk with him. I want to get the fuck out of here and never speak about this moment again. Ever. Only I'm not convinced that my mind is ready to let me forget about this just yet.

"Sure." He studies me for a moment, before continuing. "It's the weekend. I'm sure you've got a very full schedule planned. Just make sure you squeeze in some study time, okay?"

I smile tightly and then turn around, quickly making a break for the door. Just as I touch the handle, he calls out to me.

"Ms. Chambers? One more thing."

I cringe and force myself to smile as I turn around to face him again. I'm so embarrassed, it's not funny. How could I sign something when I had no idea what it was? God, how fucking stupid can I be? Who knows what else I have unwittingly signed over the years.

"Yes?"

"While I appreciate your commitment to trying new things, I can assure you that no tongue"—he pauses— "not even yours, will *ever* be going near my asshole."

Oh God. I want to die.

His eyes flicker with amusement as I struggle to breathe.

"Of course, I have no control over whether you masturbate in public, but I suggest if you do go down that path, you choose a warm night. The last thing you want to end up with is a cold."

This is not happening.

The way he's looking at me, I might as well just drop the skinny jeans it took me an hour to get into and get myself off right here in front of him. It's obvious he's imagining it anyway. I force myself to keep eye contact, because if I lose that, then I'm done.

"Thank you, Professor Sullivan."

The second I get to my car, I call Amy. I'm miffed that she didn't wait for me, but I get over it pretty fast, mainly because I need to unload all of this on somebody who'll understand. There's no better candidate than the person who put me in this position in the first place.

"So, did he throw you down on his desk and fuck you up the ass?" she teases.

"Oh, I'm totally fucked, but not in a good way." I groan and rub the bridge of my nose. "This is all your fault. You and your stupid games."

"What happened?" she asks. "What's going on?"

"Did you know the IMs sent through the internal system are monitored?" I accuse her. Then I cringe again. I want the world to swallow me up every time I think about it. "Every fucking message we've sent in that room, he's read."

"Of course I knew," she giggles. "I thought you knew and you just didn't care. That's why I keep messaging you, because you're so much fun."

"Didn't *care*?" I repeat, glaring at her. "Why the fuck wouldn't I care?"

The more I think about it, in all the times we'd exchanged messages, Amy had never said anything remotely incriminating. I, on the other hand, had said plenty. I sigh and force myself to calm down, knowing it's myself I need to be annoyed at. Not Amy.

"It'll be fine," she says, dismissing my concerns like she always does. "You're stressing over nothing. By Monday he'll have forgotten about it. Trust me."

I'm not so sure, but there isn't much I can do about it now anyway.

"I better go. I've got to get ready for the bachelor party."

"Okay. Call me tomorrow and let me know how it goes?" she asks. "At least this party will take your mind off it," she adds.

I nod, my mood lifting a tiny bit. She's right about one thing, at least.

Jake's party will be the perfect distraction.

"For God's sake, Becca, would you stop honking that damn horn."

Mom glares at me as she throws herself into the passenger seat of my car. I wait until she's closed the door, and then slam my foot down on the accelerator while she locks her seatbelt in.

"What? We're running late," I say, defending myself.

I told her I'd be home at six to pick her up. I even gave her until six fifteen before I started getting testy. I glance at her again, this time noticing what she's wearing—her short, navy blue dress that shows more skin than mine—but I have to admit, she looks good. With her blond hair twisted into a bun and her makeup on, you'd never guess she's in her sixties.

"Did Dad see you leave in that dress?" I ask, raising my eyebrows.

"Why do you think I was running so late?" She winks at me and I shudder.

Yes. My sixty-seven-year-old mother, loyal member of the gardening club and regular churchgoer, just insinuated that she was late because she was having sex. I should be used to it by now, but the older I get it, seems the worse *they* get.

My parents lead a very relaxed lifestyle, which was both good and bad when I was growing up. Having the freedom as a teenager to explore myself was fantastic, but bringing a guy home to discover your parents naked in the living room, experimenting with another couple? Not so fantastic. I was mortified. Actually, that doesn't even begin to cover it.

That incident took me years to get over. It wasn't helped by the fact that the next day, the entire school referred to me as *Chandelier* because my parents liked swinging. That name stuck like glue right through until graduation.

"You didn't have to come tonight. Remember?" I say, gritting my teeth.

"Jake's like the son I never had." She looks at me like I'm the crazy one. "Why would I miss his bachelor party?"

Um, because you weren't invited?

I bite back on that comment, deciding it's not worth the trouble. I don't even know how she ended up inviting herself along. One minute Jake and I were arguing about my choice of venue, and the next, Mom was accepting an invitation that he never actually gave her. While we're on it, if Jake is the son she never had, then it's probably a good thing I don't have a brother, because she really doesn't know Jake all that well. Our friendship started in high school when Jake changed schools. Back then, my parents respected my privacy a little too much. Where other parents would want to know the ins and outs of where their child was going, mine just went with the flow. At the time of graduation, Mom had met Jake twice. Then we were both away at college, and after that, I had my own place. It was only recently, being back at home, that my parents and Jake had begun to cross paths more.

Even before I finished high school, I knew I wanted to work with animals, but my grades were nowhere near good enough to get me into veterinary science. Still, I lucked out and got my dream job, handling animals on set for a production company. Thanks to a very well-endowed admissions officer named Barry Pumpfist, who was moonlighting as a porn star, I got an interview and a glowing recommendation for mature-age entry into a bridging course at UCLA. I kicked ass in that course and managed to score myself a scholarship into veterinary science.

Leaving a job I loved was a huge risk, but when I walked into that lecture room on that very first day, I knew I'd made the right decision. It felt right, and not just because my professor was incredibly hot. Watching him perform chest compressions on that cat, I knew that was what I wanted to be doing. Any reservations I'd had about my career change being some kind of midlife crisis evaporated in that moment. I wanted it more than anything, and I was prepared to do whatever it took to get there —even if it meant moving back home.

Going home wasn't a choice; it was a sacrifice I had to make in order to get what I wanted. I couldn't work at the studio *and* study, because my scholarship required me to work part of my tuition off within the university. That left me with barely enough time to study as it was, without throwing another job into the mix. I didn't love working in the president of the university's office—technology and I have a love-hate relationship—but I didn't have a choice. I'm pretty sure the president hates me, but I suppose I've given him good reason to, between wiping the entire system clean of all the mid-year results and forwarding his personal emails to the whole alumni. It took a lot of convincing that I wasn't a terrorist, or a cheat. I was just a very talented klutz.

Slowing down just before the exit to the freeway, I turn into the strip of shops where Sexytime Land is. If I'd known Mom was going to be running so late, I would've stopped here first. I park the car outside the drugstore, which is a few doors down, hoping I can fool Mom into thinking I'm going in there. It's not that I don't want her to know where I'm really going. I just don't want her following me in there and embarrassing me, which is exactly what she'd do.

"Becca, is that a *sex* store?" Mom whispers. "Can we go in?"

"What? No. Well, it *is* a sex shop, but we're not going in there. Isn't it enough that we're going to a strip club?" I grumble.

"Then what are we doing here?" she presses.

"I just need to go into the drugstore for a second," I say, hoping she leaves it at that.

"What for?" she asks.

Jesus, is nothing off limits?

"Extra-large condoms," I snap. "And something to get rid of this headache."

The one forming at the thought of going into a strip club with my mother.

"Just stay here, okay?" I force myself to smile as I climb out of the car. "I won't be long."

I half expect her to follow me, but to my relief, she stays put. Increasing my pace, I stroll inside, wanting to get this over with as quickly as possible. I casually walk over to their expansive toy section, not embarrassed that I know exactly where it is. Embarrassing my friends is what I do, and nothing does it better than sex toys.

I frown as I try to decide which option to go with: the fist or the more traditional penis-shaped dildo. My concentration is interrupted when I hear an all-too-familiar voice calling my name. I cringe and poke my head around the side of the aisle. Sure enough, there's Mom, flailing up and down the center of the store, calling out to me.

"Becca! There you are. How cool is this place?" She giggles. "It's *huge*. Not like the pokey little back-room sex shops I'm used to. Then again, the last time I was in one was when your father and I got one of those—"

"*Really* not something I want to hear," I growl, cutting her off.

She looks hurt. "But I thought we were friends."

"Nope. We can never be the kind of friends who talk about this shit, because *you're my mother*," I reply. I sigh, knowing that I sound harsh, but I've put up with this kind of shit too many times. "You're wonderful and you know I love you, but I'm sorry. I draw the line at anything that is going to scar me for life. Which, coincidentally, is pretty much everything that comes out of your mouth."

She sniffs and lifts her head, like I've offended her. Probably because I have.

"You're as bad as Midge," she finally huffs. Midge being her ninety-three-year-old friend from church. "You should've heard her react when I suggested a swinger's—"

"*Mother!* I'll leave you here," I threaten, glaring at her. "And what kind of church are you going to, anyway?"

"Being left here wouldn't necessarily be a *bad* thing..." She giggles and glances around. "Can I be honest with you about something?"

Oh God, she's whispering. This can't be good. I'm terrified as to what is coming next.

"Uh—"

"The ceremony we're having next weekend?" She cuts me off.

"The recommitment ceremony for your wedding anniversary?" I clarify.

She nods. "It's not the *marriage* that we're celebrating..." Her green eyes dance as they stare into mine. "Your father and I have finally...reconnected, after years of having to satisfy myself." She sighs and stares off into the distance, a dreamy smile on her face. "I wanted to celebrate it and our anniversary was the perfect cover. I can't tell you how much I've missed that thick, stiff—"

"Mother!" I gasp, a little part of me dying inside with every word she utters. "Are you kidding me? You've invited fifty relatives to help you celebrate the fact that you and your husband are fuck—"

"Watch your language, Rebecca," Mom warns me.

Ha. My language is the least of my worries. I feel sick. And betrayed. How am I supposed to sit through this, knowing what I do? I offered to read a poem for this thing, for God's sake. That's why she kept pushing me to read a poem entitled "The Seed That Lasts Forever." I cover my mouth with my hand.

Oh God, I'm going to be sick.

"I can't..." I close my eyes and take a deep breath. "We'll talk about this later."

I stalk back over to my dildos. I'm doing my best to push my mother's words from my mind, but they refuse to leave. *My parents are having a sex ceremony.* That's what it comes down to. Let's just hope they don't decide to do an interpretive dance.

Just forget about it and choose a damn dildo.

I need to get out of here before she does something to really embarrass—I wince when I hear a loud crash.

Too late.

I turn around, my eyes widening at the sight of Mom sprawled out on the floor, surrounded by hundreds of tiny little motorized Pac-Man-style penises. I watch as these tiny little erect penises snap their oversized mouths at her legs, like blood-thirsty piranhas, and I can't help myself—I lose it. Gasping, I clutch my stomach as tears stream down my cheeks.

Mom glares at me. "Becca, stop laughing and help me."

I step forward to help her up—but not before I drag my phone out of my jacket pocket and take a photo. If all else fails for finding an appropriate poem for the ceremony, I'll be able to create an awesome photo montage.

We work quickly to shove the tiny little critters back in their box. I smirk. How cute. Their own little box to play in. I grin and tuck one in behind my dildo. I'll keep it as a souvenir for whenever I need cheering up. I wipe the smile off my face and turn back to Mom.

"We're going. *Now.*"

I take her by the arm and lead her to the checkout, placing my purchases down on the counter. I give my mother a stern look.

"*You* can explain to Mandi what you did to her display," I add, reading the shop assistant's name tag.

"I took one off the shelf." Her cheeks flush bright red. "It's not my fault they all fell off."

"It only takes one mistake to ruin everything." I smirk, echoing the words I used to hear from her all the time when I was growing up.

"A piece of advice that *you* never listened to," she grumbles.

"Well, it was hard to take you seriously. You didn't exactly set a fine example for me, did you?"

I thank the cashier and take the bag in one hand and Mom in the other, dragging her out to the car. She climbs in and crosses her arms, glaring at the floor of the car.

"Quit pouting like a sulky teenager or I'll take you home," I warn. "You need to own up to your mistakes, Mother." Okay, so I may be enjoying this a little too much.

"That wasn't my fault," she insists.

"Oh? The tiny penises just jumped off the shelf to attack you, did they?" I rub my temples, mainly to try and hide my smirk. "God knows what you'll do next to embarrass me."

"What's that supposed to mean?" she asks.

"It means I'm capping you at two drinks. And no lap dances, no stripping, and no hitting on Jake's friends," I warn her. "No hitting on the strippers, either."

"Rebecca, I'm your sixty-seven-year-old mother—"

"Who gets a few drinks into her and suddenly thinks she's a twenty-year-old hornbag," I retort. "You were escorted out of Aunt Minnie's wake, Mom. Remember that?"

"Oh, Minnie was the biggest minx of them all," Mom protests. "She would've been dancing right there with me, if she could."

"I don't think it was the dancing they had a problem with," I remind her gently. Watching Mom trying to wrestle that coffin open while screaming "Free Minnie" was both hysterical and horrifying. "Just tone it down. *Please?*" I beg her.

She's about to reply when her phone rings. I pull into the parking lot while she answers the call. I'm only half paying attention as I reverse into a spot near the door, but when I hear the word *hospital*, she has my full attention.

"Why? What happened? Are you okay?" She pauses while I study her face and try and figure out what's going on. "No, we haven't gone in yet. It's fine."

Mom glances at me and rolls her eyes, which only slightly eases my anxieties. Mom has been known for playing down the seriousness of medical emergencies, on occasion. I have vague memories of age five, when she insisted on waiting until after her show finished before taking my grandad to the hospital. It turned out he had suffered a pretty serious heart attack.

Luckily, he was okay—well, until he died six weeks later after choking on a Twinkie.

"Oh shut up, Peter. Of course I'm going to come to the hospital. I'd never hear the end of it if I didn't."

She turns to me and shakes her head. I smirk, feeling sorry for Dad, because somehow, I feel like he's the one who's not going to hear the end of it.

"What's going on?" I ask her when she finally hangs up.

"Oh, it's fine." She waves her hand dismissively. "Your father *insisted* on trying to change the brake pads instead of calling the mechanic, like I told him to. Of course he ran over his foot and he's pretty sure it's broken in two places."

I start the car up.

Mom looks at me in alarm. "What are you doing?"

"Driving you to the hospital, what does it look like?" I frown.

"No, you're going in there." She points to the club. "You can't miss this. Jake would be crushed. It's bad enough that I'm missing it. We can't both not be there."

I don't have the heart to tell her Jake probably won't care if she's there or not.

"What about Dad—"

"He's fine," she says, waving her hand. "If he wasn't so stupid and had just listened to me in the first place, then *I* wouldn't be missing this, too, would I?"

"I guess not. Okay, so how are you going to get there?" I ask.

"I'll catch a cab."

"No way." What kind of daughter would I be if I let my

mother drive herself to the hospital, after my father broke his foot? "At least let me drive you over there."

"Tell you what: you get out and I'll give you the money to catch a cab home and I'll take your car," Mom suggests.

I hesitate.

"Go on, Becca," she coaxes, knowing she almost has me. "It's fine, I promise. It's not going to kill you to have a few drinks and loosen up a little."

I stifle a laugh. Only to Mom do I appear uptight.

"Fine," I say. "But if you have any trouble at all, just call me and I'll be right over there."

"Okay, but I'll be fine."

Get your copy!

ABOUT THE AUTHOR

A New York Times and USA Today bestselling author, Missy lives in a small town in Victoria, Australia with her husband and her confused pets (a dog who thinks that she is a cat, a cat who thinks he is a dog...you get the picture).

When she's not writing, she can usually be found looking for something to read.

Visit her website or subscribe to her newsletter for updates.

facebook.com/MissycJohnson

twitter.com/missycjohnson

instagram.com/authormissyj

amazon.com/Missy-Johnson

bookbub.com/authors/missy-johnson

ALSO BY MISSY JOHNSON

Love Hurts Series

Always You

Out of Reach

Words Left Unsaid

Don't Hold Back

Fade to Black

Awkward Love Series

It's Complicated

I Can Explain

Too Much Information

Comfort Zone

Don't Go There

Standalones

Rewriting History

Resist

Absolution

13087021R00184